BOOKS BY

MARK TWAIN

ST. JOAN OF ARC
THE INNOCENTS ABROAD
ROUGHING IT
THE GILDED AGE
A TRAMP ABROAD
FOLLOWING THE EQUATOR
PUDD'NHEAD WILSON
SKETCHES NEW AND OLD
THE AMERICAN CLAIMANT
CHRISTIAN SCIENCE
A CONNECTICUT YANKEE AT THE COURT OF KING ARTHUR
THE ADVENTURES OF HUCKLEBERRY FINN
PERSONAL RECOLLECTIONS OF JOAN OF ARC
LIFE ON THE MISSISSIPPI
THE MAN THAT CORRUPTED HADLEYBURG
THE PRINCE AND THE PAUPER
THE $30,000 BEQUEST
THE ADVENTURES OF TOM SAWYER
TOM SAWYER ABROAD
WHAT IS MAN?
THE MYSTERIOUS STRANGER

ADAM'S DIARY
A DOG'S TALE
A DOUBLE-BARRELED DETECTIVE STORY
EDITORIAL WILD OATS
EVE'S DIARY
IN DEFENSE OF HARRIET SHELLEY AND OTHER ESSAYS
IS SHAKESPEARE DEAD?
CAPT. STORMFIELD'S VISIT TO HEAVEN
A HORSE'S TALE
THE JUMPING FROG
THE £1,000,000 BANK-NOTE
TRAVELS AT HOME
TRAVELS IN HISTORY

MARK TWAIN'S LETTERS
MARK TWAIN'S SPEECHES

---

HARPER & ROW, PUBLISHERS
[ESTABLISHED 1817]

ON THE FOURTH DAY COMES THE ASTROLOGER FROM HIS CRUMBLING OLD TOWER

# THE MYSTERIOUS STRANGER

## AND OTHER STORIES

Samuel L. Clemens.

By
MARK TWAIN

HARPER & ROW, PUBLISHERS
NEW YORK, EVANSTON, AND LONDON

Printed in the United States of America
H-N

# CONTENTS

# THE MYSTERIOUS STRANGER

# THE MYSTERIOUS STRANGER*

## CHAPTER I

IT was in 1590—winter. Austria was far away from the world, and asleep; it was still the Middle Ages in Austria, and promised to remain so forever. Some even set it away back centuries upon centuries and said that by the mental and spiritual clock it was still the Age of Belief in Austria. But they meant it as a compliment, not a slur, and it was so taken, and we were all proud of it. I remember it well, although I was only a boy; and I remember, too, the pleasure it gave me.

Yes, Austria was far from the world, and asleep, and our village was in the middle of that sleep, being in the middle of Austria. It drowsed in peace in the deep privacy of a hilly and woodsy solitude where news from the world hardly ever came to disturb its dreams, and was infinitely content. At its front flowed the tranquil river, its surface painted with cloud-forms and the reflections of drifting arks and stone-boats; behind it rose the woody steeps to the base of the lofty precipice; from the top of the precipice frowned a vast castle, its long stretch of towers and bastions mailed in vines; beyond the river, a league to the left, was a tumbled expanse of forest-clothed hills cloven by winding gorges where the sun never penetrated; and to the right a precipice overlooked the river, and between it and the hills just spoken of lay a far-reaching plain dotted with little homesteads nested among orchards and shade trees.

The whole region for leagues around was the hereditary property of a prince, whose servants kept the castle always in perfect condition for occupancy, but neither he nor his family came there oftener than once in five years. When they came it was as if the lord of the world had arrived, and had brought all the glories of its kingdoms along; and when they went they left a calm behind which was like the deep sleep which follows an orgy.

Eseldorf was a paradise for us boys. We were not overmuch pestered with schooling. Mainly we were trained to be good Christians; to revere the Virgin, the Church, and the saints above everything. Beyond these matters we were not required to know much; and, in fact, not allowed to. Knowledge was not good for the common people, and could make them discontented with the lot which God had appointed for them, and God would not endure discontentment with His plans. We had two priests. One of them, Father Adolf, was a very zealous and strenuous priest, much considered.

There may have been better priests, in some ways, than Father Adolf, but there was never one in our commune who was held in more solemn and awful respect. This was because he had absolutely no fear of the Devil. He was the only Christian I have ever known of whom that could be truly said. People stood in deep dread of him on that account; for they thought that there must be something supernatural about him, else he could not be so bold and so confident. All men speak in bitter disapproval of the Devil, but they do it reverently, not flippantly; but Father Adolf's way was very different; he called him by every name he could lay his tongue to, and it made everyone shudder that heard him; and often he would even speak of him scornfully and scoffingly; then the people crossed themselves and went quickly out of his presence, fearing that something fearful might happen.

Father Adolf had actually met Satan face to face more than once, and defied him. This was known to be so. Father Adolf said it himself. He never made any secret of it, but spoke it right out. And that he was speaking true there was proof in at least one instance, for on that occasion he quarreled with the enemy, and intrepidly threw his bottle at him; and there, upon the wall of his study, was the ruddy splotch where it struck and broke.

But it was Father Peter, the other priest, that we all loved best and were sorriest for. Some people charged him with talking around in conversation that God was all goodness and would find a way to save all his poor human children. It was a horrible thing to say, but there was never any absolute proof that Father Peter said it; and it was out of character for him to say it, too, for he was always good and gentle and truthful. He wasn't charged with saying it in the pulpit, where all the congregation could hear and testify, but only outside, in talk; and it is easy for enemies to manufacture *that.* Father Peter had an enemy and a very powerful one, the astrologer who lived in a tumbled old tower up the valley, and put in his nights studying the stars. Every one knew he could foretell wars and famines, though that was not so hard, for there was always a war and generally a famine somewhere. But he could also read any man's life through the stars in a big book he had, and find lost property, and every one in the village except Father Peter stood in awe of him. Even Father Adolf, who had defied the Devil, had a wholesome respect for the astrologer when he came through our village wearing his tall, pointed hat and his long, flowing robe with stars on it, carrying his big book, and a staff which was known to have magic power. The bishop himself sometimes listened to the astrologer, it was said, for, besides studying the stars and prophesying, the astrologer made a great show of piety, which would impress the bishop, of course.

But Father Peter took no stock in the astrologer. He denounced him openly as a charlatan—a fraud with no valuable knowledge of any kind, or powers beyond those of an ordinary and rather inferior human being, which naturally made the astrologer hate Father Peter and wish to ruin him. It was the astrologer, as we all believed, who originated the story about Father Peter's shocking remark and carried it to the bishop. It was said that Father Peter had made the remark to his niece, Marget, though Marget denied it and implored the bishop to believe her and spare her old uncle from poverty and disgrace. But the bishop wouldn't listen. He suspended Father Peter indefinitely, though he wouldn't go so far as to excommunicate him on the evidence of only one witness; and now Father Peter had been out a couple of years, and our other priest, Father Adolf, had his flock.

Those had been hard years for the old priest and Marget. They had been favorites, but of course that changed when they came under the shadow of the bishop's frown. Many of their friends fell away entirely, and the rest became cool and distant. Marget was a lovely girl of eighteen when the trouble came, and she had the best head in the village, and the most in it. She taught the harp, and earned all her clothes and pocket money by her own industry. But her scholars fell off one by one now; she was forgotten when there were dances and parties among the youth of the village; the young fellows stopped coming to the house, all except Wilhelm Meidling—and he could have been spared; she and her uncle were sad and forlorn in their neglect and disgrace, and the sunshine was gone out of their lives. Matters went worse and worse, all through the two years. Clothes were wearing out, bread was harder and harder to get. And now, at last, the very end was come. Solomon Isaacs had lent all the money he was willing to put on the house, and gave notice that to-morrow he would foreclose.

## CHAPTER II

THREE of us boys were always together, and had been so from the cradle, being fond of one another from the beginning, and this affection deepened as the years went on—Nikolaus Bauman, son of the principal judge of the local court; Seppi Wohlmeyer, son of the keeper of the principal inn, the "Golden Stag," which had a nice garden, with shade trees reaching down to the riverside, and pleasure boats for hire; and I was the third—Theodor Fischer, son of the church organist, who was also leader of the village musicians, teacher of the violin, composer, tax-collector of the commune, sexton, and in other ways a useful citizen, and respected by all. We knew the hills and the woods as well as the birds knew them; for we were always roaming them when we had leisure—at least, when we were not swimming or boating or fishing, or playing on the ice or sliding down hill.

And we had the run of the castle park, and very few had that. It was because we were pets of the oldest servingman in the castle—Felix Brandt; and often we went there, nights, to hear him talk about old times and strange things, and to smoke with him (he taught us that) and to drink coffee; for he had served in the wars, and was at the siege of Vienna; and there, when the Turks were defeated and driven away, among the captured things were bags of coffee, and the Turkish prisoners explained the character of it and how to make a pleasant drink out of it, and now he always kept coffee by him, to drink himself and also to astonish the ignorant with. When it stormed he kept us all night; and while it thundered and lightened outside he told us about ghosts and horrors of every kind, and of battles and murders and mutilations, and such things, and made it pleasant and cozy inside; and he told these things from his own experience largely. He had seen many ghosts in his time, and witches and enchanters, and once he was lost in a fierce storm at midnight in the mountains, and by the glare of the lightning had seen the Wild Huntsman rage on the blast with his specter dogs chasing after him through the driving cloud-rack. Also he had seen an incubus once, and several times he had seen the great bat that sucks the blood from the necks of people while they are asleep, fanning them softly with its wings and so keeping them drowsy till they die.

He encouraged us not to fear supernatural things, such as ghosts, and said they did no harm, but only wandered about because they were lonely and distressed and wanted kindly notice and compassion; and in time we learned not to be afraid, and even went down with him in the night to the haunted chamber in the dungeons of the castle. The ghost appeared only once, and it went by very dim to the sight and floated noiseless through the air, and then disappeared; and we scarcely trembled, he had taught us so well. He said it came up sometimes in the night and woke him by passing its clammy hand over his face, but it did him no hurt; it only wanted sympathy and notice. But the strangest thing was that he had seen angels—actual angels out of heaven—and had talked with them. They had no wings, and wore clothes, and talked and looked and acted just like any natural person, and you would never know them for angels except for the wonderful things they did which a mortal could not do, and the way they suddenly disappeared while you were talking with them, which was also a thing which no mortal could do. And he said they were pleasant and cheerful, not gloomy and melancholy, like ghosts.

It was after that kind of a talk one May night that we got up next morning and had a good breakfast with him and then went down and crossed the bridge and went away up into the hills on the left to a woody hill-top which was a favorite place of ours, and there we stretched out on the grass in the shade to rest and smoke and talk over these strange things, for they were in our minds yet, and impressing us. But we couldn't smoke, because we had been heedless and left our flint and steel behind.

Soon there came a youth strolling toward us through the trees, and he sat down and began to talk in a friendly way, just as if he knew us. But we did not answer him, for he was a stranger and we were not used to strangers and were shy of them. He had new and good clothes on, and was handsome and had a winning face and a pleasant voice, and was easy and graceful and unembarrassed, not slouchy and awkward and diffident, like other boys. We wanted to be friendly with him, but didn't know how to begin. Then I thought of the pipe, and wondered if it would be taken as kindly meant if I offered it to him. But I remembered that we had no fire, so I was sorry and disappointed. But he looked up bright and pleased, and said:

"Fire? Oh, that is easy; I will furnish it."

I was so astonished I couldn't speak; for I had not said anything. He took the pipe and blew his breath on it, and the tobacco glowed red, and spirals of blue smoke rose up. We jumped up and were going to run, for that was natural; and we did run a few steps, although he was yearningly pleading for us to stay, and giving us his word that he would not do us any harm, but only wanted to be friends with us and have company. So we stopped and stood, and wanted to go back, being full of curiosity and wonder, but afraid to venture. He went on coaxing, in his soft, persuasive way; and when we saw that the pipe did not blow up and nothing happened, our confidence returned by little and little, and presently our curiosity got to be stronger than our fear, and we ventured back—but slowly, and ready to fly at any alarm.

He was bent on putting us at ease, and he had the right art; one could not remain doubtful and timorous where a person was so earnest and simple and gentle, and talked so alluringly as he did; no, he won us over, and it was not long before we were content and comfortable and chatty, and glad we had found this new friend. When the feeling of constraint was all gone we asked him how he had learned to do that strange thing, and he said he hadn't learned it at all; it came natural to him—like other things—other curious things.

"What ones?"

"Oh, a number; I don't know how many."

"Will you let us see you do them?"

"Do—please!" the others said.

"You won't run away again?"

"No—indeed we won't. Please do. Won't you?"

"Yes, with pleasure; but you mustn't forget your promise, you know."

We said we wouldn't, and he went to a puddle and came back with water in a cup which he had made out of a leaf, and blew upon it and threw it out, and it was a lump of ice the shape of the cup. We were astonished and charmed, but not afraid any more; we were very glad to be there, and asked him to go on and do some more things. And he did. He said he would give us any kind of fruit we liked, whether it was in season or not. We all spoke at once:

"Orange!"

"Apple!"

"Grapes!"

"They are in your pockets," he said, and it was true. And they were of the best, too, and we ate them and wished we had more, though none of us said so.

"You will find them where those came from," he said, "and everything else your appetites call for; and you need not name the thing you wish; as long as I am with you, you have only to wish and find."

And he said true. There was never anything so wonderful and so interesting. Bread, cakes, sweets, nuts—whatever one wanted, it was there. He ate nothing himself, but sat and chatted, and did one curious thing after another to amuse us. He made a tiny toy squirrel out of clay, and it ran up a tree and sat on a limb overhead and barked down at us. Then he made a dog that was not much larger than a mouse, and it treed the squirrel and danced about the tree, excited and barking, and was as alive as any dog could be. It frightened the squirrel from tree to tree and followed it up until both were out of sight in the forest. He made birds out of clay and set them free, and they flew away, singing.

At last I made bold to ask him to tell us who he was.

"An angel," he said, quite simply, and set another bird free and clapped his hands and made it fly away.

A kind of awe fell upon us when we heard him say that, and we were afraid again; but he said we need not be troubled, there was no occasion for us to be afraid of an angel, and he liked us, anyway. He went on chatting as simply and unaffectedly as ever; and while he talked he made a crowd of little men and women the size of your finger, and they went diligently to work and cleared and leveled off a space a couple of yards square in the grass and began to build a cunning little castle in it, the women mixing the mortar and carrying it up the scaffoldings in pails on their heads, just as our work-women have always done, and the men laying the courses of masonry—five hundred of these toy people swarming briskly about and working diligently and wiping the sweat off their faces as natural as life.

In the absorbing interest of watching those five hundred little people make the castle grow step by step and course by course, and take shape and symmetry, that feeling and awe soon passed away and we were quite comfortable and at home again. We asked if we might make some people, and he said yes, and told Seppi to make some cannon for the walls, and told Nikolaus to make some halberdiers, with breastplates and greaves and helmets, and I was to make some cavalry, with horses, and in allotting these tasks he called us by our names, but did not say how he knew them. Then Seppi asked him what his own name was, and he said, tranquilly, "Satan," and held out a chip and caught a little woman on it who was falling from the scaffolding and put her back where she belonged, and said, "She is an idiot to step backward like that and not notice what she is about."

It caught us suddenly, that name did, and our work dropped out of our hands and broke to pieces—a cannon, a halberdier, and a horse. Satan laughed, and asked what was the matter. I said, "Nothing, only it seemed a strange name for an angel." He asked why.

"Because it's—it's—well, it's his name, you know."

"Yes—he is my uncle."

He said it placidly, but it took our breath for a moment and made our hearts beat. He did not seem to notice that, but mended our halberdiers and things with a touch, handing them to us finished, and said, "Don't you remember?—he was an angel himself, once."

"Yes—it's true," said Seppi; "I didn't think of that."

"Before the Fall he was blameless."

"Yes," said Nikolaus, "he was without sin."

"It is a good family—ours," said Satan; "there is not a better. He is the only member of it that has ever sinned."

I should not be able to make any one understand how exciting it all was. You know that kind of quiver that trembles around through you when you are seeing something so strange and enchanting and wonderful that it is just a fearful joy to be alive and look at it; and you know how you gaze, and your lips turn dry and your breath comes short, but you wouldn't be anywhere but there, not for the world. I was bursting to ask one question—I had it on my tongue's end and could hardly hold it back—but I was ashamed to ask it; it might be a rudeness. Satan set an ox down that he had been making, and smiled up at me and said:

"It wouldn't be a rudeness, and I should forgive it if it was. Have I seen him? Millions of times. From the time that I was a little child a thousand years old I was his second favorite among the nursery angels of our blood and lineage—to use a human phrase—yes, from that time until the Fall, eight thousand years, measured as you count time."

"Eight—thousand!"

"Yes." He turned to Seppi, and went on as if answering something that was in Seppi's mind: "Why, naturally I look like a boy, for that is what I am. With us what you call time is a spacious thing; it takes a long stretch of it to grow an angel to full age." There was a question in my mind, and he turned to me and answered it, "I am sixteen thousand years old—counting as you count." Then he turned to Nikolaus and said: "No, the Fall did not affect me nor the rest of the relationship. It was only he that I was named for who ate of the fruit of the tree and then beguiled the man and the woman with it. We others are still ignorant of sin; we are not able to commit it; we are without blemish, and shall abide in that estate always. We—" Two of the little workmen were quarreling, and in buzzing little bumblebee voices they were cursing and swearing at each other; now came blows and blood; then they locked themselves together in a life-and-death struggle. Satan reached out his hand and crushed the life out of them with his fingers, threw them away, wiped the red from his fingers on his handkerchief, and went on talking where he had left off: "We cannot do wrong; neither have we any disposition to do it, for we do not know what it is."

It seemed a strange speech, in the circumstances, but we barely noticed that, we were so shocked and grieved at the wanton murder he had committed—for murder it was, that was its true name, and it was without palliation or excuse, for the men had not wronged him in any way. It made us miserable, for we loved him, and had thought him so noble and so beautiful and gracious, and had honestly believed he was an angel; and to have him do this cruel thing—ah, it lowered him so, and we had had such pride in him. He went right on talking, just as if nothing had happened, telling about his travels, and the interesting things he had seen in the big worlds of our solar systems and of other solar systems far away in the remotenesses of space, and about the customs of the immortals that inhabit them, somehow fascinating us, enchanting us, charming us in spite of the pitiful scene that was now under our eyes, for the wives of the little dead men had found the crushed and shapeless bodies and were crying over them, and sobbing and lamenting, and a priest was kneeling there with his hands crossed upon his breast, praying; and crowds and crowds of pitying friends were massed about them, reverently uncovered, with their bare heads bowed, and many with the tears running down—a scene which Satan paid no attention to until the small noise of the weeping and praying began to annoy them, then he reached out and took the heavy board seat out of our swing and brought it down and mashed all those people into the earth just as if they had been flies, and went on talking just the same.

An angel, and kill a priest! An angel who did not know how to do wrong, and yet destroys in cold blood hundreds of helpless poor men and women who had never done him any harm! It made us sick to see that awful deed, and to think that none of those poor creatures was prepared except the priest, for none of them had ever heard a mass or seen a church. And we were witnesses; we had seen these murders done and it was our duty to tell, and let the law take its course.

But he went on talking right along, and worked his enchantments upon us again with that fatal music of his voice. He made us forget everything; we could only listen to him, and love him, and be his slaves, to do with us as he would. He made us drunk with the joy of being with him, and of looking into the heaven of his eyes, and of feeling the ecstasy that thrilled along our veins from the touch of his hand.

## CHAPTER III

THE Stranger had seen everything, he had been everywhere, he knew everything, and he forgot nothing. What another must study, he learned at a glance; there were no difficulties for him. And he made things live before you when he told about them. He saw the world made; he saw Adam created; he saw Samson surge against the pillars and bring the temple down in ruins about him; he saw Cæsar's death; he told of the daily life in heaven; he had seen the damned writhing in the red waves of hell; and he made us see all these things, and it was as if we were on the spot and looking at them with our own eyes. And we felt them, too, but there was no sign that they were anything to him beyond mere entertainments. Those visions of hell, those poor babes and women and girls and lads and men shrieking and supplicating in anguish—why, we could hardly bear it, but he was as bland about it as if it had been so many imitation rats in an artificial fire.

And always when he was talking about men and women here on the earth and their doings—even their grandest and sublimest—we were secretly ashamed, for his manner showed that to him they and their doings were of paltry poor consequence; often you would think he was talking about flies, if you didn't know. Once he even said, in so many words, that our people down here were quite interesting to him, notwithstanding they were so dull and ignorant and trivial and conceited, and so diseased and rickety, and such a shabby, poor, worthless lot all around. He said it in a quite matter-of-course way and without bitterness, just as a person might talk about bricks or manure or any other thing that was of no consequence and hadn't feelings. I could see he meant no offense, but in my thoughts I set it down as not very good manners.

"Manners!" he said. "Why, it is merely the truth, and truth is good manners; manners are a fiction. The castle is done. Do you like it?"

Any one would have been obliged to like it. It was lovely to look at, it was so shapely and fine, and so cunningly perfect in all its particulars, even to the little flags waving from the turrets. Satan said we must put the artillery in place now, and station the halberdiers and display the cavalry. Our men and horses were a spectacle to see, they were so little like what they were intended for; for, of course, we had no art in making such things. Satan said they were the worst he had seen; and when he touched them and made them alive, it was just ridiculous the way they acted, on account of their legs not being of uniform lengths. They reeled and sprawled around as if they were drunk, and endangered everybody's lives around them, and finally fell over and lay helpless and kicking. It made us all laugh, though it was a shameful thing to see. The guns were charged with dirt, to fire a salute, but they were so crooked and so badly made that they all burst when they went off, and killed some of the gunners and crippled the others. Satan said we would have a storm now, and an earthquake, if we liked, but we must stand off a piece, out of danger. We wanted to call the people away, too, but he said never mind them; they were of no consequence, and we could make more, some time or other, if we needed them.

A small storm-cloud began to settle down black over the castle, and the miniature lightning and thunder began to play, and the ground to quiver, and the wind to pipe and wheeze, and the rain to fall, and all the people flocked into the castle for shelter. The cloud settled down blacker and blacker, and one could see the castle only dimly through it; the lightning blazed out flash upon flash and pierced the castle and set it on fire, and the flames shone out red and fierce through the cloud, and the people came flying out, shrieking, but Satan brushed them back, paying no attention to our begging and crying and imploring; and in the midst of the howling of the wind and volleying of the thunder the magazine blew up, the earthquake rent the ground wide, and the castle's wreck and ruin tumbled into the chasm, which swallowed it from sight, and closed upon it, with all that innocent life, not one of the five hundred poor creatures escaping. Our hearts were broken; we could not keep from crying.

"Don't cry," Satan said; "they were of no value."

"But they are gone to hell!"

"Oh, it is no matter; we can make plenty more."

It was of no use to try to move him; evidently he was wholly without feeling, and could not understand. He was full of bubbling spirits, and as gay as if this were a wedding instead of a fiendish massacre. And he was bent on making us feel as he did, and of course his magic accomplished his desire. It was no trouble to him; he did whatever he pleased with us. In a little while we were dancing on that grave, and he was playing to us on a strange, sweet instrument which he took out of his pocket; and the music—but there is no music like that, unless perhaps in heaven, and that was where he brought it from, he said. It made one mad, for pleasure; and we could not take our eyes from him, and the looks that went out of our eyes came from our hearts, and their dumb speech was worship. He brought the dance from heaven, too, and the bliss of paradise was in it.

Presently he said he must go away on an errand. But we could not bear the thought of it, and clung to him, and pleaded with him to stay; and that pleased him, and he said so, and said he would not go yet, but would wait a little while and we would sit down and talk a few minutes longer; and he told us Satan was only his real name, and he was to be known by it to us alone, but he had chosen another one to be called by in the presence of others; just a common one, such as people have—Philip Traum.

It sounded so odd and mean for such a being! But it was his decision, and we said nothing; his decision was sufficient.

We had seen wonders this day; and my thoughts began to run on the pleasure it would be to tell them when I got home, but he noticed those thoughts, and said:

"No, all these matters are a secret among us four. I do not mind your trying to tell them, if you like, but I will protect your tongues, and nothing of the secret will escape from them."

It was a disappointment, but it couldn't be helped, and it cost us a sigh or two. We talked pleasantly along, and he was always reading our thoughts and responding to them, and it seemed to me that this was the most wonderful of all the things he did, but he interrupted my musings and said:

"No, it would be wonderful for you, but it is not wonderful for me. I am not limited like you. I am not subject to human conditions. I can measure and understand your human weaknesses, for I have studied them; but I have none of them. My flesh is not real, although it would seem firm to your touch; my clothes are not real; I am a spirit. Father Peter is coming. We looked around, but did not see any one. "He is not in sight yet, but you will see him presently."

"Do you know him, Satan?"

"No."

"Won't you talk with him when he comes? He is not ignorant and dull, like us, and he would so like to talk with you. Will you?"

"Another time, yes, but not now. I must go on my errand after a little. There he is now; you can see him. Sit still, and don't say anything."

We looked up and saw Father Peter approaching through the chestnuts. We three were sitting together in the grass, and Satan sat in front of us in the path. Father Peter came slowly along with his head down, thinking, and stopped within a couple of yards of us and took off his hat and got out his silk handkerchief, and stood there mopping his face and looking as if he were going to speak to us, but he didn't. Presently he muttered, "I can't think what brought me here; it seems as if I were in my study a minute ago—but I suppose I have been dreaming along for an hour and have come all this stretch without noticing; for I am not myself in these troubled days." Then he went mumbling along to himself and walked straight through Satan, just as if nothing were there. It made us catch our breath to see it. We had the impulse to cry out, the way you nearly always do when a startling thing happens, but something mysteriously restrained us and we remained quiet, only breathing fast. Then the trees hid Father Peter after a little, and Satan said:

"It is as I told you—I am only a spirit."

"Yes, one perceives it now," said Nikolaus, "but we are not spirits. It is plain he did not see you, but were we invisible, too? He looked at us, but he didn't seem to see us."

"No, none of us was visible to him, for I wished it so."

It seemed almost too good to be true, that we were actually seeing these romantic and wonderful things, and that it was not a dream. And there he sat, looking just like anybody—so natural and simple and charming, and chatting along again the same as ever, and—well, words cannot make you understand what we felt. It was an ecstasy; and an ecstasy is a thing that will not go into words; it feels like music, and one cannot tell about music so that another person can get the feeling of it. He was back in the old ages once more now, and making them live before us. He had seen so much, so much! It was just a wonder to look at him and try to think how it must seem to have such experience behind one.

But it made you seem sorrowfully trivial, and the creature of a day, and such a short and paltry day, too. And he didn't say anything to raise up your drooping pride—no, not a word. He always spoke of men in the same old indifferent way—just as one speaks of bricks and manure-piles and such things; you could see that they were of no consequence to him, one way or the other. He didn't mean to hurt us, you could see that; just as we don't mean to insult a brick when we disparage it; a brick's emotions are nothing to us; it never occurs to us to think whether it has any or not.

Once when he was bunching the most illustrious kings and conquerors and poets and prophets and pirates and beggars together—just a brick-pile—I was shamed into putting in a word for man, and asked him why he made so much difference between men and himself. He had to struggle with that a moment; he didn't seem to understand how I could ask such a strange question. Then he said:

"The difference between man and me? The difference between a mortal and an immortal? between a cloud and a spirit?" He picked up a wood-louse that was creeping along a piece of bark: "What is the difference between Cæsar and this?"

I said, "One cannot compare things which by their nature and by the interval between them are not comparable."

"You have answered your own question," he said. "I will expand it. Man is made of dirt—I saw him made. I am not made of dirt. Man is a museum of diseases, a home of impurities; he comes to-day and is gone to-morrow; he begins as dirt and departs as stench; I am of the aristocracy of the Imperishables. And man has the *Moral Sense.* You understand? He has the *Moral Sense.* That would seem to be difference enough between us, all by itself."

He stopped there, as if that settled the matter. I was sorry, for at that time I had but a dim idea of what the Moral Sense was. I merely knew that we were proud of having it, and when he talked like that about it, it wounded me, and I felt as a girl feels who thinks her dearest finery is being admired and then overhears strangers making fun of it. For a while we were all silent, and I, for one, was depressed. Then Satan began to chat again, and soon he was sparkling along in such a cheerful and vivacious vein that my spirits rose once more. He told some very cunning things that put us in a gale of laughter; and when he was telling about the time that Samson tied the torches to the foxes' tails and set them loose in the Philistines' corn, and Samson sitting on the fence slapping his thighs and laughing, with the tears running down his cheeks, and lost his balance and fell off the fence, the memory of that picture got him to laughing, too, and we did have a most lovely and jolly time. By and by he said:

"I am going on my errand now."

"Don't!" we all said. "Don't go; stay with us. You won't come back."

"Yes, I will; I give you my word."

"When? To-night? Say when."

"It won't be long. You will see."

"We like you."

"And I you. And as a proof of it I will show you something fine to see. Usually when I go I merely vanish; but now I will dissolve myself and let you see me do it."

He stood up, and it was quickly finished. He thinned away and thinned away until he was a soap-bubble, except that he kept his shape. You could see the bushes through him as clearly as you see things through a soap-bubble, and all over him played and flashed the delicate iridescent colors of the bubble, and along with them was that thing shaped like a window-sash which you always see on the globe of the bubble. You have seen a bubble strike the carpet and lightly bound along two or three times before it bursts. He did that. He sprang—touched the grass—bounded—floated along—touched again—and so on, and presently exploded—puff! and in his place was vacancy.

It was a strange and beautiful thing to see. We did not say anything, but sat wondering and dreaming and blinking; and finally Seppi roused up and said, mournfully sighing:

"I suppose none of it has happened."

Nikolaus sighed and said about the same.

I was miserable to hear them say it, for it was the same cold fear that was in my own mind. Then we saw poor old Father Peter wandering along back, with his head bent down, searching the ground. When he was pretty close to us he looked up and saw us, and said, "How long have you been here, boys?"

"A little while, Father."

"Then it is since I came by, and maybe you can help me. Did you come up by the path?"

"Yes, Father."

"That is good. I came the same way. I have lost my wallet. There wasn't much in it, but a very little is much to me, for it was all I had. I suppose you haven't seen anything of it?"

"No, Father, but we will help you hunt."

"It is what I was going to ask you. Why, here it is!"

We hadn't noticed it; yet there it lay, right where Satan stood when he began to melt—if he did melt and it wasn't a delusion. Father Peter picked it up and looked very much surprised.

"It is mine," he said, "but not the contents. This is fat; mine was flat; mine was light; this is heavy." He opened it; it was stuffed as full as it could hold with gold coins. He let us gaze our fill; and of course we did gaze, for we had never seen so much money at one time before. All our mouths came open to say "Satan did it!" but nothing came out. There it was, you see—we couldn't tell what Satan didn't want told; he had said so himself.

"Boys, did you do this?"

It made us laugh. And it made him laugh, too, as soon as he thought what a foolish question it was.

"Who has been here?"

Our mouths came open to answer, but stood so for a moment, because we couldn't say "Nobody," for it wouldn't be true, and the right word didn't seem to come; then I thought of the right one, and said it:

"Not a human being."

"That is so," said the others, and let their mouths go shut.

"It is not so," said Father Peter, and looked at us very severely. "I came by here a while ago, and there was no one here, but that is nothing; some one has been here since. I don't mean to say that the person didn't pass here before you came, and I don't mean to say you saw him, but some one did pass, that I know. On your honor—you saw no one?"

"Not a human being."

"That is sufficient; I know you are telling me the truth."

He began to count the money on the path, we on our knees eagerly helping to stack it in little piles.

"It's eleven hundred ducats odd!" he said. "Oh dear! if it were only mine—and I need it so!" and his voice broke and his lips quivered.

"It is yours, sir!" we all cried out at once, "every heller!"

"No—it isn't mine. Only four ducats are mine; the rest . . . !" He fell to dreaming, poor old soul, and caressing some of the coins in his hands, and forgot where he was, sitting there on his heels with his old gray head bare; it was pitiful to see. "No," he said, waking up, "it isn't mine. I can't account for it. I think some enemy . . . it must be a trap."

Nikolaus said: "Father Peter, with the exception of the astrologer you haven't a real enemy in the village—nor Marget, either. And not even a half-enemy that's rich enough to chance eleven hundred ducats to do you a mean turn. I'll ask you if that's so or not?"

He couldn't get around that argument, and it cheered him up. "But it isn't mine, you see—it isn't mine, in any case."

He said it in a wistful way, like a person that wouldn't be sorry, but glad, if anybody would contradict him.

"It is yours, Father Peter, and we are witness to it. Aren't we, boys?"

"Yes, we are—and we'll stand by it, too."

"Bless your hearts, you do almost persuade me; you do, indeed. If I had only a hundred-odd ducats of it! The house is mortgaged for it, and we've no home for our heads if we don't pay to-morrow. And that four ducats is all we've got in the—"

"It's yours, every bit of it, and you've got to take it—we are bail that it's all right. Aren't we, Theodor? Aren't we, Seppi?"

We two said yes, and Nikolaus stuffed the money back into the shabby old wallet and made the owner take it. So he said he would use two hundred of it, for his house was good enough security for that, and would put the rest at interest till the rightful owner came for it; and on our side we must sign a paper showing how he got the money—a paper to show to the villagers as proof that he had not got out of his troubles dishonestly.

## CHAPTER IV

IT made immense talk next day, when Father Peter paid Solomon Isaacs in gold and left the rest of the money with him at interest. Also, there was a pleasant change; many people called at the house to congratulate him, and a number of cool old friends became kind and friendly again; and, to top all, Marget was invited to a party.

And there was no mystery; Father Peter told the whole circumstance just as it happened, and said he could not account for it, only it was the plain hand of Providence, so far as he could see.

One or two shook their heads and said privately it looked more like the hand of Satan; and really that seemed a surprisingly good guess for ignorant people like that. Some came slyly buzzing around and tried to coax us boys to come out and "tell the truth;" and promised they wouldn't ever tell, but only wanted to know for their own satisfaction, because the whole thing was so curious. They even wanted to buy the secret, and pay money for it; and if we could have invented something that would answer—but we couldn't; we hadn't the ingenuity, so we had to let the chance go by, and it was a pity.

We carried that secret around without any trouble, but the other one, the big one, the splendid one, burned the very vitals of us, it was so hot to get out and we so hot to let it out and astonish people with it. But we had to keep it in; in fact, it kept itself in. Satan said it would, and it did. We went off every day and got to ourselves in the woods so that we could talk about Satan, and really that was the only subject we thought of or cared anything about; and day and night we watched for him and hoped he would come, and we got more and more impatient all the time. We hadn't any interest in the other boys any more, and wouldn't take part in their games and enterprises. They seemed so tame, after Satan; and their doings so trifling and commonplace after his adventures in antiquity and the constellations, and his miracles and meltings and explosions, and all that.

During the first day we were in a state of anxiety on account of one thing, and we kept going to Father Peter's house on one pretext or another to keep track of it. That was the gold coin; we were afraid it would crumble and turn to dust, like fairy money. If it did— But it didn't. At the end of the day no complaint had been made about it, so after that we were satisfied that it was real gold, and dropped the anxiety out of our minds.

There was a question which we wanted to ask Father Peter, and finally we went there the second evening, a little diffidently, after drawing straws, and I asked it as casually as I could, though it did not sound as casual as I wanted, because I didn't know how:

"What is the Moral Sense, sir?"

He looked down, surprised, over his great spectacles, and said, "Why, it is the faculty which enables us to distinguish good from evil."

It threw some light, but not a glare, and I was a little disappointed, also to some degree embarrassed. He was waiting for me to go on, so, in default of anything else to say, I asked, "Is it valuable?"

"Valuable? Heavens! lad, it is the one thing that lifts man above the beasts that perish and makes him heir to immortality!"

This did not remind me of anything further to say, so I got out, with the other boys, and we went away with that indefinite sense you have often had of being filled but not fatted. They wanted me to explain, but I was tired.

We passed out through the parlor, and there was Marget at the spinnet teaching Marie Lueger. So one of the deserting pupils was back; and an influential one, too; the others would follow. Marget jumped up and ran and thanked us again, with tears in her eyes—this was the third time—for saving her and her uncle from being turned into the street, and we told her again we hadn't done it; but that was her way, she never could be grateful enough for anything a person did for her; so we let her have her say. And as we passed through the garden, there was Wilhelm Meidling sitting there waiting, for it was getting toward the edge of the evening, and he would be asking Marget to take a walk along the river with him when she was done with the lesson. He was a young lawyer, and succeeding fairly well and working his way along, little by little. He was very fond of Marget, and she of him. He had not deserted along with the others, but had stood his ground all through. His faithfulness was not lost on

Marget and her uncle. He hadn't so very much talent, but he was handsome and good, and these are a kind of talents themselves and help along. He asked us how the lesson was getting along, and we told him it was about done. And maybe it was so; we didn't know anything about it, but we judged it would please him, and it did, and didn't cost us anything.

## CHAPTER V

ON the fourth day comes the astrologer from his crumbling old tower up the valley, where he had heard the news, I reckon. He had a private talk with us, and we told him what we could, for we were mightily in dread of him. He sat there studying and studying awhile to himself; then he asked:

"How many ducats did you say?"

"Eleven hundred and seven, sir."

Then he said, as if he were talking to himself: "It is ver-y singular. Yes . . . very strange. A curious coincidence." Then he began to ask questions, and went over the whole ground from the beginning, we answering. By and by he said: "Eleven hundred and six ducats. It is a large sum."

"Seven," said Seppi, correcting him.

"Oh, seven, was it? Of course a ducat more or less isn't of consequence, but you said eleven hundred and six before."

It would not have been safe for us to say he was mistaken, but we knew he was. Nikolaus said, "We ask pardon for the mistake, but we meant to say seven."

"Oh, it is no matter, lad; it was merely that I noticed the discrepancy. It is several days, and you cannot be expected to remember precisely. One is apt to be inexact when there is no particular circumstance to impress the count upon the memory."

"But there was one, sir," said Seppi, eagerly.

"What was it, my son?" asked the astrologer, indifferently.

"First, we all counted the piles of coin, each in turn, and all made it the same—eleven hundred and six. But I had slipped one out, for fun, when the count began, and now I slipped it back and said, 'I think there is a mistake—there are eleven hundred and seven; let us count again.' We did, and of course I was right. They were astonished; then I told how it came about."

The astrologer asked us if this was so, and we said it was.

"That settles it," he said. "I know the thief now. Lads, the money was stolen."

Then he went away, leaving us very much troubled, and wondering what he could mean. In about an hour we found out; for by that time it was all over the village that Father Peter had been arrested for stealing a great sum of money from the astrologer. Everybody's tongue was loose and going. Many said it was not in Father Peter's character and must be a mistake; but the others shook their heads and said misery and want could drive a suffering man to almost anything. About one detail there were no differences; all agreed that Father Peter's account of how the money came into his hands was just about unbelievable—it had such an impossible look. They said it might have come into the astrologer's hands in some such way, but into Father Peter's, never! Our characters began to suffer now. We were Father Peter's only witnesses; how much did he probably pay us to back up his fantastic tale? People talked that kind of talk to us pretty freely and frankly, and were full of scoffings when we begged them to believe really we had told only the truth. Our parents were harder on us than any one else. Our fathers said we were disgracing our families, and they commanded us to purge ourselves of our lie, and there was no limit to their anger when we continued to say we had spoken true. Our mothers cried over us and begged us to give back our bribe and get back our honest names and save our families from shame, and come out and honorably confess. And at last we were so worried and harassed that we tried to tell the whole thing, Satan and all—but no, it wouldn't come out. We were hoping and longing all the time that Satan would come and help us out of our trouble, but there was no sign of him.

Within an hour after the astrologer's talk with us, Father Peter was in prison and the money sealed up and in the hands of the officers of the law. The money was in a bag, and Solomon Isaacs said he had not touched it since he had counted it; his oath was taken that it was the same money, and that the amount was eleven hundred and seven ducats. Father Peter claimed trial by the ecclesiastical court, but our other priest, Father Adolf, said an ecclesiastical court hadn't jurisdiction over a suspended priest. The bishop upheld him. That settled it; the case would go to trial in the civil court. The court would not sit for some time to come. Wilhelm Meidling would be Father Peter's lawyer and do the best he could, of course, but he told us privately that a weak case on his side and all the power and prejudice on the other made the outlook bad.

So Marget's new happiness died a quick death. No friends came to condole with her, and none were expected; an unsigned note withdrew her invitation to the party. There would be no scholars to take lessons. How could she support herself? She could remain in the house, for the mortgage was paid off, though the government and not poor Solomon Isaacs had the mortgage-money in its grip for the present. Old Ursula, who was cook, chambermaid, housekeeper, laundress, and everything else for Father Peter, and had been Marget's nurse in earlier years, said God would provide. But she said that from habit, for she was a good Christian. She meant to help in the providing, to make sure, if she could find a way.

We boys wanted to go and see Marget and show friendliness for her, but our parents were afraid of offending the community and wouldn't let us. The astrologer was going around inflaming everybody against Father Peter, and saying he was an abandoned thief and had stolen eleven hundred and seven gold ducats from him. He said he knew he was a thief from that fact, for it was exactly the sum he had lost and which Father Peter pretended he had "found."

In the afternoon of the fourth day after the catastrophe old Ursula appeared at our house and asked for some washing to do, and begged my mother to keep this secret, to save Marget's pride, who would stop this project if she found it out, yet Marget had not enough to eat and was growing weak. Ursula was growing weak herself, and showed it; and she ate of the food that was offered her like a starving person, but could not be persuaded to carry any home, for Marget would not eat charity food. She took some clothes down to the stream to wash them, but we saw from the window that handling the bat was too much for her strength; so she was called back and a trifle of money offered her, which she was afraid to take lest Marget should suspect; then she took it, saying she would explain that she found it in the road. To keep it from being a lie and damning her soul, she got me to drop it while she watched; then she went along by there and found it, and exclaimed with surprise and joy, and picked it up and went her way. Like the rest of the village, she could tell every-day lies fast enough and without taking any precautions against fire and brimstone on their account; but this was a new kind of lie, and it had a dangerous look because she hadn't had any practice in it. After a week's practice it wouldn't have given her any trouble. It is the way we are made.

I was in trouble, for how would Marget live? Ursula could not find a coin in the road every day—perhaps not even a second one. And I was ashamed, too, for not having been near Marget, and she so in need of friends; but that was my parents' fault, not mine, and I couldn't help it.

I was walking along the path, feeling very down-hearted, when a most cheery and tingling freshening-up sensation went rippling through me, and I was too glad for any words, for I knew by that sign that Satan was by. I had noticed it before. Next moment he was alongside of me and I was telling him all my trouble and what had been happening to Marget and her uncle. While we were talking we turned a curve and saw old Ursula resting in the shade of a tree, and she had a lean stray kitten in her lap and was petting it. I asked her where she got it, and she said it came out of the woods and followed her; and she said it probably hadn't any mother or any friends and she was going to take it home and take care of it. Satan said:

"I understand you are very poor. Why do you want to add another mouth to feed? Why don't you give it to some rich person?"

Ursula bridled at this and said: "Perhaps you would like to have it. You must be rich, with your fine clothes and quality airs." Then she sniffed and said: "Give it to the rich—the idea! The rich don't care for anybody but themselves; it's only the poor that have feeling for the poor, and help them. The poor and God. God will provide for this kitten."

"What makes you think so?"

Ursula's eyes snapped with anger. "Because I know it!" she said. "Not a sparrow falls to the ground without His seeing it."

"But it falls, just the same. What good is seeing it fall?"

Old Ursula's jaws worked, but she could not get any word out for the moment, she was so horrified. When she got her tongue she stormed out, "Go about your business, you puppy, or I will take a stick to you!"

I could not speak, I was so scared. I knew that with his notions about the human race Satan would consider it a matter of no consequence to strike her dead, there being "plenty more;" but my tongue stood still, I could give her no warning. But nothing happened; Satan remained tranquil—tranquil and indifferent. I suppose he could not be insulted by Ursula any more than the king could be insulted by a tumble-bug. The old woman jumped to her feet when she made her remark, and did it as briskly as a young girl. It had been many years since she had done the like of that. That was Satan's influence; he was a fresh breeze to the weak and the sick, wherever he came. His presence affected even the lean kitten, and it skipped to the ground and began to chase a leaf. This surprised Ursula, and she stood looking at the creature and nodding her head wonderingly, her anger quite forgotten.

"What's come over it?" she said. "Awhile ago it could hardly walk."

"You have not seen a kitten of that breed before," said Satan.

Ursula was not proposing to be friendly with the mocking stranger, and she gave him an ungentle look and retorted: "Who asked you to come here and pester me, I'd like to know? And what do you know about what I've seen and what I haven't seen?"

"You haven't seen a kitten with the hair-spines on its tongue pointing to the front, have you?"

"No—nor you, either."

"Well, examine this one and see."

Ursula was become pretty spry, but the kitten was spryer, and she could not catch it, and had to give it up. Then Satan said:

"Give it a name, and maybe it will come."

Ursula tried several names, but the kitten was not interested.

"Call it Agnes. Try that."

The creature answered to the name and came. Ursula examined its tongue. "Upon my word, it's true!" she said. "I have not seen this kind of a cat before. Is it yours?"

"No."

"Then how did you know its name so pat?"

"Because all cats of that breed are named Agnes; they will not answer to any other."

Ursula was impressed. "It is the most wonderful thing!" Then a shadow of trouble came into her face, for her superstitions were aroused, and she reluctantly put the creature down, saying: "I suppose I must let it go; I am not afraid—no, not exactly that, though the priest—well, I've heard people—indeed, many people . . . And, besides, it is quite well now and can take care of itself." She sighed, and turned to go, murmuring: "It is such a pretty one, too, and would be such company—and the house is so sad and lonesome these troubled days . . . Miss Marget so mournful and just a shadow, and the old master shut up in jail."

"It seems a pity not to keep it," said Satan.

Ursula turned quickly—just as if she were hoping some one would encourage her.

"Why?" she asked, wistfully.

"Because this breed brings luck."

"Does it? Is it true? Young man, do you know it to be true? How does it bring luck?

"Well, it brings money, anyway."

Ursula looked disappointed. "Money? A cat bring money? The idea! You could never sell it here; people do not buy cats here; one can't even give them away." She turned to go.

"I don't mean sell it. I mean have an income from it. This kind is called the Lucky Cat. Its owner finds four silver groschen in his pocket every morning.

I saw the indignation rising in the old woman's face. She was insulted. This boy was making fun of her. That was her thought. She thrust her hands into her pockets and straightened up to give him a piece of her mind. Her temper was all up, and hot. Her mouth came open and let out three words of a bitter sentence, . . . then it fell silent, and the anger in her face turned to surprise or wonder or fear, or something, and she slowly brought out her hands from her pockets and opened them and held them so. In one was my piece of money, in the other lay four silver groschen. She gazed a little while, perhaps to see if the groschen would vanish away; then she said, fervently:

"It's true—it's true—and I'm ashamed and beg forgiveness, O dear master and benefactor!" And she ran to Satan and kissed his hand, over and over again, according to the Austrian custom.

In her heart she probably believed it was a witch-cat and an agent of the Devil; but no matter, it was all the more certain to be able to keep its contract and furnish a daily good living for the family, for in matters of finance even the piousest of our peasants would have more confidence in an arrangement with the Devil than with an archangel. Ursula started homeward, with Agnes in her arms, and I said I wished I had her privilege of seeing Marget.

Then I caught my breath, for we were there. There in the parlor, and Marget standing looking at us, astonished. She was feeble and pale, but I knew that those conditions would not last in Satan's atmosphere, and it turned out so. I introduced Satan—that is, Philip Traum—and we sat down and talked. There was no constraint. We were simple folk, in our village, and when a stranger was a pleasant person we were soon friends. Marget wondered how we got in without her hearing us. Traum said the door was open, and we walked in and waited until she should turn around and greet us. This was not true; no door was open; we entered through the walls or the roof or down the chimney, or somehow; but no matter, what Satan wished a person to believe, the person was sure to believe, and so Marget was quite satisfied with that explanation. And then the main part of her mind was on Traum, anyway; she couldn't keep her eyes off him, he was so beautiful. That gratified me, and made me proud. I hoped he would show off some, but he didn't. He seemed only interested in being friendly and telling lies. He said he was an orphan. That made Marget pity him. The water came into her eyes. He said he had never known his mamma; she passed away while he was a young thing; and said his papa was in shattered health, and had no property to speak of—in fact, none of any earthly value—but he had an uncle in business down in the tropics, and he was very well off and had a monopoly, and it was from this uncle that he drew his support. The very mention of a kind uncle was enough to remind Marget of her own, and her eyes filled again. She said she hoped their two uncles would meet, some day. It made me shudder. Philip said he hoped so, too; and that made me shudder again.

"Maybe they will," said Marget. "Does your uncle travel much?"

"Oh yes, he goes all about; he has business everywhere."

And so they went on chatting, and poor Marget forgot her sorrow for one little while, anyway. It was probably the only really bright and cheery hour she had known lately. I saw she liked Philip, and I knew she would. And when he told her he was studying for the ministry I could see that she liked him better than ever. And then, when he promised to get her admitted to the jail so that she could see her uncle, that was the capstone. He said he would give the guards a little present, and she must always go in the evening after dark, and say nothing, "but just show this paper and pass in, and show it again when you come out"—and he scribbled some queer marks on the paper and gave it to her, and she was ever so thankful, and right away was in a fever for the sun to go down; for in that old, cruel time prisoners were not allowed to see their friends, and sometimes they spent years in the jails without ever seeing a friendly face. I judged that the marks on the paper were an enchantment, and that the guards would not know what they were doing, nor have any memory of it afterward; and that was indeed the way of it. Ursula put her head in at the door now and said:

"Supper's ready, miss." Then she saw us and looked frightened, and motioned me to come to her, which I did, and she asked if we had told about the cat. I said no, and she was relieved, and said please don't; for if Miss Marget knew, she would think it was an unholy cat and would send for a priest and have its gifts all purified out of it, and then there wouldn't be any more dividends. So I said we wouldn't tell, and she was satisfied. Then I was beginning to say good-by to Marget, but Satan interrupted and said, ever so politely—well, I don't remember just the words, but anyway he as good as invited himself to supper, and me, too. Of course Marget was miserably embarrassed, for she had no reason to suppose there would be half enough for a sick bird. Ursula heard him, and she came straight into the room, not a bit pleased. At first she was astonished to see Marget looking so fresh and rosy, and said so; then she spoke up in her native tongue, which was Bohemian, and said—as I learned afterward—"Send him away, Miss Marget; there's not victuals enough."

Before Marget could speak, Satan had the word, and was talking back to Ursula in her own language

—which was a surprise to her, and for her mistress, too. He said, "Didn't I see you down the road awhile ago?"

"Yes, sir."

"Ah, that pleases me; I see you remember me." He stepped to her and whispered: "I told you it is a Lucky Cat. Don't be troubled; it will provide."

That sponged the slate of Ursula's feelings clean of its anxieties, and a deep, financial joy shone in her eyes. The cat's value was augmenting. It was getting full time for Marget to take some sort of notice of Satan's invitation, and she did it in the best way, the honest way that was natural to her. She said she had little to offer, but that we were welcome if we would share it with her.

We had supper in the kitchen, and Ursula waited at table. A small fish was in the frying-pan, crisp and brown and tempting, and one could see that Marget was not expecting such respectable food as this. Ursula brought it, and Marget divided it between Satan and me, declining to take any of it herself; and was beginning to say she did not care for fish to-day, but she did not finish the remark. It was because she noticed that another fish had appeared in the pan. She looked surprised, but did not say anything. She probably meant to inquire of Ursula about this later. There were other surprises: flesh and game and wines and fruits—things which had been strangers in that house lately; but Marget made no exclamations, and now even looked unsurprised, which was Satan's influence, of course. Satan talked right along, and was entertaining, and made the time pass pleasantly and cheerfully; and although he told a good many lies, it was no harm in him, for he was only an angel and did not know any better. They do not know right from wrong; I knew this, because I remembered what he had said about it. He got on the good side of Ursula. He praised her to Marget, confidentially, but speaking just loud enough for Ursula to hear. He said she was a fine woman, and he hoped some day to bring her and his uncle together. Very soon Ursula was mincing and simpering around in a ridiculous girly way, and smoothing out her gown and prinking at herself like a foolish old hen, and all the time pretending she was not hearing what Satan was saying. I was ashamed, for it showed us to be what Satan considered us, a silly race and trivial. Satan said his uncle entertained a great deal, and to have a clever woman presiding over the festivities would double the attractions of the place.

"But your uncle is a gentleman, isn't he?" asked Marget.

"Yes," said Satan indifferently; "some even call him a Prince, out of compliment, but he is not bigoted; to him personal merit is everything, rank nothing."

My hand was hanging down by my chair; Agnes came along and licked it; by this act a secret was revealed. I started to say, "It is all a mistake; this is just a common, ordinary cat; the hair-needles on her tongue point inward, not outward." But the words did not come, because they couldn't. Satan smiled upon me, and I understood.

When it was dark Marget took food and wine and fruit, in a basket, and hurried away to the jail, and Satan and I walked toward my home. I was thinking to myself that I should like to see what the inside of the jail was like; Satan overheard the thought, and the next moment we were in the jail. We were in the torture-chamber, Satan said. The rack was there, and the other instruments, and there was a smoky lantern or two hanging on the walls and helping to make the place look dim and dreadful. There were people there—and executioners—but as they took no notice of us, it meant that we were invisible. A young man lay bound, and Satan said he was suspected of being a heretic, and the executioners were about to inquire into it. They asked the man to confess to the charge, and he said he could not, for it was not true. Then they drove splinter after splinter under his nails, and he shrieked with the pain. Satan was not disturbed, but I could not endure it, and had to be whisked out of there. I was faint and sick, but the fresh air revived me, and we walked toward my home. I said it was a brutal thing.

"No, it was a human thing. You should not insult the brutes by such a misuse of that word; they have not deserved it," and he went on talking like that. "It is like your paltry race—always lying, always claiming virtues which it hasn't got, always denying them to the higher animals, which alone possess them. No brute ever does a cruel thing—that is the monopoly of those with the Moral Sense. When a brute inflicts pain he does it innocently; it is not wrong; for him there is no such thing as wrong. And he does not inflict pain for the pleasure of inflicting it—only man does that. Inspired by that mongrel Moral Sense of his! A sense whose function is to distinguish between right and wrong, with liberty to choose which of them he will do. Now what advantage can he get out of that? He is always choosing, and in nine cases out of ten he prefers the wrong. There shouldn't be any wrong; and without the Moral Sense there couldn't be any. And yet he is such an unreasoning creature that he is not able to perceive that the Moral Sense degrades him to the bottom layer of animated beings and is a shameful possession. Are you feeling better? Let me show you something."

## CHAPTER VI

IN a moment we were in a French village. We walked through a great factory of some sort, where men and women and little children were toiling in heat and dirt and a fog of dust; and they were clothed in rags, and drooped at their work, for they were worn and half starved, and weak and drowsy. Satan said:

"It is some more Moral Sense. The proprietors are rich, and very holy; but the wage they pay to these poor brothers and sisters of theirs is only enough to keep them from dropping dead with hunger. The work-hours are fourteen per day, winter and summer—from six in the morning till eight at night—little children and all. And they walk to and from the pigsties which they inhabit—four miles each way, through mud and slush, rain, snow, sleet, and storm, daily, year in and year out. They get four hours of sleep. They kennel together, three families in a room, in unimaginable filth and stench; and disease comes, and they die off like flies. Have they committed a crime, these mangy things? No. What have they done, that they are punished so? Nothing at all, except getting themselves born into your foolish race. You have seen how they treat a misdoer there in the jail; now you see how they treat the innocent and the worthy. Is your race logical? Are these ill-smelling innocents better off than that heretic? Indeed, no; his punishment is trivial compared with theirs. They broke him on the wheel and smashed him to rags and pulp after we left, and he is dead now, and free of your precious race; but these poor slaves here—why, they have been dying for years, and some of them will not escape from life for years to come. It is the Moral Sense which teaches the factory proprietors the difference between right and wrong—you perceive the result. They think themselves better than dogs. Ah, you are such an illogical, unreasoning race! And paltry—oh, unspeakably!"

Then he dropped all seriousness and just overstrained himself making fun of us, and deriding our pride in our warlike deeds, our great heroes, our imperishable fames, our mighty kings, our ancient aristocracies, our venerable history—and laughed and laughed till it was enough to make a person sick to hear him; and finally he sobered a little and said, "But, after all, it is not all ridiculous; there is a sort of pathos about it when one remembers how few are your days, how childish your pomps, and what shadows you are!"

Presently all things vanished suddenly from my sight, and I knew what it meant. The next moment we were walking along in our village; and down toward the river I saw the twinkling lights of the Golden Stag. Then in the dark I heard a joyful cry:

"He's come again!"

It was Seppi Wohlmeyer. He had felt his blood leap and his spirits rise in a way that could mean only one thing, and he knew Satan was near, although it was too dark to see him. He came to us, and we walked along together, and Seppi poured out his gladness like water. It was as if he were a lover and had found his sweetheart who had been lost. Seppi was a smart and animated boy, and had enthusiasm and expression, and was a contrast to Nikolaus and me. He was full of the last new mystery, now—the disappearance of Hans Oppert, the village loafer. People were beginning to be curious about it, he said. He did not say anxious—curious was the right word, and strong enough. No one had seen Hans for a couple of days.

"Not since he did that brutal thing, you know," he said.

"What brutal thing?" It was Satan that asked.

"Well, he is always clubbing his dog, which is a good dog, and his only friend, and is faithful, and loves him, and does no one any harm; and two days ago he was at it again, just for nothing—just for pleasure—and the dog was howling and begging, and Theodor and I begged, too, but he threatened us, and struck the dog again with all his might and knocked one of his eyes out, and he said to us, 'There, I hope you are satisfied now; that's what you have got for him by your damned meddling'—and he laughed, the heartless brute." Seppi's voice trembled with pity and anger. I guessed what Satan would say, and he said it.

"There is that misused word again—that shabby slander. Brutes do not act like that, but only men."

"Well, it was inhuman, anyway."

"No, it wasn't, Seppi; it was human—quite distinctly human. It is not pleasant to hear you libel the higher animals by attributing to them dispositions which they are free from, and which are found nowhere but in the human heart. None of the higher animals is tainted with the disease called the Moral Sense. Purify your language, Seppi; drop those lying phrases out of it."

He spoke pretty sternly—for him—and I was sorry I hadn't warned Seppi to be more particular about the word he used. I knew how he was feeling. He would not want to offend Satan; he would rather offend all his kin. There was an uncomfortable silence, but relief soon came, for that poor dog came along now, with his eye hanging down, and went straight to Satan, and began to moan and mutter brokenly, and Satan began to answer in the same way, and it was plain that they were talking together in the dog language. We all sat down in the grass, in the moonlight, for the clouds were breaking away now, and Satan took the dog's head in his lap and put the eye back in its place, and the dog was comfortable, and he wagged his tail and licked Satan's hand, and looked thankful and said the same; I knew he was saying it, though I did not understand the words. Then the two talked together a bit, and Satan said:

"He says his master was drunk."

"Yes, he was," said we.

"And an hour later he fell over the precipice there beyond the Cliff Pasture."

"We know the place; it is three miles from here."

"And the dog has been often to the village, begging people to go there, but he was only driven away and not listened to."

We remembered it, but hadn't understood what he wanted.

"He only wanted help for the man who had misused him, and he thought only of that, and has had no food nor sought any. He has watched by his master two nights. What do you think of your race? Is heaven reserved for it, and this dog ruled out, as your teachers tell you? Can your race add anything to this dog's stock of morals and magnanimities?" He spoke to the creature, who jumped up, eager and happy, and apparently ready for orders and impatient to execute them. "Get some men; go with the dog—he will show you that carrion; and take a priest along to arrange about insurance, for death is near."

With the last word he vanished, to our sorrow and disappointment. We got the men and Father Adolf, and we saw the man die. Nobody cared but the dog; he mourned and grieved, and licked the dead face, and could not be comforted. We buried him where he was, and without a coffin, for he had no money, and no friend but the dog. If we had been an hour earlier the priest would have been in time to send that poor creature to heaven, but now he was gone down into the awful fires, to burn forever. It seemed such a pity that in a world where so many people have difficulty to put in their time, one little hour could not have been spared for this poor creature who needed it so much, and to whom it would have made the difference between eternal joy and eternal pain. It gave an appalling idea of the value of an hour, and I thought I could never waste one again without remorse and terror. Seppi was depressed and grieved, and said it must be so much better to be a dog and not run such awful risks. We took this one home with us and kept him for our own. Seppi had a very good thought as we were walking along, and it cheered us up and made us feel much better. He said the dog had forgiven the man that had wronged him so, and maybe God would accept that absolution.

There was a very dull week, now, for Satan did not come, nothing much was going on, and we boys could not venture to go and see Marget, because the nights were moonlit and our parents might find us out if we tried. But we came across Ursula a couple of times taking a walk in the meadows beyond the river to air the cat, and we learned from her that things were going well. She had natty new clothes on and bore a prosperous look. The four groschen a day were arriving without a break, but were not being spent for food and wine and such things—the cat attended to all that.

Marget was enduring her forsakenness and isolation fairly well, all things considered, and was cheerful, by help of Wilhelm Meidling. She spent an hour or two every night in the jail with her uncle, and had fattened him up with the cat's contributions. But she was curious to know more about Philip Traum, and hoped I would bring him again. Ursula was curious about him herself, and asked a good many questions about his uncle. It made the boys laugh, for I had told them the nonsense Satan had been stuffing her with. She got no satisfaction out of us, our tongues being tied.

Ursula gave us a small item of information: money being plenty now, she had taken on a servant to help about the house and run errands. She tried to tell it in a commonplace, matter-of-course way, but she was so set up by it and so vain of it that her pride in it leaked out pretty plainly. It was beautiful to see her veiled delight in this grandeur, poor old thing, but when we heard the name of the servant we wondered if she had been altogether wise; for although we were young, and often thoughtless, we had fairly good perception on some matters. This boy was Gottfried Narr, a dull, good creature, with no harm in him and nothing against him personally; still, he was under a cloud, and properly so, for it had not been six months since a social blight had mildewed the family—his grandmother had been burned as a witch. When that kind of a malady is in the blood it does not always come out with just one burning. Just now was not a good time for Ursula and Marget to be having dealings with a member of such a family, for the witch-terror had risen higher during the past year than it had ever reached in the memory of the oldest villagers. The mere mention of a witch was almost enough to frighten us out of our wits. This was natural enough, because of late years there were more kinds of witches than there used to be; in old times it had been only old women, but of late years they were of all ages—even children of eight and nine; it was getting so that anybody might turn out to be a familiar of the Devil—age and sex hadn't anything to do with it. In our little region we had tried to extirpate the witches, but the more of them we burned the more of the breed rose up in their places.

Once, in a school for girls only ten miles away, the teachers found that the back of one of the girls was all red and inflamed, and they were greatly frightened, believing it to be the Devil's marks. The girl was scared, and begged them not to denounce her, and said it was only fleas; but of course it would not do to let the matter rest there. All the girls were examined, and eleven out of the fifty were badly marked, the rest less so. A commission was appointed, but the eleven only cried for their mothers and would not confess. Then they were shut up, each by herself, in the dark, and put on black bread and water for ten days and nights; and by that time they were haggard and wild, and their eyes were dry and they did not cry any more, but only sat and mumbled, and would not take the food. Then one of them confessed, and said they had often ridden through the air on broomsticks to the witches' Sabbath, and in a bleak place high up in the mountains had danced and drunk and caroused with several hundred other witches and the Evil One, and all had conducted themselves in a scandalous way and had reviled the priests and blasphemed God. That is what she said—not in narrative form, for she was not able to remember any of the details without having them called to her mind one after the other; but the commission did that, for they knew just what questions to ask, they being all written down for the use of witch-commissioners two centuries before. They asked, "Did you do so and so?" and she always said yes, and looked weary and tired, and took no interest in it. And so when the other ten heard that this one confessed, they confessed, too, and answered yes to the questions. Then they were burned at the stake all together, which was just and right; and everybody went from all the countryside to see it. I went, too; but when I saw that one of them was a bonny, sweet girl I used to play with, and looked so pitiful there chained to the stake, and her mother crying over her and devouring her with kisses and clinging around her neck, and saying, "Oh, my God! oh, my God!" it was too dreadful, and I went away.

It was bitter cold weather when Gottfried's grandmother was burned. It was charged that she had cured bad headaches by kneading the person's head and neck with her fingers—as she said—but really by the Devil's help, as everybody knew. They were going to examine her, but she stopped them, and confessed straight off that her power was from the Devil. So they appointed to burn her next morning, early, in our market-square. The officer who was to prepare the fire was there first, and prepared it. She was there next—brought by the constables, who left her and went to fetch another witch. Her family did not come with her. They might be reviled, maybe stoned, if the people were excited. I came, and gave her an apple. She was squatting at the fire, warming herself and waiting; and her old lips and hands were blue with the cold. A stranger came next. He was a traveler, passing through; and he spoke to her gently, and, seeing nobody but me there to hear, said he was sorry for her. And he asked if what she confessed was true, and she said no. He looked surprised and still more sorry then, and asked her:

"Then why did you confess?"

"I am old and very poor," she said, "and I work for my living. There was no way but to confess. If I hadn't they might have set me free. That would ruin me, for no one would forget that I had been suspected of being a witch, and so I would get no more work, and wherever I went they would set the dogs on me. In a little while I would starve. The fire is best; it is soon over. You have been good to me, you two, and I thank you."

She snuggled closer to the fire, and put out her hands to warm them, the snow-flakes descending soft and still on her old gray head and making it white and whiter. The crowd was gathering now, and an egg came flying and struck her in the eye, and broke and ran down her face. There was a laugh at that.

I told Satan all about the eleven girls and the old woman, once, but it did not affect him. He only said it was the human race, and what the human race did was of no consequence. And he said he had seen it made; and it was not made of clay; it was made of mud—part of it was, anyway. I knew what he meant by that—the Moral Sense. He saw the thought in my head, and it tickled him and made him laugh. Then he called a bullock out of a pasture and petted it and talked with it, and said:

"There—he wouldn't drive children mad with hunger and fright and loneliness, and then burn them for confessing to things invented for them which had never happened. And neither would he break the hearts of innocent, poor old women and make them afraid to trust themselves among their own race; and he would not insult them in their death-agony. For he is not besmirched with the Moral Sense, but is as the angels are, and knows no wrong, and never does it."

Lovely as he was, Satan could be cruelly offensive when he chose; and he always chose when the human race was brought to his attention. He always turned up his nose at it, and never had a kind word for it.

Well, as I was saying, we boys doubted if it was a good time for Ursula to be hiring a member of the Narr family. We were right. When the people found it out they were naturally indignant. And, moreover, since Marget and Ursula hadn't enough to eat themselves, where was the money coming from to feed another mouth? That is what they wanted to know; and in order to find out they stopped avoiding Gottfried and began to seek his society and have sociable conversations with him. He was pleased—not thinking any harm and not seeing the trap—and so he talked innocently along, and was no discreeter than a cow.

"Money!" he said; "they've got plenty of it. They pay me two groschen a week, besides my keep. And they live on the fat of the land, I can tell you; the prince himself can't beat their table."

This astonishing statement was conveyed by the astrologer to Father Adolf on a Sunday morning when he was returning from mass. He was deeply moved, and said:

"This must be looked into."

He said there must be witchcraft at the bottom of it, and told the villagers to resume relations with Marget and Ursula in a private and unostentatious way, and keep both eyes open. They were told to keep their own counsel, and not rouse the suspicions of the household. The villagers were at first a bit reluctant to enter such a dreadful place, but the priest said they would be under his protection while there, and no harm could come to them, particularly if they carried a trifle of holy water along and kept their beads and crosses handy. This satisfied them and made them willing to go; envy and malice made the baser sort even eager to go.

And so poor Marget began to have company again, and was as pleased as a cat. She was like 'most anybody else—just human, and happy in her prosperities and not averse from showing them off a little; and she was humanly grateful to have the warm shoulder turned to her and be smiled upon by her friends and the village again; for of all the hard things to bear, to be cut by your neighbors and left in contemptuous solitude is maybe the hardest.

The bars were down, and we could all go there now, and we did—our parents and all—day after day. The cat began to strain herself. She provided the top of everything for those companies, and in abundance—among them many a dish and many a wine which they had not tasted before and which they had not even heard of except at second-hand from the prince's servants. And the tableware was much above ordinary, too.

Marget was troubled at times, and pursued Ursula with questions to an uncomfortable degree; but Ursula stood her ground and stuck to it that it was Providence, and said no word about the cat. Marget knew that nothing was impossible to Providence, but she could not help having doubts that this effort was from there, though she was afraid to say so, lest disaster come of it. Witchcraft occurred to her, but she put the thought aside, for this was before Gottfried joined the household, and she knew Ursula was pious and a bitter hater of witches. By the time Gottfried arrived Providence was established, unshakably intrenched, and getting all the gratitude. The cat made no murmur, but went on composedly improving in style and prodigality by experience.

In any community, big or little, there is always a fair proportion of people who are not malicious or unkind by nature, and who never do unkind things except when they are overmastered by fear, or when their self-interest is greatly in danger, or some such matter as that. Eseldorf had its proportion of such people, and ordinarily their good and gentle influence was felt, but these were not ordinary times—on account of the witch-dread—and so we did not seem to have any gentle and compassionate hearts left, to speak of. Every person was frightened at the unaccountable state of things at Marget's house, not doubting that witchcraft was at the bottom of it, and fright frenzied their reason. Naturally there were some who pitied Marget and Ursula for the danger that was gathering about them, but naturally they did not say so; it would not have been safe. So the others had it all their own way, and there was none to advise the ignorant girl and the foolish woman and warn them to modify their doings. We boys wanted to warn them, but we backed down when it came to the pinch, being afraid. We found that we were not manly enough nor brave enough to do a generous action when there was a chance that it could get us into trouble. Neither of us confessed this poor spirit to the others, but did as other people would have done—dropped the subject and talked about something else. And I knew we all felt mean, eating and drinking Marget's fine things along with those companies of spies, and petting her and complimenting her with the rest, and seeing with self-reproach how foolishly happy she was, and never saying a word to put her on her guard. And, indeed, she was happy, and as proud as a princess, and so grateful to have friends again. And all the time these people were watching with all their eyes and reporting all they saw to Father Adolf.

But he couldn't make head or tail of the situation. There must be an enchanter somewhere on the premises, but who was it? Marget was not seen to do any jugglery, nor was Ursula, nor yet Gottfried; and still the wines and dainties never ran short, and a guest could not call for a thing and not get it. To produce these effects was usual enough with witches and enchanters—that part of it was not new; but to do it without any incantations, or even any rumblings or earthquakes or lightnings or apparitions—that was new, novel, wholly irregular. There was nothing in the books like this. Enchanted things were always unreal. Gold turned to dirt in an unenchanted atmosphere, food withered away and vanished. But this test failed in the present case. The spies brought samples: Father Adolf prayed over them, exorcised them, but it did no good; they remained sound and real, they yielded to natural decay only, and took the usual time to do it.

Father Adolf was not merely puzzled, he was also exasperated; for these evidences very nearly convinced him—privately—that there was no witchcraft in the matter. It did not wholly convince him, for this could be a new kind of witchcraft. There was a way to find out as to this: if this prodigal abundance of provender was not brought in from the outside, but produced on the premises, there was witchcraft, sure.

# CHAPTER VII

MARGET announced a party, and invited forty people; the date for it was seven days away. This was a fine opportunity. Marget's house stood by itself, and it could be easily watched. All the week it was watched night and day. Marget's household went out and in as usual, but they carried nothing in their hands, and neither they nor others brought anything to the house. This was ascertained. Evidently rations for forty people were not being fetched. If they were furnished any sustenance it would have to be made on the premises. It was true that Marget went out with a basket every evening, but the spies ascertained that she always brought it back empty.

The guests arrived at noon and filled the place. Father Adolf followed; also, after a little, the astrologer, without invitation. The spies had informed him that neither at the back nor the front had any parcels been brought in. He entered, and found the eating and drinking going on finely, and everything progressing in a lively and festive way. He glanced around and perceived that many of the cooked delicacies and all of the native and foreign fruits were of a perishable character, and he also recognized that these were fresh and perfect. No apparitions, no incantations, no thunder. That settled it. This was witchcraft. And not only that, but of a new kind—a kind never dreamed of before. It was a prodigious power, an illustrious power; he resolved to discover its secret. The announcement of it would resound throughout the world, penetrate to the remotest lands, paralyze all the nations with amazement—and carry his name with it, and make him renowned forever. It was a wonderful piece of luck, a splendid piece of luck; the glory of it made him dizzy.

All the house made room for him; Marget politely seated him; Ursula ordered Gottfried to bring a special table for him. Then she decked it and furnished it, and asked for his orders.

"Bring me what you will," he said.

The two servants brought supplies from the pantry, together with white wine and red—a bottle of each. The astrologer, who very likely had never seen such delicacies before, poured out a beaker of red wine, drank it off, poured another, then began to eat with a grand appetite.

I was not expecting Satan, for it was more than a week since I had seen or heard of him, but now he came in—I knew it by the feel, though people were in the way and I could not see him. I heard him apologizing for intruding; and he was going away, but Marget urged him to stay, and he thanked her and stayed. She brought him along, introducing him to the girls, and to Meidling, and to some of the elders; and there was quite a rustle of whispers: "It's the young stranger we hear so much about and can't get sight of, he is away so much." "Dear, dear, but he is beautiful—what is his name?" "Philip Traum." "Ah, it fits him!" (You see,

"Traum" is German for "Dream.") "What does he do?" "Studying for the ministry, they say." "His face is his fortune—he'll be a cardinal some day." "Where is his home?" "Away down somewhere in the tropics, they say—has a rich uncle down there." And so on. He made his way at once; everybody was anxious to know him and talk with him. Everybody noticed how cool and fresh it was, all of a sudden, and wondered at it, for they could see that the sun was beating down the same as before, outside, and the sky was clear of clouds, but no one guessed the reason, of course.

The astrologer had drunk his second beaker; he poured out a third. He set the bottle down, and by accident overturned it. He seized it before much was spilled, and held it up to the light, saying, "What a pity—it is royal wine." Then his face lighted with joy or triumph, or something, and he said, "Quick! Bring a bowl."

It was brought—a four-quart one. He took up that two-pint bottle and began to pour; went on pouring, the red liquor gurgling and gushing into the white bowl and rising higher and higher up its sides, everybody staring and holding their breath—and presently the bowl was full to the brim.

"Look at the bottle," he said, holding it up; "it is full yet!" I glanced at Satan, and in that moment he vanished. Then Father Adolf rose up, flushed and excited, crossed himself, and began to thunder in his great voice, "This house is bewitched and accursed!" People began to cry and shriek and crowd toward the door. "I summon this detected household to—"

His words were cut off short. His face became red, then purple, but he could not utter another sound. Then I saw Satan, a transparent film, melt into the astrologer's body; then the astrologer put up his hand, and apparently in his own voice said, "Wait—remain where you are." All stopped where they stood. "Bring a funnel!" Ursula brought it, trembling and scared, and he stuck it in the bottle and took up the great bowl and began to pour the wine back, the people gazing and dazed with astonishment, for they knew the bottle was already full before he began. He emptied the whole of the bowl into the bottle, then smiled out over the room, chuckled, and said, indifferently: "It is nothing—anybody can do it! With my powers I can even do much more."

A frightened cry burst out everywhere. "Oh, my God, he is possessed!" and there was a tumultuous rush for the door which swiftly emptied the house of all who did not belong in it except us boys and Meidling. We boys knew the secret, and would have told it if we could, but we couldn't. We were very thankful to Satan for furnishing that good help at the needful time.

Marget was pale, and crying; Meidling looked kind of petrified; Ursula the same; but Gottfried was the worst—he couldn't stand, he was so weak and scared. For he was of a witch family, you know, and it would be bad for him to be suspected. Agnes came loafing in, looking pious and unaware, and wanted to rub up against Ursula and be petted, but Ursula was afraid of her and shrank away from her, but pretending she was not meaning any incivility, for she knew very well it wouldn't answer to have strained relations with that kind of a cat. But we boys took Agnes and petted her, for Satan would not have befriended her if he had not had a good opinion of her, and that was indorsement enough for us. He seemed to trust anything that hadn't the Moral Sense.

Outside, the guests, panic-stricken, scattered in every direction and fled in a pitiable state of terror; and such a tumult as they made with their running and sobbing and shrieking and shouting that soon all the village came flocking from their houses to see what had happened, and they thronged the street and shouldered and jostled one another in excitement and fright; and then Father Adolf appeared, and they fell apart in two walls like the cloven Red Sea, and presently down this lane the astrologer came striding and mumbling, and where he passed the lanes surged back in packed masses, and fell silent with awe, and their eyes stared and their breasts heaved, and several women fainted; and when he was gone by the crowd swarmed together and followed him at a distance, talking excitedly and asking questions and finding out the facts. Finding out the facts and passing them on to others, with improvements—improvements which soon enlarged the bowl of wine to a barrel, and made the one bottle hold it all and yet remain empty to the last.

When the astrologer reached the market-square he went straight to a juggler, fantastically dressed, who was keeping three brass balls in the air, and took them from him and faced around upon the approaching crowd and said: "This poor clown is ignorant of his art. Come forward and see an expert perform."

So saying, he tossed the balls up one after another and set them whirling in a slender bright oval in the air, and added another, then another and another, and soon—no one seeing whence he got them—adding, adding, adding, the oval lengthening all the time, his hands moving so swiftly that they were just a web or a blur and not distinguishable as hands; and such as counted said there were now a hundred balls in the air. The spinning great oval reached up twenty feet in the air and was a shining and glinting and wonderful sight. Then he folded his arms and told the balls to go on spinning without his help—and they did it. After a couple of minutes he said, "There, that will do," and the oval broke and came crashing down, and the balls scattered abroad and rolled every whither. And wherever one of them came the people fell back in dread, and no one would touch it. It made him laugh, and he scoffed at the people and called them cowards and old women. Then he turned and saw the tight-rope, and said foolish people were daily wasting their money to see a clumsy and ignorant varlet degrade that beautiful art; now they should see the work of a master. With that he made a spring into the air and lit firm on his feet on the rope. Then he hopped the whole length of it back and forth on one foot, with his hands clasped over his eyes; and next he began to throw somersaults, both backward and forward, and threw twenty-seven.

The people murmured, for the astrologer was old, and always before had been halting of movement and at times even lame, but he was nimble enough now and went on with his antics in the liveliest manner. Finally he sprang lightly down and walked away, and passed up the road and around the corner and disappeared. Then that great, pale, silent, solid crowd drew a deep breath and looked into one another's faces as if they said: "Was it real? Did you see it, or was it only I—and I was dreaming?" Then they broke into a low murmur of talking, and fell apart in couples, and moved toward their homes, still talking in that awed way, with faces close together and laying a hand on an arm and making other such gestures as people make when they have been deeply impressed by something.

We boys followed behind our fathers, and listened, catching all we could of what they said; and when they sat down in our house and continued their talk they still had us for company. They were in a sad mood, for it was certain, they said, that disaster for the village must follow this awful visitation of witches and devils. Then my father remembered that Father Adolf had been struck dumb at the moment of his denunciation.

"They have not ventured to lay their hands upon an anointed servant of God before," he said; "and how they could have dared it this time I cannot make out, for he wore his crucifix. Isn't it so?"

"Yes," said the others, "we saw it."

"It is serious, friends, it is very serious. Always before, we had a protection. It has failed."

The others shook, as with a sort of chill, and muttered those words over—"It has failed." "God has forsaken us."

"It is true," said Seppi Wohlmeyer's father; there is nowhere to look for help."

"The people will realize this," said Nikolaus's father, the judge, "and despair will take away their courage and their energies. We have indeed fallen upon evil times."

He sighed, and Wohlmeyer said, in a troubled voice: "The report of it all will go about the country, and our village will be shunned as being under the displeasure of God. The Golden Stag will know hard times."

"True, neighbor," said my father; "all of us will suffer—all in repute, many in estate. And, good God!—"

"What is it?"

"That can come—to finish us!"

"Name it—um Gottes Willen!"

"The Interdict!"

It smote like a thunderclap, and they were like to swoon with the terror of it. Then the dread of this calamity roused their energies, and they stopped brooding and began to consider ways to avert it. They discussed this, that, and the other way, and talked till the afternoon was far spent, then confessed that at present they could arrive at no decision. So they parted sorrowfully, with oppressed hearts which were filled with bodings.

While they were saying their parting words I slipped out and set my course for Marget's house to see what was happening there. I met many people, but none of them greeted me. It ought to have been surprising, but it was not, for they were so distraught with fear and dread that they were not in their right minds, I think; they were white and haggard, and walked like persons in a dream, their eyes open but seeing nothing, their lips moving but uttering nothing, and worriedly clasping and unclasping their hands without knowing it.

At Marget's it was like a funeral. She and Wilhelm sat together on the sofa, but said nothing, and not even holding hands. Both were steeped in gloom, and Marget's eyes were red from the crying she had been doing. She said:

"I have been begging him to go, and come no more, and so save himself alive. I cannot bear to be his murderer. This house is bewitched, and no inmate will escape the fire. But he will not go, and he will be lost with the rest."

Wilhelm said he would not go; if there was danger for her, his place was by her, and there he would remain. Then she began to cry again, and it was all so mournful that I wished I had stayed away. There was a knock, now, and Satan came in, fresh and cheery and beautiful, and brought that winy atmosphere of his and changed the whole thing. He never said a word about what had been happening, nor about the awful fears which were freezing the blood in the hearts of the community, but began to talk and rattle on about all manner of gay and pleasant things: and next about music—an artful stroke which cleared away the remnant of Marget's depression and brought her spirits and her interests broad awake. She had not heard any one talk so well and so knowingly on that subject before, and she was so uplifted by it and so charmed that what she was feeling lit up her face and came out in her words; and Wilhelm noticed it and did not look as pleased as he ought to have done. And next Satan branched off into poetry, and recited some, and did it well, and Marget was charmed again; and again Wilhelm was not as pleased as he ought to have been, and this time Marget noticed it and was remorseful.

I fell asleep to pleasant music that night—the patter of rain upon the panes and the dull growling of distant thunder. Away in the night Satan came and roused me and said: "Come with me. Where shall we go?"

"Anywhere—so it is with you."

Then there was a fierce glare of sunlight, and he said, "This is China."

That was a grand surprise, and made me sort of drunk with vanity and gladness to think I had come so far—so much, much farther than anybody else in our village, including Bartel Sperling, who had such a great opinion of his travels. We buzzed around over that empire for more than half an hour, and saw the whole of it. It was wonderful, the spectacles we saw; and some were beautiful, others too horrible to think. For instance— However, I may go into that by and by, and also why Satan chose China for this excursion instead of another place; it would interrupt my tale to do it now. Finally we stopped flitting and lit.

We sat upon a mountain commanding a vast landscape of mountain-range and gorge and valley and plain and river, with cities and villages slumbering in the sunlight, and a glimpse of blue sea on the farther verge. It was a tranquil and dreamy picture, beautiful to the eye and restful to the spirit. If we could only make a change like that whenever we wanted to, the world would be easier to live in than it is, for change of scene shifts the mind's burdens to the other shoulder and banishes old, shop-worn wearinesses from mind and body both.

We talked together, and I had the idea of trying to reform Satan and persuade him to lead a better life. I told him about all those things he had been doing, and begged him to be more considerate and stop making people unhappy. I said I knew he did not mean any harm, but that he ought to stop and consider the possible consequences of a thing before launching it in that impulsive and random way of his; then he would not make so much trouble. He was not hurt by this plain speech; he only looked amused and surprised, and said:

"What? I do random things? Indeed, I never do. I stop and consider possible consequences? Where is the need? I know what the consequences are going to be—always."

"Oh, Satan, then how could you do these things?"

"Well, I will tell you, and you must understand if you can. You belong to a singular race. Every man is a suffering-machine and a happiness-machine combined. The two functions work together harmoniously, with a fine and delicate precision, on the give-and-take principle. For every happiness turned out in the one department the other stands ready to modify it with a sorrow or a pain—maybe a dozen. In most cases the man's life is about equally divided between happiness and unhappiness. When this is not the case the unhappiness predominates—always; never the other. Sometimes a man's make and disposition are such that his misery-machine is able to do nearly all the business. Such a man goes through life almost ignorant of what happiness is. Everything he touches, everything he does, brings a misfortune upon him. You have seen such people? To that kind of a person life is not an advantage, is it? It is only a disaster. Sometimes for an hour's happiness a man's machinery makes him pay years of misery. Don't you know that? It happens every now and then. I will give you a case or two presently. Now the people of your village are nothing to me—you know that, don't you?"

I did not like to speak out too flatly, so I said I had suspected it.

"Well, it is true that they are nothing to me. It is not possible that they should be. The difference between them and me is abysmal, immeasurable. They have no intellect."

"No intellect?"

"Nothing that resembles it. At a future time I will examine what man calls his mind and give you the details of that chaos, then you will see and understand. Men have nothing in common with me—there is no point of contact; they have foolish little feelings and foolish little vanities and impertinences and ambitions; their foolish little life is but a laugh, a sigh, and extinction; and they have no sense. Only the Moral Sense. I will show you what I mean. Here is a red spider, not so big as a pin's head. Can you imagine an elephant being interested in him—caring whether he is happy or isn't, or whether he is wealthy or poor, or whether his sweetheart returns his love or not, or whether his mother is sick or well, or whether he is looked up to in society or not, or whether his enemies will smite him or his friends desert him, or whether his hopes will suffer blight or his political ambitions fail, or whether he shall die in the bosom of his family or neglected and despised in a foreign land? These things can never be important to the elephant; they are nothing to him; he cannot shrink his sympathies to the microscopic size of them. Man is to me as the red spider is to the elephant. The elephant has nothing against the spider—he cannot get down to that remote level; I have nothing against man. The elephant is indifferent; I am indifferent. The elephant would not take the trouble to do the spider an ill turn; if he took the notion he might do him a good turn, if it came in his way and cost nothing. I have done men good service, but no ill turns.

"The elephant lives a century, the red spider a day; in power, intellect, and dignity the one creature is separated from the other by a distance which is simply astronomical. Yet in these, as in all qualities, man is immeasurably further below me than is the wee spider below the elephant.

"Man's mind clumsily and tediously and laboriously patches little trivialities together and gets a result—such as it is. My mind creates! Do you get the force of that? Creates anything it desires—and in a moment. Creates without material. Creates fluids, solids, colors—anything, everything—out of the airy nothing which is called Thought. A man imagines a silk thread, imagines a machine to make it, imagines a picture, then by weeks of labor embroiders it on canvas with the thread. I think the whole thing, and in a moment it is before you—created.

"I think a poem, music, the record of a game of chess—anything—and it is there. This is the immortal mind—nothing is beyond its reach. Nothing can obstruct my vision; the rocks are transparent to me, and darkness is daylight. I do not need to open a book; I take the whole of its contents into my mind at a single glance, through the cover; and in a million years I could not forget a single word of it, or its place in the volume. Nothing goes on in the skull of man, bird, fish, insect, or other creature which can be hidden from me. I pierce the learned man's brain with a single glance, and the treasures which cost him threescore years to accumulate are mine; he can forget, and he does forget, but I retain.

"Now, then, I perceive by your thoughts that you are understanding me fairly well. Let us proceed. Circumstances might so fall out that the elephant could like the spider—supposing he can see it—but he could not love it. His love is for his own kind—for his equals. An angel's love is sublime, adorable, divine, beyond the imagination of man—infinitely beyond it! But it is limited to his own august order. If it fell upon one of your race for only an instant, it would consume its object to ashes. No, we cannot love men, but we can be harmlessly indifferent to them; we can also like them, sometimes. I like you and the boys, I like Father Peter, and for your sakes I am doing all these things for the villagers."

He saw that I was thinking a sarcasm, and he explained his position.

"I have wrought well for the villagers, though it does not look like it on the surface. Your race never know good fortune from ill. They are always mistaking the one for the other. It is because they cannot see into the future. What I am doing for the villagers will bear good fruit some day; in some cases to themselves; in others, to unborn generations of men. No one will ever know that I was the cause, but it will be none the less true, for all that. Among you boys you have a game: you stand a row of bricks on end a few inches apart; you push a brick, it knocks its neighbor over, the neighbor knocks over the next brick—and so on till all the row is prostrate. That is human life. A child's first act knocks over the initial brick, and the rest will follow inexorably. If you could see into the future, as I can, you would see everything that was going to happen to that creature; for nothing can change the order of its life after the first event has determined it. That is, nothing will change it, because each act unfailingly begets an act, that act begets another, and so on to the end, and the seer can look forward down the line and see just when each act is to have birth, from cradle to grave."

"Does God order the career?"

"Foreordain it? No. The man's circumstances and environment order it. His first act determines the second and all that follow after. But suppose, for argument's sake, that the man should skip one of these acts; an apparently trifling one, for instance; suppose that it had been appointed that on a certain day, at a certain hour and minute and second and fraction of a second he should go to the well, and he didn't go. That man's career would change utterly, from that moment; thence to the grave it would be wholly different from the career which his first act as a child had arranged for him. Indeed, it might be that if he had gone to the well he would have ended his career on a throne, and that omitting to do it would set him upon a career that would lead to beggary and a pauper's grave. For instance: if at any time—say in boyhood—Columbus had skipped the triflingest little link in the chain of acts projected and made inevitable by his first childish act, it would have changed his whole subsequent life, and he would have become a priest and died obscure in an Italian village, and America would not have been discovered for two centuries afterward. I know this. To skip any one of the billion acts in Columbus's chain would have wholly changed his life. I have examined his billion of possible careers, and in only one of them occurs the discovery of America. You people do not suspect that all of your acts are of one size and importance, but it is true; to snatch at an appointed fly is as big with fate for you as in any other appointed act—"

"As the conquering of a continent, for instance?"

"Yes. Now, then, no man ever does drop a link—the thing has never happened! Even when he is trying to make up his mind as to whether he will do a thing or not, that itself is a link, an act, and has its proper place in his chain; and when he finally decides an act, that also was the thing which he was absolutely certain to do. You see, now, that a man will never drop a link in his chain. He cannot. If he made up his mind to try, that project would itself be an unavoidable link—a thought bound to occur to him at that precise moment, and made certain by the first act of his babyhood."

It seemed so dismal!

"He is a prisoner for life," I said sorrowfully, "and cannot get free."

"No, of himself he cannot get away from the consequences of his first childish act. But I can free him."

I looked up wistfully.

"I have changed the careers of a number of your villagers."

I tried to thank him, but found it difficult, and let it drop.

"I shall make some other changes. You know that little Lisa Brandt?"

"Oh yes, everybody does. My mother says she is so sweet and so lovely that she is not like any other child. She says she will be the pride of the village when she grows up; and its idol, too, just as she is now."

"I shall change her future."

"Make it better?" I asked.

"Yes. And I will change the future of Nikolaus."

I was glad, this time, and said, "I don't need to ask about his case; you will be sure to do generously by him."

"It is my intention."

Straight off I was building that great future of Nicky's in my imagination, and had already made a renowned general of him and hofmeister at the court, when I noticed that Satan was waiting for me to get ready to listen again. I was ashamed of having exposed my cheap imaginings to him, and was expecting some sarcasms, but it did not happen. He proceeded with his subject:

"Nicky's appointed life is sixty-two years."

"That's grand!" I said.

"Lisa's, thirty-six. But, as I told you, I shall change their lives and those ages. Two minutes and a quarter from now Nikolaus will wake out of his sleep and find the rain blowing in. It was appointed that he should turn over and go to sleep again. But I have appointed that he shall get up and close the window first. That trifle will change his career entirely. He will rise in the morning two minutes later than the chain of his life had appointed him to rise. By consequence, thenceforth nothing will ever happen to him in accordance with the details of the old chain." He took out his watch and sat looking at it a few moments, then said: "Nikolaus has risen to close the window. His life is changed, his new career has begun. There will be consequences."

It made me feel creepy; it was uncanny.

"But for this change certain things would happen twelve days from now. For instance, Nikolaus would save Lisa from drowning. He would arrive on the scene at exactly the right moment—four minutes past ten, the long-ago appointed instant of time—and the water would be shoal, the achievement easy and certain. But he will arrive some seconds too late, now; Lisa will have struggled into deeper water. He will do his best, but both will drown."

"Oh, Satan! oh, dear Satan!" I cried, with the tears rising in my eyes, "save them! Don't let it happen. I can't bear to lose Nikolaus, he is my loving playmate and friend; and think of Lisa's poor mother!"

I clung to him and begged and pleaded, but he was not moved. He made me sit down again, and told me I must hear him out.

"I have changed Nikolaus's life, and this has changed Lisa's. If I had not done this, Nikolaus would save Lisa, then he would catch cold from his drenching; one of your race's fantastic and desolating scarlet fevers would follow, with pathetic after-effects; for forty-six years he would lie in his bed a paralytic log, deaf, dumb, blind, and praying night and day for the blessed relief of death. Shall I change his life back?"

"Oh no! Oh, not for the world! In charity and pity leave it as it is."

"It is best so. I could not have changed any other link in his life and done him so good a service.

He had a billion possible careers, but not one of them was worth living; they were charged full with miseries and disasters. But for my intervention he would do his brave deed twelve days from now—a deed begun and ended in six minutes—and get for all reward those forty-six years of sorrow and suffering I told you of. It is one of the cases I was thinking of awhile ago when I said that sometimes an act which brings the actor an hour's happiness and self-satisfaction is paid for—or punished—by years of suffering."

I wondered what poor little Lisa's early death would save her from. He answered the thought:

"From ten years of pain and slow recovery from an accident, and then from nineteen years' pollution, shame, depravity, crime, ending with death at the hands of the executioner. Twelve days hence she will die; her mother would save her life if she could. Am I not kinder than her mother?"

"Yes—oh, indeed yes; and wiser."

"Father Peter's case is coming on presently. He will be acquitted, through unassailable proofs of his innocence."

"Why, Satan, how can that be? Do you really think it?"

"Indeed, I know it. His good name will be restored, and the rest of his life will be happy."

"I can believe it. To restore his good name will have that effect."

"His happiness will not proceed from that cause. I shall change his life that day, for his good. He will never know his good name has been restored."

In my mind—and modestly—I asked for particulars, but Satan paid no attention to my thought. Next, my mind wandered to the astrologer, and I wondered where he might be.

"In the moon," said Satan, with a fleeting sound which I believed was a chuckle. "I've got him on the cold side of it, too. He doesn't know where he is, and is not having a pleasant time; still, it is good enough for him, a good place for his star studies. I shall need him presently; then I shall bring him back and possess him again. He has a long and cruel and odious life before him, but I will change that, for I have no feeling against him and am quite willing to do him a kindness. I think I shall get him burned."

He had such strange notions of kindness! But angels are made so, and do not know any better. Their ways are not like our ways; and, besides, human beings are nothing to them; they think they are only freaks. It seems to me odd that he should put the astrologer so far away; he could have dumped him in Germany just as well, where he would be handy.

"Far away?" said Satan. "To me no place is far away; distance does not exist for me. The sun is less than a hundred million miles from here, and the light that is falling upon us has taken eight minutes to come; but I can make that flight, or any other, in a fraction of time so minute that it cannot be measured by a watch. I have but to think the journey, and it is accomplished."

I held out my hand and said, "The light lies upon it; think it into a glass of wine, Satan."

He did it. I drank the wine.

"Break the glass," he said.

I broke it.

"There—you see it is real. The villagers thought the brass balls were magic stuff and as perishable as smoke. They were afraid to touch them. You are a curious lot—your race. But come along; I have business. I will put you to bed." Said and done. Then he was gone; but his voice came back to me through the rain and darkness saying, "Yes, tell Seppi, but no other."

It was the answer to my thought.

## CHAPTER VIII

SLEEP would not come. It was not because I was proud of my travels and excited about having been around the big world to China, and feeling contemptuous of Bartel Sperling, "the traveler," as he called himself, and looked down upon us others because he had been to Vienna once and was the only Eseldorf boy who had made such a journey and seen the world's wonders. At another time that would have kept me awake, but it did not affect me now. No, my mind was filled with Nikolaus, my thoughts ran upon him only, and the good days we had seen together at romps and frolics in the woods and the fields and the river in the long summer days, and skating and sliding in the winter when our parents thought we were in school. And now he was going out of this young life, and the summers and winters would come and go, and we others would rove and play as before, but his place would be vacant; we should see him no more. To-morrow he would not suspect, but would be as he had always been, and it would shock me to hear him laugh, and see him do lightsome and frivolous things, for to me he would be a corpse, with waxen hands and dull eyes, and I should see the shroud around his face; and next day he would not suspect, nor the next, and all the time his handful of days would be wasting swiftly away and that awful thing coming nearer and nearer, his fate closing steadily around him and no one knowing it but Seppi and me. Twelve days—only twelve days. It was awful to think of. I noticed that in my thoughts I was not calling him by his familiar names, Nick and Nicky, but was speaking of him by his full name, and reverently, as one speaks of the dead. Also, as incident after incident of our comradeship came thronging into my mind out of the past, I noticed that they were mainly cases where I had wronged him or hurt him, and they rebuked me and reproached me, and my heart was wrung with remorse, just as it is when we remember our unkindnesses to friends who have passed beyond the veil, and we wish we could have them back again, if only for a moment, so that we could go on our knees to them and say, "Have pity, and forgive."

Once when we were nine years old he went a long errand of nearly two miles for the fruiterer, who gave him a splendid big apple for reward, and he was flying home with it, almost beside himself with astonishment and delight, and I met him, and he let me look at the apple, not thinking of treachery, and I ran off with it, eating it as I ran, he following me and begging; and when he overtook me I offered him the core, which was all that was left; and I laughed. Then he turned away, crying, and said he had meant to give it to his little sister. That smote me, for she was slowly getting well of a sickness, and it would have been a proud moment for him, to see her joy and surprise and have her caresses. But I was ashamed to say I was ashamed, and only said something rude and mean, to pretend I did not care, and he made no reply in words, but there was a wounded look in his face as he turned away toward his home which rose before me many times in after years, in the night, and reproached me and made me ashamed again. It had grown dim in my mind, by and by, then it disappeared; but it was back now, and not dim.

Once at school, when we were eleven, I upset my ink and spoiled four copy-books, and was in danger of severe punishment; but I put it upon him, and he got the whipping.

And only last year I had cheated him in a trade, giving him a large fish-hook which was partly broken through for three small sound ones. The first fish he caught broke the hook, but he did not know I was blamable, and he refused to take back one of the small hooks which my conscience forced me to offer him, but said, "A trade is a trade; the hook was bad, but that was not your fault."

No, I could not sleep. These little, shabby wrongs upbraided me and tortured me, and with a pain much sharper than one feels when the wrongs have been done to the living. Nikolaus was living, but no matter; he was to me as one already dead. The wind was still moaning about the eaves, the rain still pattering upon the panes.

In the morning I sought out Seppi and told him. It was down by the river. His lips moved, but he did not say anything, he only looked dazed and stunned, and his face turned very white. He stood like that a few moments, the tears welling into his eyes, then he turned away and I locked my arm in his and we walked along thinking, but not speaking. We crossed the bridge and wandered through the meadows and up among the hills and the woods, and at last the talk came and flowed freely, and it was all about Nikolaus and was a recalling of the life we had lived with him. And every now and then Seppi said, as if to himself:

"Twelve days!—less than twelve days."

We said we must be with him all the time; we must have all of him we could; the days were precious now. Yet we did not go to seek him. It would be like meeting the dead, and we were afraid. We did not say it, but that was what we were feeling. And so it gave us a shock when we turned a curve and came upon Nikolaus face to face. He shouted, gaily:

"Hi-hi! What is the matter? Have you seen a ghost?"

We couldn't speak, but there was no occasion; he was willing to talk for us all, for he had just seen Satan and was in high spirits about it. Satan had told him about our trip to China, and he had begged Satan to take him a journey, and Satan had promised. It was to be a far journey, and wonderful and beautiful; and Nikolaus had begged him to take us, too, but he said no, he would take us some day, maybe, but not now. Satan would come for him on the 13th, and Nikolaus was already counting the hours, he was so impatient.

That was the fatal day. We were already counting the hours, too.

We wandered many a mile, always following paths which had been our favorites from the days when we were little, and always we talked about the old times. All the blitheness was with Nikolaus; we others could not shake off our depression. Our tone toward Nikolaus was so strangely gentle and tender and yearning that he noticed it, and was pleased; and we were constantly doing him deferential little offices of courtesy, and saying, "Wait, let me do that for you," and that pleased him, too. I gave him seven fish-hooks—all I had—and made him take them; and Seppi gave him his new knife and a humming-top painted red and yellow—atonements for swindles practised upon him formerly, as I learned later, and probably no longer remembered by Nikolaus now. These things touched him, and he could not have believed that we loved him so; and his pride in it and gratefulness for it cut us to the heart, we were so undeserving of them. When we parted at last, he was radiant, and said he had never had such a happy day.

As we walked along homeward, Seppi said, "We always prized him, but never so much as now, when we are going to lose him."

Next day and every day we spent all of our spare time with Nikolaus; and also added to it time which we (and he) stole from work and other duties, and this cost the three of us some sharp scoldings, and some threats of punishment. Every morning two of us woke with a start and a shudder, saying, as the days flew along, "Only ten days left;" "only nine days left;" "only eight;" "only seven." Always it was narrowing. Always Nikolaus was gay and happy, and always puzzled because we were not.

He wore his invention to the bone trying to invent ways to cheer us up, but it was only a hollow success; he could see that our jollity had no heart in it, and that the laughs we broke into came up against some obstruction or other and suffered damage and decayed into a sigh. He tried to find out what the matter was, so that he could help us out of our trouble or make it lighter by sharing it with us; so we had to tell many lies to deceive him and appease him.

But the most distressing thing of all was that he was always making plans, and often they went beyond the 13th! Whenever that happened it made us groan in spirit. All his mind was fixed upon finding some way to conquer our depression and cheer us up; and at last, when he had but three days to live, he fell upon the right idea and was jubilant over it—a boys-and-girls' frolic and dance in the woods, up there where we first met Satan, and this was to occur on the 14th. It was ghastly, for that was his funeral day. We couldn't venture to protest; it would only have brought a "Why?" which we could not answer. He wanted us to help him invite his guests, and we did it—one can refuse nothing to a dying friend. But it was dreadful, for really we were inviting them to his funeral.

It was an awful eleven days; and yet, with a lifetime stretching back between to-day and then, they are still a grateful memory to me, and beautiful. In effect they were days of companionship with one's sacred dead, and I have known no comradeship that was so close or so precious. We clung to the hours and the minutes, counting them as they wasted away, and parting with them with that pain and bereavement which a miser feels who sees his hoard filched from him coin by coin by robbers and is helpless to prevent it.

When the evening of the last day came we stayed out too long; Seppi and I were in fault for that; we could not bear to part with Nikolaus; so it was very late when we left him at his door. We lingered near awhile, listening; and that happened which we were fearing. His father gave him the promised punishment, and we heard his shrieks. But we listened only a moment, then hurried away, remorseful for this thing which we had caused. And sorry for the father, too; our thought being, "If he only knew—if he only knew!"

In the morning Nikolaus did not meet us at the appointed place, so we went to his home to see what the matter was. His mother said:

"His father is out of all patience with these goings-on, and will not have any more of it. Half the time when Nick is needed he is not to be found; then it turns out that he has been gadding around with you two. His father gave him a flogging last night. It always grieved me before, and many's the time I have begged him off and saved him, but this time he appealed to me in vain, for I was out of patience myself."

"I wish you had saved him just this one time," I said, my voice trembling a little; "it would ease a pain in your heart to remember it some day."

She was ironing at the time, and her back was partly toward me. She turned about with a startled or wondering look in her face and said, "What do you mean by that?"

I was not prepared, and didn't know anything to say; so it was awkward, for she kept looking at me; but Seppi was alert and spoke up:

"Why, of course it would be pleasant to remember, for the very reason we were out so late was that Nikolaus got to telling how good you are to him, and how he never got whipped when you were by to save him; and he was so full of it, and we were so full of the interest of it, that none of us noticed how late it was getting."

"Did he say that? Did he?" and she put her apron to her eyes.

"You can ask Theodor—he will tell you the same."

"It is a dear, good lad, my Nick," she said. "I am sorry I let him get whipped; I will never do it again. To think—all the time I was sitting here last night, fretting and angry at him, he was loving me and praising me! Dear, dear, if we could only know! Then we shouldn't ever go wrong; but we are only poor, dumb beasts groping around and making mistakes. I sha'n't ever think of last night without a pang."

She was like all the rest; it seemed as if nobody could open a mouth, in these wretched days, without saying something that made us shiver. They were "groping around," and did not know what true, sorrowfully true things they were saying by accident.

Seppi asked if Nikolaus might go out with us.

"I am sorry," she answered, "but he can't. To punish him further, his father doesn't allow him to go out of the house to-day."

We had a great hope! I saw it in Seppi's eyes. We thought, "If he cannot leave the house, he cannot be drowned." Seppi asked, to make sure:

"Must he stay in all day, or only the morning?"

"All day. It's such a pity, too; it's a beautiful day, and he is so unused to being shut up. But he is busy planning his party, and maybe that is company for him. I do hope he isn't too lonesome."

Seppi saw that in her eye which emboldened him to ask if we might go up and help him pass his time.

"And welcome!" she said, right heartily. "Now I call that real friendship, when you might be abroad in the fields and the woods, having a happy time. You are good boys, I'll allow that, though you don't always find satisfactory ways of improving it. Take these cakes—for yourselves—and give him this one, from his mother."

The first thing we noticed when we entered Nikolaus's room was the time—a quarter to 10. Could that be correct? Only such a few minutes to live! I felt a contraction at my heart. Nikolaus jumped up and gave us a glad welcome. He was in good spirits over his plannings for his party and had not been lonesome.

"Sit down," he said, "and look at what I've been doing. And I've finished a kite that you will say is a beauty. It's drying, in the kitchen; I'll fetch it."

He had been spending his penny savings in fanciful trifles of various kinds, to go as prizes in the games, and they were marshaled with fine and showy effect upon the table. He said:

"Examine them at your leisure while I get mother to touch up the kite with her iron if it isn't dry enough yet."

Then he tripped out and went clattering downstairs, whistling.

We did not look at the things; we couldn't take any interest in anything but the clock. We sat staring at it in silence, listening to the ticking, and every time the minute-hand jumped we nodded recognition—one minute fewer to cover in the race for life or for death. Finally Seppi drew a deep breath and said:

"Two minutes to ten. Seven minutes more and he will pass the death-point. Theodor, he is going to be saved! He's going to—"

"Hush! I'm on needles. Watch the clock and keep still."

Five minutes more. We were panting with the strain and the excitement. Another three minutes, and there was a footstep on the stair.

"Saved!" And we jumped up and faced the door.

The old mother entered, bringing the kite. "Isn't it a beauty?" she said. "And, dear me, how he has slaved over it—ever since daylight, I think, and only finished it awhile before you came." She stood it against the wall, and stepped back to take a view of it. "He drew the pictures his own self, and I think they are very good. The church isn't so very good, I'll have to admit, but look at the bridge—any one can recognize the bridge in a minute. He asked me to bring it up. . . . Dear me! it's seven minutes past ten, and I—"

"But where is he?"

"He? Oh, he'll be here soon; he's gone out a minute."

"Gone out?"

"Yes. Just as he came down-stairs little Lisa's mother came in and said the child had wandered off somewhere, and as she was a little uneasy I told Nikolaus to never mind about his father's orders—go and look her up. . . . Why, how white you two do look! I do believe you are sick. Sit down; I'll fetch something. That cake has disagreed with you. It is a little heavy, but I thought—"

She disappeared without finishing her sentence, and we hurried at once to the back window and looked toward the river. There was a great crowd at the other end of the bridge, and people were flying toward that point from every direction.

"Oh, it is all over—poor Nikolaus! Why, oh, why did she let him get out of the house!"

"Come away," said Seppi, half sobbing, "come quick—we can't bear to meet her; in five minutes she will know."

But we were not to escape. She came upon us at the foot of the stairs, with her cordials in her hands, and made us come in and sit down and take the medicine. Then she watched the effect, and it did not satisfy her; so she made us wait longer, and kept upbraiding herself for giving us the unwholesome cake.

Presently the thing happened which we were dreading. There was a sound of tramping and scraping outside, and a crowd came solemnly in, with heads uncovered, and laid the two drowned bodies on the bed.

"Oh, my God!" that poor mother cried out, and fell on her knees, and put her arms about her dead boy and began to cover the wet face with kisses. "Oh, it was I that sent him, and I have been his death. If I had obeyed, and kept him in the house, this would not have happened. And I am rightly punished; I was cruel to him last night, and him begging me, his own mother, to be his friend."

And so she went on and on, and all the women cried, and pitied her, and tried to comfort her, but she could not forgive herself and could not be comforted, and kept on saying if she had not sent him out he would be alive and well now, and she was the cause of his death.

It shows how foolish people are when they blame themselves for anything they have done. Satan knows, and he said nothing happens that your first act hasn't arranged to happen and made inevitable; and so, of your own motion you can't ever alter the scheme or do a thing that will break a link. Next we heard screams, and Frau Brandt came wildly plowing and plunging through the crowd with her dress in disorder and hair flying loose, and flung herself upon her dead child with moans and kisses and pleadings and endearments; and by and by she rose up almost exhausted with her outpourings of passionate emotion, and clenched her fist and lifted it toward the sky, and her tear-drenched face grew hard and resentful, and she said:

"For nearly two weeks I have had dreams and presentiments and warnings that death was going to strike what was most precious to me, and day and night and night and day I have groveled in the dirt before Him praying Him to have pity on my innocent child and save it from harm—and here is His answer!"

Why, He had saved it from harm—but she did not know.

She wiped the tears from her eyes and cheeks, and stood awhile gazing down at the child and caressing its face and its hair with her hands; then she spoke again in that bitter tone: "But in His hard heart is no compassion. I will never pray again."

She gathered her dead child to her bosom and strode away, the crowd falling back to let her pass, and smitten dumb by the awful words they had heard. Ah, that poor woman! It is as Satan said, we do not know good fortune from bad, and are always mistaking the one for the other. Many a time since I have heard people pray to God to spare the life of sick persons, but I have never done it.

Both funerals took place at the same time in our little church next day. Everybody was there, including the party guests. Satan was there, too; which was proper, for it was on account of his efforts that the funerals had happened. Nikolaus had departed this life without absolution, and a collection was taken up for masses, to get him out of purgatory. Only two-thirds of the required money was gathered, and the parents were going to try to borrow the rest, but Satan furnished it. He told us privately that there was no purgatory, but he had contributed in order that Nikolaus's parents and their friends might be saved from worry and distress. We thought it very good of him, but he said money did not cost him anything.

At the graveyard the body of little Lisa was seized for debt by a carpenter to whom the mother owed fifty groschen for work done the year before. She had never been able to pay this, and was not able now. The carpenter took the corpse home and kept it four days in his cellar, the mother weeping and imploring about his house all the time; then he buried it in his brother's cattle-yard, without religious ceremonies. It drove the mother wild with grief and shame, and she forsook her work and went daily about the town, cursing the carpenter and blaspheming the laws of the emperor and the church, and it was pitiful to see. Seppi asked Satan to interfere, but he said the carpenter and the rest were members of the human race and were acting quite neatly for that species of animal. He would interfere if he found a horse acting in such a way, and we must inform him when we came across that kind of horse doing that kind of a human thing, so that he could stop it. We believed this was sarcasm, for of course there wasn't any such horse.

But after a few days we found that we could not abide that poor woman's distress, so we begged Satan to examine her several possible careers, and see if he could not change her, to her profit, to a new one. He said the longest of her careers as they now stood gave her forty-two years to live, and her shortest one twenty-nine, and that both were charged with grief and hunger and cold and pain. The only improvement he could make would be to enable her to skip a certain three minutes from now; and he asked us if he should do it. This was such a short time to decide in that we went to pieces with nervous excitement, and before we could pull ourselves together and ask for particulars he said the time would be up in a few more seconds; so then we gasped out, "Do it!"

"It is done," he said; "she was going around a corner; I have turned her back; it has changed her career."

"Then what will happen, Satan?"

"It is happening now. She is having words with Fischer, the weaver. In his anger Fischer will straightway do what he would not have done but for this accident. He was present when she stood over her child's body and uttered those blasphemies."

"What will he do?"

"He is doing it now—betraying her. In three days she will go to the stake."

We could not speak; we were frozen with horror, for if we had not meddled with her career she would have been spared this awful fate. Satan noticed these thoughts, and said:

"What you are thinking is strictly human-like—that is to say, foolish. The woman is advantaged. Die when she might, she would go to heaven. By this prompt death she gets twenty-nine years more of heaven than she is entitled to, and escapes twenty-nine years of misery here."

A moment before we were bitterly making up our minds that we would ask no more favors of Satan for friends of ours, for he did not seem to know any way to do a person a kindness but by killing him; but the whole aspect of the case was changed now, and we were glad of what we had done and full of happiness in the thought of it.

After a little I began to feel troubled about Fischer, and asked, timidly, "Does this episode change Fischer's life-scheme, Satan?"

"Change it? Why, certainly. And radically. If he had not met Frau Brandt awhile ago he would die next year, thirty-four years of age. Now he will live to be ninety, and have a pretty prosperous and comfortable life of it, as human lives go."

We felt a great joy and pride in what we had done for Fischer, and were expecting Satan to sympathize with this feeling; but he showed no sign and this made us uneasy. We waited for him to speak, but he didn't; so, to assuage our solicitude we had to ask him if there was any defect in Fischer's good luck. Satan considered the question a moment, then said, with some hesitation:

"Well, the fact is, it is a delicate point. Under his several former possible life-careers he was going to heaven."

We were aghast. "Oh, Satan! and under this one—"

"There, don't be so distressed. You were sincerely trying to do him a kindness; let that comfort you."

"Oh, dear, dear, that cannot comfort us. You ought to have told us what we were doing, then we wouldn't have acted so."

But it made no impression on him. He had never felt a pain or a sorrow, and did not know what they were, in any really informing way. He had no knowledge of them except theoretically—that is to say, intellectually. And of course that is no good. One can never get any but a loose and ignorant notion of such things except by experience. We tried our best to make him comprehend the awful thing that had been done and how we were compromised by it, but he couldn't seem to get hold of it. He said he did not think it important where Fischer went to; in heaven he would not be missed, there were "plenty there." We tried to make him see that he was missing the point entirely; that Fischer, and not other people, was the proper one to decide about the importance of it; but it all went for nothing; he said he did not care for Fischer—there were plenty more Fischers.

The next minute Fischer went by on the other side of the way, and it made us sick and faint to see him, remembering the doom that was upon him, and we the cause of it. And how unconscious he was that anything had happened to him! You could see by his elastic step and his alert manner that he was well satisfied with himself for doing that hard turn for poor Frau Brandt. He kept glancing back over his shoulder expectantly. And, sure enough, pretty soon Frau Brandt followed after, in charge of the officers and wearing jingling chains. A mob was in her wake, jeering and shouting, "Blasphemer and heretic!" and some among them were neighbors and friends of her happier days. Some were trying to strike her, and the officers were not taking as much trouble as they might to keep them from it.

"Oh, stop them, Satan!" It was out before we remembered that he could not interrupt them for a moment without changing their whole after-lives. He puffed a little puff toward them with his lips and they began to reel and stagger and grab at the empty air; then they broke apart and fled in every direction, shrieking, as if in intolerable pain. He had crushed a rib of each of them with that little puff. We could not help asking if their life-chart was changed.

"Yes, entirely. Some have gained years, some have lost them. Some few will profit in various ways by the change, but only that few."

We did not ask if we had brought poor Fischer's luck to any of them. We did not wish to know. We fully believed in Satan's desire to do us kindnesses, but we were losing confidence in his judgment. It was at this time that our growing anxiety to have him look over our life-charts and suggest improvements began to fade out and give place to other interests.

For a day or two the whole village was a chattering turmoil over Frau Brandt's case and over the mysterious calamity that had overtaken the mob, and at her trial the place was crowded. She was easily convicted of her blasphemies, for she uttered those terrible words again and said she would not take them back. When warned that she was imperiling her life, she said they could take it in welcome, she did not want it, she would rather live with the professional devils in perdition than with these imitators in the village. They accused her of breaking all those ribs by witchcraft, and asked her if she was not a witch? She answered scornfully:

"No. If I had that power would any of you holy hypocrites be alive five minutes? No; I would strike you all dead. Pronounce your sentence and let me go; I am tired of your society."

So they found her guilty, and she was excommunicated and cut off from the joys of heaven and doomed to the fires of hell; then she was clothed in a coarse robe and delivered to the secular arm, and conducted to the market-place, the bell solemnly tolling the while. We saw her chained to the stake, and saw the first film of blue smoke rise on the still air. Then her hard face softened, and she looked upon the packed crowd in front of her and said, with gentleness:

"We played together once, in long-agone days when we were innocent little creatures. For the sake of that, I forgive you."

We went away then, and did not see the fires consume her, but we heard the shrieks, although we put our fingers in our ears. When they ceased we knew she was in heaven, notwithstanding the excommunication; and we were glad of her death and not sorry that we had brought it about.

One day, a little while after this, Satan appeared again. We were always watching out for him, for life was never very stagnant when he was by. He came upon us at that place in the woods where we had first met him. Being boys, we wanted to be entertained; we asked him to do a show for us.

"Very well," he said; "would you like to see a history of the progress of the human race?—its development of that product which it calls civilization?"

We said we should.

So, with a thought, he turned the place into the Garden of Eden, and we saw Abel praying by his altar; then Cain came walking toward him with his club, and did not seem to see us, and would have stepped on my foot if I had not drawn it in. He spoke to his brother in a language which we did not understand; then he grew violent and threatening, and we knew what was going to happen, and turned away our heads for the moment; but we heard the crash of the blows and heard the shrieks and the groans; then there was silence, and we saw Abel lying in his blood and gasping out his life, and Cain standing over him and looking down at him, vengeful and unrepentant.

Then the vision vanished, and was followed by a long series of unknown wars, murders, and massacres. Next we had the Flood, and the Ark tossing around in the stormy waters, with lofty mountains in the distance showing veiled and dim through the rain. Satan said:

"The progress of your race was not satisfactory. It is to have another chance now."

The scene changed, and we saw Noah overcome with wine.

Next, we had Sodom and Gomorrah, and "the attempt to discover two or three respectable persons there," as Satan described it. Next, Lot and his daughters in the cave.

Next came the Hebraic wars, and we saw the victors massacre the survivors and their cattle, and save the young girls alive and distribute them around.

Next we had Jael; and saw her slip into the tent and drive the nail into the temple of her sleeping guest; and we were so close that when the blood gushed out it trickled in a little, red stream to our feet, and we could have stained our hands in it if we had wanted to.

Next we had Egyptian wars, Greek wars, Roman wars, hideous drenchings of the earth with blood; and we saw the treacheries of the Romans toward the Carthaginians, and the sickening spectacle of the massacre of those brave people. Also we saw Cæsar invade Britain—"not that those barbarians had done him any harm, but because he wanted their land, and desired to confer the blessings of civilization upon their widows and orphans," as Satan explained.

Next, Christianity was born. Then ages of Europe passed in review before us, and we saw Christianity and Civilization march hand in hand through those ages, "leaving famine and death and desolation in their wake, and other signs of the progress of the human race," as Satan observed.

And always we had wars, and more wars, and still other wars—all over Europe, all over the world. "Sometimes in the private interest of royal families," Satan said, "sometimes to crush a weak nation; but never a war started by the aggressor for any clean purpose—there is no such war in the history of the race."

"Now," said Satan, "you have seen your progress down to the present, and you must confess that it is wonderful—in its way. We must now exhibit the future."

He showed us slaughters more terrible in their destruction of life, more devastating in their engines of war, than any we had seen.

"You perceive," he said, "that you have made continual progress. Cain did his murder with a club; the Hebrews did their murders with javelins and swords; the Greeks and Romans added protective armor and the fine arts of military organization and generalship; the Christian has added guns and gunpowder; a few centuries from now he will have so greatly improved the deadly effectiveness of his weapons of slaughter that all men will confess that without Christian civilization war must have remained a poor and trifling thing to the end of time."

Then he began to laugh in the most unfeeling way, and make fun of the human race, although he knew that what he had been saying shamed us and wounded us. No one but an angel could have acted so; but suffering is nothing to them; they do not know what it is, except by hearsay.

More than once Seppi and I had tried in a humble and diffident way to convert him, and as he had remained silent we had taken his silence as a sort of encouragement; necessarily, then, this talk of his was a disappointment to us, for it showed that we had made no deep impression upon him. The thought made us sad, and we knew then how the missionary must feel when he has been cherishing a glad hope and has seen it blighted. We kept our grief to ourselves, knowing that this was not the time to continue our work.

Satan laughed his unkind laugh to a finish; then he said: "It is a remarkable progress. In five or six thousand years five or six high civilizations have risen, flourished, commanded the wonder of the world, then faded out and disappeared; and not one of them except the latest ever invented any sweeping and adequate way to kill people. They all did their best—to kill being the chiefest ambition of the human race and the earliest incident in its history—but only the Christian civilization has scored a triumph to be proud of. Two or three centuries from now it will be recognized that all the competent killers are Christians; then the pagan world will go to school to the Christian—not to acquire his religion, but his guns. The Turk and the Chinaman will buy those to kill missionaries and converts with."

By this time his theater was at work again, and before our eyes nation after nation drifted by, during two or three centuries, a mighty procession, an endless procession, raging, struggling, wallowing through seas of blood, smothered in battle-smoke through which the flags glinted and the red jets from the cannon darted; and always we heard the thunder of the guns and the cries of the dying.

"And what does it amount to?" said Satan, with his evil chuckle. "Nothing at all. You gain nothing; you always come out where you went in. For a million years the race has gone on monotonously propagating itself and monotonously reperforming this dull nonsense—to what end? No wisdom can guess! Who gets a profit out of it? Nobody but a parcel of usurping little monarchs and nobilities who despise you; would feel defiled if you touched them; would shut the door in your face if you proposed to call; whom you slave for, fight for, die for, and are not ashamed of it, but proud; whose existence is a perpetual insult to you and you are afraid to resent it; who are mendicants supported by your alms, yet assume toward you the airs of benefactor toward beggar; who address you in the language of master to slave, and are answered in the language of slave to master; who are worshiped by you with your mouth, while in your heart—if you have one—you despise yourselves for it. The first man was a hypocrite and a coward, qualities which have not yet failed in his line; it is the foundation upon which all civilizations have been built. Drink to their perpetuation! Drink to their augmentation! Drink to—" Then he saw by our faces how much we were hurt, and he cut his sentence short and stopped chuckling, and his manner changed. He said, gently: "No, we will drink one another's health, and let civilization go. The wine which has flown to our hands out of space by desire is earthly, and good enough for that other toast; but throw away the glasses; we will drink this one in wine which has not visited this world before."

We obeyed, and reached up and received the new cups as they descended. They were shapely and beautiful goblets, but they were not made of any material that we were acquainted with. They seemed to be in motion, they seemed to be alive; and certainly the colors in them were in motion. They were very brilliant and sparkling, and of every tint, and they were never still, but flowed to and fro in rich tides which met and broke and flashed out dainty explosions of enchanting color. I think it was most like opals washing about in waves and flashing out their splendid fires. But there is nothing to compare the wine with. We drank it, and felt a strange and witching ecstasy as of heaven go stealing through us, and Seppi's eyes filled and he said worshipingly:

"We shall be there some day, and then—"

He glanced furtively at Satan, and I think he hoped Satan would say, "Yes, you will be there some day," but Satan seemed to be thinking about something else, and said nothing. This made me feel ghastly, for I knew he had heard; nothing. spoken or unspoken, ever escaped him. Poor Seppi looked distressed, and did not finish his remark. The goblets rose and clove their way into the sky, a triplet of radiant sundogs, and disappeared. Why didn't they stay? It seemed a bad sign, and depressed me. Should I ever see mine again? Would Seppi ever see his?

## CHAPTER IX

It was wonderful, the mastery Satan had over time and distance. For him they did not exist. He called them human inventions, and said they were artificialities. We often went to the most distant parts of the globe with him, and stayed weeks and months, and yet were gone only a fraction of a second, as a rule. You could prove it by the clock. One day when our people were in such awful distress because the witch commission were afraid to proceed against the astrologer and Father Peter's household, or against any, indeed, but the poor and the friendless, they lost patience and took to witch-hunting on their own score, and began to chase a born lady who was known to have the habit of curing people by devilish arts, such as bathing them, washing them, and nourishing them instead of bleeding them and purging them through the ministrations of a barber-surgeon in the proper way. She came flying down, with the howling and cursing mob after her, and tried to take refuge in houses, but the doors were shut in her face. They chased her more than half an hour, we following to see it, and at last she was exhausted and fell, and they caught her. They dragged her to a tree and threw a rope over the limb, and began to make a noose in it, some holding her, meantime, and she crying and begging, and her young daughter looking on and weeping, but afraid to say or do anything.

They hanged the lady, and I threw a stone at her, although in my heart I was sorry for her; but all were throwing stones and each was watching his neighbor, and if I had not done as the others did it would have been noticed and spoken of. Satan burst out laughing.

All that were near by turned upon him, astonished and not pleased. It was an ill time to laugh, for his free and scoffing ways and his supernatural music had brought him under suspicion all over the town and turned many privately against him. The big blacksmith called attention to him now, raising his voice so that all should hear, and said:

"What are you laughing at? Answer! Moreover, please explain to the company why you threw no stone."

"Are you sure I did not throw a stone?"

"Yes. You needn't try to get out of it; I had my eye on you."

"And I—I noticed you!" shouted two others.

"Three witnesses," said Satan: "Mueller, the blacksmith; Klein, the butcher's man; Pfeiffer, the weaver's journeyman. Three very ordinary liars. Are there any more?"

"Never mind whether there are others or not, and never mind about what you consider us—three's enough to settle your matter for you. You'll prove that you threw a stone, or it shall go hard with you."

"That's so!" shouted the crowd, and surged up as closely as they could to the center of interest.

"And first you will answer that other question," cried the blacksmith, pleased with himself for being mouthpiece to the public and hero of the occasion. "What are you laughing at?"

Satan smiled and answered, pleasantly: "To see three cowards stoning a dying lady when they were so near death themselves."

You could see the superstitious crowd shrink and catch their breath, under the sudden shock. The blacksmith, with a show of bravado, said:

"Pooh! What do you know about it?"

"I? Everything. By profession I am a fortune-teller, and I read the hands of you three—and some others—when you lifted them to stone the woman. One of you will die to-morrow week; another of you will die to-night; the third has but five minutes to live—and yonder is the clock!"

It made a sensation. The faces of the crowd blanched, and turned mechanically toward the clock. The butcher and the weaver seemed smitten with an illness, but the blacksmith braced up and said, with spirit:

"It is not long to wait for prediction number one. If it fails, young master, you will not live a whole minute after, I promise you that."

No one said anything; all watched the clock in a deep stillness which was impressive. When four and a half minutes were gone the blacksmith gave a sudden gasp and clapped his hands upon his heart, saying, "Give me breath! Give me room!" and began to sink down. The crowd surged back, no one offering to support him, and he fell lumbering to the ground and was dead. The people stared at him, then at Satan, then at one another; and their lips moved, but no words came. Then Satan said:

"Three saw that I threw no stone. Perhaps there are others; let them speak."

It struck a kind of panic into them, and, although no one answered him, many began to violently accuse one another, saying, "You said he didn't throw," and getting for reply, "It is a lie, and I will make you eat it!" And so in a moment they were in a raging and noisy turmoil, and beating and banging one another; and in the midst was the only indifferent one—the dead lady hanging from her rope, her troubles forgotten, her spirit at peace.

So we walked away, and I was not at ease, but was saying to myself, "He told them he was laughing at them, but it was a lie—he was laughing at me."

That made him laugh again, and he said, "Yes, I was laughing at you, because, in fear of what others might report about you, you stoned the woman when your heart revolted at the act—but I was laughing at the others, too."

"Why?"

"Because their case was yours."

"How is that?"

"Well, there were sixty-eight people there, and sixty-two of them had no more desire to throw a stone than you had."

"Satan!"

"Oh, it's true. I know your race. It is made up of sheep. It is governed by minorities, seldom or never by majorities. It suppresses its feelings and its beliefs and follows the handful that makes the most noise. Sometimes the noisy handful is right, sometimes wrong; but no matter, the crowd follows it. The vast majority of the race, whether savage or civilized, are secretly kind-hearted and shrink from inflicting pain, but in the presence of the aggressive and pitiless minority they don't dare to assert themselves. Think of it! One kind-hearted creature spies upon another, and sees to it that he loyally helps in iniquities which revolt both of them. Speaking as an expert, I know that ninety-nine out of a hundred of your race were strongly against the killing of witches when that foolishness was first agitated by a handful of pious lunatics in the long ago. And I know that even to-day, after ages of transmitted prejudice and silly teaching, only one person in twenty puts any real heart into the harrying of a witch. And yet apparently everybody hates witches and wants them killed. Some day a handful will rise up on the other side and make the most noise—perhaps even a single daring man with a big voice and a determined front will do it—and in a week all the sheep will wheel and follow him, and witch-hunting will come to a sudden end.

Monarchies, aristocracies, and religions are all based upon that large defect in your race—the individual's distrust of his neighbor, and his desire, for safety's or comfort's sake, to stand well in his neighbor's eye. These institutions will always remain, and always flourish, and always oppress you, affront you, and degrade you, because you will always be and remain slaves of minorities. There was never a country where the majority of the people were in their secret hearts loyal to any of these institutions."

I did not like to hear our race called sheep, and said I did not think they were.

"Still, it is true, lamb," said Satan. "Look at you in war—what mutton you are, and how ridiculous!"

"In war? How?"

"There has never been a just one, never an honorable one—on the part of the instigator of the war. I can see a million years ahead, and this rule will never change in so many as half a dozen instances. The loud little handful—as usual—will shout for the war. The pulpit will—warily and cautiously—object—at first; the great, big, dull bulk of the nation will rub its sleepy eyes and try to make out why there should be a war, and will say, earnestly and indignantly, "It is unjust and dishonorable, and there is no necessity for it." Then the handful will shout louder. A few fair men on the other side will argue and reason against the war with speech and pen, and at first will have a hearing and be applauded; but it will not last long; those others will outshout them, and presently the anti-war audiences will thin out and lose popularity. Before long you will see this curious thing: the speakers stoned from the platform, and free speech strangled by hordes of furious men who in their secret hearts are still at one with those stoned speakers—as earlier—but do not dare to say so. And now the whole nation—pulpit and all—will take up the war-cry, and shout itself hoarse, and mob any honest man who ventures to open his mouth; and presently such mouths will cease to open. Next the statesmen will invent cheap lies, putting the blame upon the nation that is attacked, and every man will be glad of those conscience-soothing falsities, and will diligently study them, and refuse to examine any refutations of them; and thus he will by and by convince himself that the war is just, and will thank God for the better sleep he enjoys after this process of grotesque self-deception."

## CHAPTER X

DAYS and days went by now, and no Satan. It was dull without him. But the astrologer, who had returned from his excursion to the moon, went about the village, braving public opinion, and getting a stone in the middle of his back now and then when some witch-hater got a safe chance to throw it and dodge out of sight. Meantime two influences had been working well for Marget. That Satan, who was quite indifferent to her, had stopped going to her house after a visit or two had hurt her pride, and she had set herself the task of banishing him from her heart. Reports of Wilhelm Meidling's dissipation brought to her from time to time by old Ursula had touched her with remorse, jealousy of Satan being the cause of it; and so now, these two matters working upon her together, she was getting a good profit out of the combination—her interest in Satan was steadily cooling, her interest in Wilhelm as steadily warming. All that was needed to complete her conversion was that Wilhelm should brace up and do something that should cause favorable talk and incline the public toward him again.

The opportunity came now. Marget sent and asked him to defend her uncle in the approaching trial, and he was greatly pleased, and stopped drinking and began his preparations with diligence. With more diligence than hope, in fact, for it was not a promising case. He had many interviews in his office with Seppi and me, and threshed out our testimony pretty thoroughly, thinking to find some valuable grains among the chaff, but the harvest was poor, of course.

If Satan would only come! That was my constant thought. He could invent some way to win the case; for he had said it would be won, so he necessarily knew how it could be done. But the days dragged on, and still he did not come. Of course I did not doubt that it would win, and that Father Peter would be happy for the rest of his life, since Satan had said so; yet I knew I should be much more comfortable if he would come and tell us how to manage it. It was getting high time for Father Peter to have a saving change toward happiness, for by general report he was worn out with his imprisonment and the ignominy that was burdening him, and was like to die of his miseries unless he got relief soon.

At last the trial came on, and the people gathered from all around to witness it; among them many strangers from considerable distances. Yes, everybody was there except the accused. He was too feeble in body for the strain. But Marget was present, and keeping up her hope and her spirit the best she could. The money was present, too. It was emptied on the table, and was handled and caressed and examined by such as were privileged.

The astrologer was put in the witness-box. He had on his best hat and robe for the occasion.

*Question.* You claim that this money is yours?

*Answer.* I do.

*Q.* How did you come by it?

*A.* I found the bag in the road when I was returning from a journey.

*Q.* When?

*A.* More than two years ago.

*Q.* What did you do with it?

*A.* I brought it home and hid it in a secret place in my observatory, intending to find the owner if I could.

*Q.* You endeavored to find him?

*A.* I made diligent inquiry during several months, but nothing came of it.

*Q.* And then?

*A.* I thought it not worth while to look further, and was minded to use the money in finishing the wing of the foundling-asylum connected with the priory and nunnery. So I took it out of its hiding-place and counted it to see if any of it was missing. And then—

*Q.* Why do you stop? Proceed.

*A.* I am sorry to have to say this, but just as I had finished and was restoring the bag to its place, I looked up and there stood Father Peter behind me.

Several murmured, "That looks bad," but others answered, "Ah, but he is such a liar!"

*Q.* That made you uneasy?

*A.* No; I thought nothing of it at the time, for Father Peter often came to me unannounced to ask for a little help in his need.

Marget blushed crimson at hearing her uncle falsely and impudently charged with begging, especially from one he had always denounced as a fraud, and was going to speak, but remembered herself in time and held her peace.

*Q.* Proceed.

*A.* In the end I was afraid to contribute the money to the foundling-asylum, but elected to wait yet another year and continue my inquiries. When I heard of Father Peter's find I was glad, and no suspicion entered my mind; when I came home a day or two later and discovered that my own money was gone I still did not suspect until three circumstances connected with Father Peter's good fortune struck me as being singular coincidences.

*Q.* Pray name them.

*A.* Father Peter had found his money in a path—I had found mine in a road. Father Peter's find consisted exclusively of gold ducats—mine also. Father Peter found eleven hundred and seven ducats—I exactly the same.

This closed his evidence, and certainly it made a strong impression on the house; one could see that.

Wilhelm Meidling asked him some questions, then called us boys, and we told our tale. It made the people laugh, and we were ashamed. We were feeling pretty badly, anyhow, because Wilhelm was hopeless, and showed it. He was doing as well as he could, poor young fellow, but nothing was in his favor, and such sympathy as there was was now plainly not with his client. It might be difficult for court and people to believe the astrologer's story, considering his character, but it was almost impossible to believe Father Peter's. We were already feeling badly enough, but when the astrologer's lawyer said he believed he would not ask us any questions—for our story was a little delicate and it would be cruel for him to put any strain upon it—everybody tittered, and it was almost more than we could bear. Then he made a sarcastic little speech, and got so much fun out of our tale, and it seemed so ridiculous and childish and every way impossible and foolish, that it made everybody laugh till the tears came; and at last Marget could not keep up her courage any longer, but broke down and cried, and I was so sorry for her.

Now I noticed something that braced me up. It was Satan standing alongside of Wilhelm! And there was such a contrast!—Satan looked so confident, had such a spirit in his eyes and face, and Wilhelm looked so depressed and despondent. We two were comfortable now, and judged that he would testify and persuade the bench and the people that black was white and white black, or any other color he wanted it. We glanced around to see what the strangers in the house thought of him, for he was beautiful, you know—stunning, in fact—but no one was noticing him; so we knew by that that he was invisible.

The lawyer was saying his last words; and while he was saying them Satan began to melt into Wilhelm. He melted into him and disappeared; and then there was a change, when his spirit began to look out of Wilhelm's eyes.

That lawyer finished quite seriously, and with dignity. He pointed to the money, and said:

"The love of it is the root of all evil. There it lies, the ancient tempter, newly red with the shame of its latest victory—the dishonor of a priest of God and his two poor juvenile helpers in crime. If it could but speak, let us hope that it would be constrained to confess that of all its conquests this was the basest and the most pathetic."

He sat down. Wilhelm rose and said:

"From the testimony of the accuser I gather that he found this money in a road more than two years ago. Correct me, sir, if I misunderstood you."

The astrologer said his understanding of it was correct.

"And the money so found was never out of his hands thenceforth up to a certain definite date—the last day of last year. Correct me, sir, if I am wrong."

The astrologer nodded his head. Wilhelm turned to the bench and said:

"If I prove that this money here was not that money, then it is not his?"

"Certainly not; but this is irregular. If you had such a witness it was your duty to give proper notice of it and have him here to—" He broke off and began to consult with the other judges. Meantime that other lawyer got up excited and began to protest against allowing new witnesses to be brought into the case at this late stage.

The judges decided that his contention was just and must be allowed.

"But this is not a new witness," said Wilhelm. "It has already been partly examined. I speak of the coin."

"The coin? What can the coin say?"

"It can say it is not the coin that the astrologer once possessed. It can say it was not in existence last December. By its date it can say this."

And it was so! There was the greatest excitement in the court while that lawyer and the judges were reaching for coins and examining them and exclaiming. And everybody was full of admiration of Wilhelm's brightness in happening to think of that neat idea. At last order was called and the court said:

"All of the coins but four are of the date of the present year. The court tenders its sincere sympathy to the accused, and its deep regret that he, an innocent man, through an unfortunate mistake, has suffered the undeserved humiliation of imprisonment and trial. The case is dismissed."

So the money could speak, after all, though that lawyer thought it couldn't. The court rose, and almost everybody came forward to shake hands with Marget and congratulate her, and then to shake with Wilhelm and praise him; and Satan had stepped out of Wilhelm and was standing around looking on full of interest, and people walking through him every which way, not knowing he was there. And Wilhelm could not explain why he only thought of the date on the coins at the last moment, instead of earlier; he said it just occurred to him, all of a sudden, like an inspiration, and he brought it right out without any hesitation, for, although he didn't examine the coins, he seemed, somehow, to know it was true. That was honest of him, and like him; another would have pretended he had thought of it earlier, and was keeping it back for a surprise.

He had dulled down a little now; not much, but still you could notice that he hadn't that luminous look in his eyes that he had while Satan was in him. He nearly got it back, though, for a moment when Marget came and praised him and thanked him and couldn't keep him from seeing how proud she was of him. The astrologer went off dissatisfied and cursing, and Solomon Isaacs gathered up the money and carried it away. It was Father Peter's for good and all, now.

Satan was gone. I judged that he had spirited himself away to the jail to tell the prisoner the news; and in this I was right. Marget and the rest of us hurried thither at our best speed, in a great state of rejoicing.

Well, what Satan had done was this: he had appeared before that poor prisoner, exclaiming, "The trial is over, and you stand forever disgraced as a thief—by verdict of the court!"

The shock unseated the old man's reason. When we arrived, ten minutes later, he was parading pompously up and down and delivering commands to this and that and the other constable or jailer, and calling them Grand Chamberlain, and Prince This and Prince That, and Admiral of the Fleet, Field Marshal in Command, and all such fustian, and was as happy as a bird. He thought he was Emperor!

Marget flung herself on his breast and cried, and indeed everybody was moved almost to heartbreak.

He recognized Marget, but could not understand why she should cry. He patted her on the shoulder and said:

"Don't do it, dear; remember, there are witnesses, and it is not becoming in the Crown Princess. Tell me your trouble—it shall be mended; there is nothing the Emperor cannot do." Then he looked around and saw old Ursula with her apron to her eyes. He was puzzled at that, and said, "And what is the matter with you?"

Through her sobs she got out words explaining that she was distressed to see him—"so." He reflected over that a moment, then muttered, as if to himself: "A singular old thing, the Dowager Duchess—means well, but is always snuffling and never able to tell what it is about. It is because she doesn't know." His eyes fell on Wilhelm. "Prince of India," he said, "I divine that it is you that the Crown Princess is concerned about. Her tears shall be dried; I will no longer stand between you; she shall share your throne; and between you you shall inherit mine. There, little lady, have I done well? You can smile now—isn't it so?"

He petted Marget and kissed her, and was so contented with himself and with everybody that he could not do enough for us all, but began to give away kingdoms and such things right and left, and the least that any of us got was a principality. And so at last, being persuaded to go home, he marched in imposing state; and when the crowds along the way saw how it gratified him to be hurrahed at, they humored him to the top of his desire, and he responded with condescending bows and gracious smiles, and often stretched out a hand and said, "Bless you, my people!"

As pitiful a sight as ever I saw. And Marget, and old Ursula crying all the way.

On my road home I came upon Satan, and reproached him with deceiving me with that lie. He was not embarrassed, but said, quite simply and composedly:

"Ah, you mistake; it was the truth. I said he would be happy the rest of his days, and he will, for he will always think he is the Emperor, and his pride in it and his joy in it will endure to the end. He is now, and will remain, the one utterly happy person in this empire."

"But the method of it, Satan, the method! Couldn't you have done it without depriving him of his reason?"

It was difficult to irritate Satan, but that accomplished it.

"What an ass you are!" he said. "Are you so unobservant as not to have found out that sanity and happiness are an impossible combination? No sane man can be happy, for to him life is real, and he sees what a fearful thing it is. Only the mad can be happy, and not many of those. The few that imagine themselves kings or gods are happy, the rest are no happier than the sane. Of course, no man is entirely in his right mind at any time, but I have been referring to the extreme cases. I have taken from this man that trumpery thing which the race regards as a Mind; I have replaced his tin life with a silver gilt fiction; you see the result—and you criticize! I said I would make him permanently happy, and I have done it. I have made him happy by the only means possible to his race—and you are not satisfied!" He heaved a discouraged sigh, and said, "It seems to me that this race is hard to please."

There it was, you see. He didn't seem to know any way to do a person a favor except by killing him or making a lunatic out of him. I apologized, as well as I could; but privately I did not think much of his processes—at that time.

Satan was accustomed to say that our race lived a life of continuous and uninterrupted self-deception. It duped itself from cradle to grave with shams and delusions which it mistook for realities, and this made its entire life a sham. Of the score of fine qualities which it imagined it had and was vain of, it really possessed hardly one. It regarded itself as gold, and was only brass. One day when he was in this vein he mentioned a detail—the sense of humor. I cheered up then, and took issue. I said we possessed it.

"There spoke the race!" he said; "always ready to claim what it hasn't got, and mistake its ounce of brass filings for a ton of gold-dust. You have a mongrel perception of humor, nothing more; a multitude of you possess that. This multitude see the comic side of a thousand low-grade and trivial things—broad incongruities, mainly; grotesqueries, absurdities, evokers of the horse-laugh. The ten thousand high-grade comicalities which exist in the world are sealed from their dull vision. Will a day come when the race will detect the funniness of these juvenilities and laugh at them—and by laughing at them destroy them? For your race, in its poverty, has unquestionably one really effective weapon—laughter. Power, money, persuasion, supplication, persecution—these can lift at a colossal humbug—push it a little—weaken it a little, century by century; but only laughter can blow it to rags and atoms at a blast. Against the assault of laughter nothing can stand. You are always fussing and fighting with your other weapons. Do you ever use that one? No; you leave it lying rusting. As a race, do you ever use it at all? No; you lack sense and the courage."

We were traveling at the time and stopped at a little city in India and looked on while a juggler did his tricks before a group of natives. They were wonderful, but I knew Satan could beat that game, and I begged him to show off a little, and he said he would. He changed himself into a native in turban and breech-cloth, and very considerately conferred on me a temporary knowledge of the language.

The juggler exhibited a seed, covered it with earth in a small flower-pot, then put a rag over the pot; after a minute the rag began to rise; in ten minutes it had risen a foot; then the rag was removed and a little tree was exposed, with leaves upon it and ripe fruit. We ate the fruit, and it was good. But Satan said:

"Why do you cover the pot? Can't you grow the tree in the sunlight?"

"No," said the juggler; "no one can do that."

"You are only an apprentice; you don't know your

trade. Give me the seed. I will show you." He took the seed and said, "What shall I raise from it?"

"It is a cherry seed; of course you will raise a cherry."

"Oh no; that is a trifle; any novice can do that. Shall I raise an orange-tree from it?"

"Oh yes!" and the juggler laughed.

"And shall I make it bear other fruits as well as oranges?"

"If God wills!" and they all laughed.

Satan put the seed in the ground, put a handful of dust on it, and said, "Rise!"

A tiny stem shot up and began to grow, and grew so fast that in five minutes it was a great tree, and we were sitting in the shade of it. There was a murmur of wonder, then all looked up and saw a strange and pretty sight, for the branches were heavy with fruits of many kinds and colors—oranges, grapes, bananas, peaches, cherries, apricots, and so on. Baskets were brought, and the unlading of the tree began; and the people crowded around Satan and kissed his hand, and praised him, calling him the prince of jugglers. The news went about the town, and everybody came running to see the wonder—and they remembered to bring baskets, too. But the tree was equal to the occasion; it put out new fruits as fast as any were removed; baskets were filled by the score and by the hundred, but always the supply remained undiminished. At last a foreigner in white linen and sun-helmet arrived, and exclaimed, angrily:

"Away from here! Clear out, you dogs; the tree is on my lands and is my property."

The natives put down their baskets and made humble obeisance. Satan made humble obeisance, too, with his fingers to his forehead, in the native way, and said:

"Please let them have their pleasure for an hour, sir—only that, and no longer. Afterward you may forbid them; and you will still have more fruit than you and the state together can consume in a year."

This made the foreigner very angry, and he cried out, "Who are you, you vagabond, to tell your betters what they may do and what they mayn't!" and he struck Satan with his cane and followed this error with a kick.

The fruits rotted on the branches, and the leaves withered and fell. The foreigner gazed at the bare limbs with the look of one who is surprised, and not gratified. Satan said:

"Take good care of the tree, for its health and yours are bound together. It will never bear again, but if you tend it well it will live long. Water its roots once in each hour every night—and do it yourself; it must not be done by proxy, and to do it in daylight will not answer. If you fail only once in any night, the tree will die, and you likewise. Do not go home to your own country any more—you would not reach there; make no business or pleasure engagements which require you to go outside your gate at night—you cannot afford the risk; do not rent or sell this place—it would be injudicious."

The foreigner was proud and wouldn't beg, but I thought he looked as if he would like to. While he stood gazing at Satan we vanished away and landed in Ceylon.

I was sorry for that man; sorry Satan hadn't been his customary self and killed him or made him a lunatic. It would have been a mercy. Satan overheard the thought, and said:

"I would have done it but for his wife, who has not offended me. She is coming to him presently from their native land, Portugal. She is well, but has not long to live, and has been yearning to see him and persuade him to go back with her next year. She will die without knowing he can't leave that place?"

"He won't tell her?"

"He? He will not trust that secret with any one; he will reflect that it could be revealed in sleep, in the hearing of some Portuguese guest's servant some time or other."

"Did none of those natives understand what you said to him?"

"None of them understood, but he will always be afraid that some of them did. That fear will be torture to him, for he has been a harsh master to them. In his dreams he will imagine them chopping his tree down. That will make his days uncomfortable—I have already arranged for his nights."

It grieved me, though not sharply, to see him take such a malicious satisfaction in his plans for this foreigner.

"Does he believe what you told him, Satan?"

"He thought he didn't, but our vanishing helped. The tree, where there had been no tree before—that helped. The insane and uncanny variety of fruits—the sudden withering—all these things are helps.

Let him think as he may, reason as he may, one thing is certain, he will water the tree. But between this and night he will begin his changed career with a very natural precaution—for him."

"What is that?"

"He will fetch a priest to cast out the tree's devil. You are such a humorous race—and don't suspect it."

"Will he tell the priest?"

"No. He will say a juggler from Bombay created it, and that he wants the juggler's devil driven out of it, so that it will thrive and be fruitful again. The priest's incantations will fail; then the Portuguese will give up that scheme and get his watering-pot ready."

"But the priest will burn the tree. I know it; he will not allow it to remain."

"Yes, and anywhere in Europe he would burn the man, too. But in India the people are civilized, and these things will not happen. The man will drive the priest away and take care of the tree."

I reflected a little, then said, "Satan, you have given him a hard life, I think."

"Comparatively. It must not be mistaken for a holiday."

We flitted from place to place around the world as we had done before, Satan showing me a hundred wonders, most of them reflecting in some way the weakness and triviality of our race. He did this now every few days—not out of malice—I am sure of that—it only seemed to amuse and interest him, just as a naturalist might be amused and interested by a collection of ants.

## CHAPTER XI

FOR as much as a year Satan continued these visits, but at last he came less often, and then for a long time he did not come at all. This always made me lonely and melancholy. I felt that he was losing interest in our tiny world and might at any time abandon his visits entirely. When one day he finally came to me I was overjoyed, but only for a little while. He had come to say good-by, he told me, and for the last time. He had investigations and undertakings in other corners of the universe, he said, that would keep him busy for a longer period than I could wait for his return.

"And you are going away, and will not come back any more?"

"Yes," he said. "We have comraded long together, and it has been pleasant—pleasant for both; but I must go now, and we shall not see each other any more."

"In this life, Satan, but in another? We shall meet in another, surely?"

Then, all tranquilly and soberly, he made the strange answer, "*There is no other.*"

A subtle influence blew upon my spirit from his, bringing with it a vague, dim, but blessed and hopeful feeling that the incredible words might be true—even *must* be true.

"Have you never suspected this, Theodor?"

"No. How could I? But if it can only be true—"

"It is true."

A gust of thankfulness rose in my breast, but a doubt checked it before it could issue in words, and I said, "But—but—we have seen that future life—seen it in its actuality, and so—"

"It was a vision—it had no existence."

I could hardly breathe for the great hope that was struggling in me. "A vision?—a vi—"

"*Life itself is only a vision, a dream.*"

It was electrical. By God! I had had that very thought a thousand times in my musings!

"*Nothing* exists; all is a dream. God—man—the world—the sun, the moon, the wilderness of stars—a dream, all a dream; they have no existence. *Nothing exists save empty space—and you!*"

"I!"

"And you are not you—you have no body, no blood, no bones, you are but a *thought.* I myself have no existence; I am but a dream—your dream, creature of your imagination. In a moment you will have realized this, then you will banish me from your visions and I shall dissolve into the nothingness out of which you made me. . . .

"I am perishing already—I am failing—I am passing away. In a little while you will be alone in shoreless space, to wander its limitless solitudes without friend or comrade forever—for you will remain a *thought,* the only existent thought, and by your nature inextinguishable, indestructible. But I, your poor servant, have revealed you to yourself and set you free. Dream other dreams, and better!

"Strange! that you should not have suspected years ago—centuries, ages, eons, ago!—for you have existed, companionless, through all the eternities. Strange, indeed, that you should not have suspected that your universe and its contents were only dreams, visions, fiction! Strange, because they are so frankly and hysterically insane—like all dreams: a God who could make good children as easily as bad, yet preferred to make bad ones; who could have made every one of them happy, yet never made a single happy one; who made them prize their bitter life, yet stingily cut it short; who gave his angels eternal happiness unearned, yet required his other children to earn it; who gave his angels painless lives, yet cursed his other children with biting miseries and maladies of mind and body; who mouths justice and invented hell—mouths mercy and invented hell—mouths Golden Rules, and forgiveness multiplied by seventy times seven, and invented hell; who mouths morals to other people and has none himself; who frowns upon crimes, yet commits them all; who created man without invitation, then tries to shuffle the responsibility for man's acts upon man, instead of honorably placing it where it belongs, upon himself; and finally, with altogether divine obtuseness, invites this poor, abused slave to worship him! . . .

"You perceive, *now*, that these things are all impossible except in a dream. You perceive that they are pure and puerile insanities, the silly creations of an imagination that is not conscious of its freaks—in a word, that they are a dream, and you the maker of it. The dream-marks are all present; you should have recognized them earlier.

"It is true, that which I have revealed to you; there is no God, no universe, no human race, no earthly life, no heaven, no hell. It is all a dream—a grotesque and foolish dream. Nothing exists but you. And you are but a *thought*—a vagrant thought, a useless thought, a homeless thought, wandering forlorn among the empty eternities!"

He vanished, and left me appalled; for I knew, and realized, that all he had said was true.

# A HORSE'S TALE

# ACKNOWLEDGMENTS

ALTHOUGH I have had several opportunities to see a bull-fight, I have never seen one; but I needed a bull-fight in this story, and a trustworthy one will be found in it. I got it out of John Hay's *Castilian Days*, reducing and condensing it to fit the requirements of this small story. Mr. Hay and I were friends from early times, and if he were still with us he would not rebuke me for the liberty I have taken.

The knowledge of military minutiæ exhibited in this story will be found to be correct, but it is not mine; I took it from *Army Regulations*, ed. 1904; *Hardy's Tactics—Cavalry*, revised ed., 1861; and *Jomini's Handbook of Military Etiquette*, West Point ed., 1905.

It would not be honest in me to encourage by silence the inference that I composed the Horse's private bugle-call, for I did not. I lifted it, as Aristotle says. It is the opening strain in *The Pizzicato* in *Sylvia*, by Delibes. When that master was composing it he did not know it was a bugle-call, it was I that found it out.

Along through the story I have distributed a few anachronisms and unborn historical incidents and such things, so as to help the tale over the difficult places. This idea is not original with me; I got it out of Herodotus. Herodotus says, "Very few things happen at the right time, and the rest do not happen at all: the conscientious historian will correct these defects."

The cats in the chair do not belong to me, but to another.

These are all the exceptions. What is left of the story is mine.

MARK TWAIN.

LONE TREE HILL, DUBLIN,
NEW HAMPSHIRE, *October*, *1905*.

# Part I

# A HORSE'S TALE*

## CHAPTER I

### SOLDIER BOY—PRIVATELY TO HIMSELF

I AM Buffalo Bill's horse. I have spent my life under his saddle—with him in it, too, and he is good for two hundred pounds, without his clothes; and there is no telling how much he does weigh when he is out on the war-path and has his batteries belted on. He is over six feet, is young, hasn't an ounce of waste flesh, is straight, graceful, springy in his motions, quick as a cat, and has a handsome face, and black hair dangling down on his shoulders, and is beautiful to look at; and nobody is braver than he is, and nobody is stronger, except myself. Yes, a person that doubts that he is fine to see should see him in his beaded buckskins, on my back and his rifle peeping above his shoulder, chasing a hostile trail, with me going like the wind and his hair streaming out behind from the shelter of his broad slouch. Yes, he is a sight to look at then—and I'm part of it myself.

I am his favorite horse, out of dozens. Big as he is, I have carried him eighty-one miles between nightfall and sunrise on the scout; and I am good for fifty, day in and day out, and all the time. I am not large, but I am built on a business basis. I have carried him thousands and thousands of miles on scout duty for the army, and there's not a gorge, nor a pass, nor a valley, nor a fort, nor a trading post, nor a buffalo-range in the whole sweep of the Rocky Mountains and the Great Plains that we don't know as well as we know the bugle-calls. He is Chief of Scouts to the Army of the Frontier, and it makes us very important. In such a position as I hold in the military service one needs to be of good family and possess an education much above the common to be worthy of the place. I am the best-educated horse outside of the hippodrome, everybody says, and the best-mannered. It may be so, it is not for me to say; modesty is the best policy, I think. Buffalo Bill taught me the most of what I know, my mother taught me much, and I taught myself the rest. Lay a row of moccasins before me—Pawnee, Sioux, Shoshone, Cheyenne, Blackfoot, and as many other tribes as you please—and I can name the tribe every moccasin belongs to by the make of it. Name it in horse-talk, and could do it in American if I had speech.

I know some of the Indian signs—the signs they make with their hands, and by signal-fires at night and columns of smoke by day. Buffalo Bill taught me how to drag wounded soldiers out of the line of fire with my teeth; and I've done it, too; at least I've dragged *him* out of the battle when he was wounded. And not just once, but twice. Yes, I know a lot of things. I remember forms, and gaits, and faces; and you can't disguise a person that's done me a kindness so that I won't know him thereafter wherever I find him. I know the art of searching for a trail, and I know the stale track from the fresh. I can keep a trail all by myself, with Buffalo Bill asleep in the saddle; ask him—he will tell you so. Many a time, when he has ridden all night, he has said to me at dawn, "Take the watch, Boy; if the trail freshens, call me." Then he goes to sleep. He knows he can trust me, because I have a reputation. A scout horse that has a reputation does not play with it.

My mother was all American—no alkali-spider about *her*, I can tell you; she was of the best blood of Kentucky, the bluest Blue-grass aristocracy, very proud and acrimonious—or maybe it is ceremonious. I don't know which it is. But it is no matter; size is the main thing about a word, and that one's up to standard. She spent her military life as colonel of the Tenth Dragoons, and saw a deal of rough service—distinguished service it was, too. I mean, she *carried* the Colonel; but it's all the same. Where would he be without his horse? He wouldn't arrive. It takes two to make a colonel of dragoons. She was a fine dragoon horse, but never got above that. She was strong enough for the scout service, and had the endurance, too, but she couldn't quite come up to the speed required; a scout horse has to have steel in his muscle and lightning in his blood.

My father was a bronco. Nothing as to lineage—that is, nothing as to recent lineage—but plenty good enough when you go a good way back. When

Professor Marsh was out here hunting bones for the chapel of Yale University he found skeletons of horses no bigger than a fox, bedded in the rocks, and he said they were ancestors of my father. My mother heard him say it; and he said those skeletons were two million years old, which astonished her and made her Kentucky pretensions look small and pretty antiphonal, not to say oblique. Let me see. . . . I used to know the meaning of those words, but . . . well, it was years ago, and 'tisn't as vivid now as it was when they were fresh. That sort of words doesn't keep, in the kind of climate we have out here. Professor Marsh said those skeletons were fossils. So that makes me part blue grass and part fossil; if there is any older or better stock, you will have to look for it among the Four Hundred, I reckon. I am satisfied with it. And am a happy horse, too, though born out of wedlock.

And now we are back at Fort Paxton once more, after a forty-day scout, away up as far as the Big Horn. Everything quiet. Crows and Blackfeet squabbling—as usual—but no outbreaks, and settlers feeling fairly easy.

The Seventh Cavalry still in garrison, here; also the Ninth Dragoons, two artillery companies, and some infantry. All glad to see me, including General Alison, commandant. The officers' ladies and children well, and called upon me—with sugar. Colonel Drake, Seventh Cavalry, said some pleasant things; Mrs. Drake was very complimentary; also Captain and Mrs. Marsh, Company B, Seventh Cavalry; also the Chaplain, who is always kind and pleasant to me, because I kicked the lungs out of a trader once. It was Tommy Drake and Fanny Marsh that furnished the sugar—nice children, the nicest at the post, I think.

That poor orphan child is on her way from France—everybody is full of the subject. Her father was General Alison's brother; married a beautiful young Spanish lady ten years ago, and has never been in America since. They lived in Spain a year or two, then went to France. Both died some months ago. This little girl that is coming is the only child. General Alison is glad to have her. He has never seen her. He is a very nice old bachelor, but is an old bachelor just the same and isn't more than about a year this side of retirement by age limit; and so what does he know about taking care of a little maid nine years old? If I could have her it would be another matter, for I know all about children, and they adore me. Buffalo Bill will tell you so himself.

I have some of this news from overhearing the garrison-gossip, the rest of it I got from Potter, the General's dog. Potter is the great Dane. He is privileged, all over the post, like Shekels, the Seventh Cavalry's dog, and visits everybody's quarters and picks up everything that is going, in the way of news. Potter has no imagination, and no great deal of culture, perhaps, but he has a historical mind and a good memory, and so he is the person I depend upon mainly to post me up when I get back from a scout. That is, if Shekels is out on depredation and I can't get hold of him.

## CHAPTER II

### LETTER FROM ROUEN—TO GENERAL ALISON

MY *dear Brother-in-law,*—Please let me write again in Spanish, I cannot trust my English, and I am aware, from what your brother used to say, that army officers educated at the Military Academy of the United States are taught our tongue. It is as I told you in my other letter: both my poor sister and her husband, when they found they could not recover, expressed the wish that you should have their little Catherine—as knowing that you would presently be retired from the army—rather than that she should remain with me, who am broken in health, or go to your mother in California, whose health is also frail.

You do not know the child, therefore I must tell you something about her. You will not be ashamed of her looks, for she is a copy in little of her beautiful mother—and it is that Andalusian beauty which is not surpassable, even in your country. She has her mother's charm and grace and good heart and sense of justice, and she has her father's vivacity and cheerfulness and pluck and spirit of enterprise, with the affectionate disposition and sincerity of both parents.

My sister pined for her Spanish home all these years of exile; she was always talking of Spain to the child, and tending and nourishing the love of Spain in the little thing's heart as a precious flower; and she died happy in the knowledge that the fruitage of her patriotic labors was as rich as even she could desire.

Cathy is a sufficiently good little scholar, for her nine years; her mother taught her Spanish herself, and kept it always fresh upon her ear and her tongue by hardly ever speaking with her in any other tongue; her father was her English teacher, and talked with her in that language almost exclusively; French has been her everyday speech for more than seven years among her playmates here; she has a good working use of governess—German and Italian. It is true that there is always a faint foreign fragrance about her speech, no matter what language she is talking, but it is only just noticeable, nothing more, and is rather a charm than a mar, I think. In the ordinary child-studies Cathy is neither before nor behind the average child of nine, I should say. But I can say this for her: in love for her friends and in high-mindedness and good-heartedness she has not many equals, and in my opinion no superiors. And I beg of you, let her have her way with the dumb animals—they are her worship. It is an inheritance from her mother. She knows but little of cruelties and oppressions—keep them from her sight if you can. She would flare up at them and make trouble, in her small but quite decided and resolute way; for she has a character of her own, and lacks neither promptness nor initiative. Sometimes her judgment is at fault, but I think her intentions are always right. Once when she was a little creature of three or four years she suddenly brought her tiny foot down upon the floor in an apparent outbreak of indignation, then fetched it a backward wipe, and stooped down to examine the result. Her mother said:

"Why, what is it, child? What has stirred you so?"

"Mamma, the big ant was trying to kill the little one."

"And so you protected the little one."

"Yes, mamma, because he had no friend, and I wouldn't let the big one kill him."

"But you have killed them both."

Cathy was distressed, and her lip trembled. She picked up the remains and laid them upon her palm, and said:

"Poor little anty, I'm so sorry; and I didn't mean to kill you, but there wasn't any other way to save you, it was such a hurry."

She is a dear and sweet little lady, and when she goes it will give me a sore heart. But she will be happy with you, and if your heart is old and tired, give it into her keeping; she will make it young again, she will refresh it, she will make it sing. Be good to her, for all our sakes!

My exile will soon be over now. As soon as I am a little stronger I shall see my Spain again; and that will make *me* young again!

MERCEDES.

# CHAPTER III

## GENERAL ALISON TO HIS MOTHER

I AM glad to know that you are all well, in San Bernardino.

. . . That grandchild of yours has been here—well, I do not quite know how many days it is; nobody can keep account of days or anything else where she is! Mother, she did what the Indians were never able to do. She took the Fort—took it the first day! Took me, too; took the colonels, the captains, the women, the children, and the dumb brutes; took Buffalo Bill, and all his scouts; took the garrison—to the last man; and in forty-eight hours the Indian encampment was hers, illustrious old Thunder-Bird and all. Do I seem to have lost my solemnity, my gravity, my poise, my dignity? You would lose your own, in my circumstances. Mother, you never saw such a winning little devil. She is all energy, and spirit, and sunshine, and interest in everybody and everything, and pours out her prodigal love upon every creature that will take it, high or low, Christian or pagan, feathered or furred; and none has declined it to date, and none ever will, I think. But she has a temper, and sometimes it catches fire and flames up, and is likely to burn whatever is near it; but it is soon over, the passion goes as quickly as it comes. Of course she has an Indian name already; Indians always rechristen a stranger early. Thunder-Bird attended to her case. He gave her the Indian equivalent for firebug, or firefly. He said:

"'Times, ver' quiet, ver' soft, like summer night, but when she mad she blaze."

Isn't it good? Can't you see the flare? She's beautiful, mother, beautiful as a picture; and there is a touch of you in her face, and of her father—poor George! and in her unresting activities, and her fearless ways, and her sunbursts and cloudbursts, she is always bringing George back to me. These impulsive natures are dramatic. George was dramatic, so is this Lightning-Bug, so is Buffalo Bill. When Cathy first arrived—it was in the forenoon—Buffalo Bill was away, carrying orders to Major Fuller, at Five Forks, up in the Clayton Hills. At mid-afternoon I was at my desk, trying to work, and this sprite had been making it impossible for half an hour. At last I said:

"Oh, you bewitching little scamp, *can't* you be quiet just a minute or two, and let your poor old uncle attend to a part of his duties?"

"I'll try, uncle; I will, indeed," she said.

"Well, then, that's a good child—kiss me. Now, then, sit up in that chair, and set your eye on that clock. There—that's right. If you stir—if you so much as wink—for four whole minutes, I'll bite you!"

It was very sweet and humble and obedient she looked, sitting there, still as a mouse; I could hardly keep from setting her free and telling her to make as much racket as she wanted to. During as much as two minutes there was a most unnatural and heavenly quiet and repose, then Buffalo Bill came thundering up to the door in all his scout finery, flung himself out of the saddle, said to his horse, "Wait for me, Boy," and stepped in, and stopped dead in his tracks—gazing at the child. She forgot orders, and was on the floor in a moment, saying:

"Oh, you are so beautiful! Do you like me?"

"No, I don't, I love you!" and he gathered her up with a hug, and then set her on his shoulder—apparently nine feet from the floor.

She was at home. She played with his long hair, and admired his big hands and his clothes and his carbine, and asked question after question, as fast as he could answer, until I excused them both for half an hour, in order to have a chance to finish my work. Then I heard Cathy exclaiming over Soldier Boy; and he was worthy of her raptures, for he is a wonder of a horse, and has a reputation which is as shining as his own silken hide.

## CHAPTER IV

### CATHY TO HER AUNT MERCEDES

OH, it is wonderful here, aunty dear, just paradise! Oh, if you could only see it! everything so wild and lovely; such grand plains, stretching such miles and miles and miles, all the most delicious velvety sand and sage-brush, and rabbits as big as a dog, and such tall and noble jackassful ears that that is what they name them by; and such vast mountains, and so rugged and craggy and lofty, with cloud-shawls wrapped around their shoulders, and looking so solemn and awful and satisfied; and the charming Indians, oh, how you would dote on them, aunty dear, and they would on you, too, and they would let you hold their babies, the way they do me, and they *are* the fattest, and brownest, and sweetest little things, and never cry, and wouldn't if they had pins sticking in them, which they haven't, because they are poor and can't afford it; and the horses and mules and cattle and dogs—hundreds and hundreds and hundreds, and not an animal that you can't do what you please with, except uncle Thomas, but *I* don't mind him, he's lovely; and oh, if you could hear the bugles: *too—too—too-too—too—too*, and so on—per-fectly beautiful! Do you recognize that one? It's the first toots of the *reveille;* it goes, dear me, *so* early in the morning!—then I and every other soldier on the whole place are up and out in a minute, except uncle Thomas, who is most unaccountably lazy, I don't know why, but I have talked to him about it, and I reckon it will be better, now. He hasn't any faults much, and is charming and sweet, like Buffalo Bill, and Thunder-Bird, and Mammy Dorcas, and Soldier Boy, and Shekels, and Potter, and Sour-Mash, and—well, they're *all* that, just angels, as you may say.

The very first day I came, I don't know how long ago it was, Buffalo Bill took me on Soldier Boy to Thunder-Bird's camp, not the big one which is out on the plain, which is White Cloud's, he took me to *that* one next day, but this one is four or five miles up in the hills and crags, where there is a great shut-in meadow, full of Indian lodges and dogs and squaws and everything that is interesting, and a brook of the clearest water running through it, with white pebbles on the bottom and trees all along the banks cool and shady and good to wade in, and as the sun goes down it is dimmish in there, but away up against the sky you see the big peaks towering up and shining bright and vivid in the sun, and sometimes an eagle sailing by them, not flapping a wing, the same as if he was asleep; and young Indians and girls romping and laughing and carrying on, around the spring and the pool, and not much clothes on except the girls, and dogs fighting, and the squaws busy at work, and the bucks busy resting, and the old men sitting in a bunch smoking, and passing the pipe not to the left but to the right, which means there's been a row in the camp and they are settling it if they can, and children playing *just* the same as any other children, and little boys shooting at a mark with bows, and I cuffed one of them because he hit a dog with a club that wasn't doing anything, and he resented it but before long he wished he hadn't: but this sentence is getting too long and I will start another. Thunder-Bird put on his Sunday-best war outfit to let me see him, and he was splendid to look at, with his face painted red and bright and intense like a fire-coal and a valance of eagle feathers from the top of his head all down his back, and he had his tomahawk, too, and his pipe, which has a stem which is longer than my arm, and I never had such a good time in an Indian camp in my life, and I learned a lot of words of the language, and next day BB took me to the camp out on the Plains, four miles, and I had another good time and got acquainted with some more Indians and dogs; and the big chief, by the name of White Cloud, gave me a pretty little bow and arrows and I gave him my red sash-ribbon, and in four days I could shoot very well with it and beat any white boy of my size at the post; and I have been to those camps plenty of times since; and I have learned to ride, too, BB taught me, and every day he practises me and praises me, and every time I do better than ever he lets me have a scamper on Soldier Boy, and *that's* the last agony of pleasure! for he is the charmingest horse, and so beautiful and shiny and black, and hasn't another color on him anywhere, except a white star in his forehead, not just an imitation star, but a real one, with four points, shaped exactly like a star that's hand-made, and if you should cover him all up but his star you would know him anywhere, even in Jerusalem or Australia, by that. And I got acquainted with a good many of the Seventh Cavalry, and the dragoons, and officers, and families, and horses, in the first few days, and some more in the next few and the next few and the next few, and now I know more soldiers and horses than you can think, no matter how hard you try. I am keeping up my studies every now and then, but there isn't much time for it. I love you so! and I send you a hug and a kiss. CATHY.

P.S.—I belong to the Seventh Cavalry and Ninth Dragoons, I am an officer, too, and do not have to work on account of not getting any wages.

## CHAPTER V

### GENERAL ALISON TO MERCEDES

SHE has been with us a good nice long time, now. You are troubled about your sprite because this is such a wild frontier, hundreds of miles from civilization, and peopled only by wandering tribes of savages? You fear for her safety? Give yourself no uneasiness about her. Dear me, she's in a nursery! and she's got more than eighteen hundred nurses. It would distress the garrison to suspect that you think they can't take care of her. They think they can. They would tell you so themselves. You see, the Seventh Cavalry has never had a child of its very own before, and neither has the Ninth Dragoons; and so they are like all new mothers, they think there is no other child like theirs, no other child so wonderful, none that is so worthy to be faithfully and tenderly looked after and protected. These bronzed veterans of mine are very good mothers, I think, and wiser than some other mothers; for they let her take lots of risks, and it is a good education for her; and the more risks she takes and comes successfully out of, the prouder they are of her. They adopted her, with grave and formal military ceremonies of their own invention—solemnities is the truer word; solemnities that were so profoundly solemn and earnest, that the spectacle would have been comical if it hadn't been so touching. It was a good show, and as stately and complex as guard-mount and the trooping of the colors; and it had its own special music, composed for the occasion by the bandmaster of the Seventh; and the child was as serious as the most serious war-worn soldier of them all; and finally when they throned her upon the shoulder of the oldest veteran, and pronounced her "well and truly adopted," and the bands struck up and all saluted and she saluted in return, it was better and more moving than any kindred thing I have seen on the stage, because stage things are make-believe, but this was real and the players' hearts were in it.

It happened several weeks ago, and was followed by some additional solemnities. The men created a couple of new ranks, thitherto unknown to the army regulations, and conferred them upon Cathy, with ceremonies suitable to a duke. So now she is Corporal-General of the Seventh Cavalry, and Flag-Lieutenant of the Ninth Dragoons, with the privilege (decreed by the men) of writing U.S.A. after her name! Also, they presented her a pair of shoulder-straps—both dark blue, the one with F. L. on it, the other with C. G. Also, a sword. She wears them. Finally, they granted her the *salute*. I am witness that that ceremony is faithfully observed by both parties—and most gravely and decorously, too. I have never seen a soldier smile yet, while delivering it, nor Cathy in returning it.

Ostensibly I was not present at these proceedings, and am ignorant of them; but I was where I could see. I was afraid of one thing—the jealousy of the other children of the post; but there is nothing of that, I am glad to say. On the contrary, they are proud of their comrade and her honors. It is a surprising thing, but it is true. The children are devoted to Cathy, for she has turned their dull frontier life into a sort of continuous festival; also they know her for a stanch and steady friend, a friend who can always be depended upon, and does not change with the weather.

She has become a rather extraordinary rider, under the tutorship of a more than extraordinary teacher—BB, which is her pet name for Buffalo Bill. She pronounces it *beeby.* He has not only taught her seventeen ways of breaking her neck, but twenty-two ways of avoiding it. He has infused into her the best and surest protection of a horseman—*confidence.* He did it gradually, systematically, little by little, a step at a time, and each step made sure before the next was essayed. And so he inched her along up through terrors that had been discounted by training before she reached them, and therefore were not recognizable as terrors when she got to them. Well, she is a daring little rider, now, and is perfect in what she knows of horsemanship. By and by she will know the art like a West Point cadet, and will exercise it as fearlessly. She doesn't know anything about sidesaddles. Does that distress you? And she is a fine performer, without any saddle at all. Does that discomfort you? Do not let it; she is not in any danger, I give you my word.

You said that if my heart was old and tired she would refresh it, and you said truly. I do not know how I got along without her, before. I was a forlorn old tree, but now that this blossoming vine has wound itself about me and become the life of my life, it is very different. As a furnisher of business for me and for Mammy Dorcas she is exhaustlessly competent, but I like my share of it and of course Dorcas likes hers, for Dorcas "raised" George, and Cathy is George over again in so many ways that she brings back Dorcas's youth and the joys of that long-vanished time. My father tried to set Dorcas free twenty years ago, when we still lived in Virginia, but without success; she considered herself a member of the family, and wouldn't go. And so, a member of the family she remained, and has held that position unchallenged ever since, and holds it now; for when my mother sent her here from San Bernardino when we learned that Cathy was coming, she only changed from one division of the family to the other. She has the warm heart of her race, and its lavish affections, and when Cathy arrived the pair were mother and child in five minutes, and that is what they are to date and will continue. Dorcas really thinks she raised George, and that is one of her prides, but perhaps it was a mutual raising, for their ages were the same—thirteen years short of mine. But they were playmates, at any rate; as regards that, there is no room for dispute.

Cathy thinks Dorcas is the best Catholic in America except herself. She could not pay any one a higher compliment than that, and Dorcas could not receive one that would please her better. Dorcas is satisfied that there has never been a more wonderful child than Cathy. She has conceived the curious idea that Cathy is *twins*, and that one of them is a boy-twin and failed to get segregated—got submerged, is the idea. To argue with her that this is nonsense is a waste of breath—her mind is made up, and arguments do not affect it. She says:

"Look at her; she loves dolls, and girl-plays, and everything a girl loves, and she's gentle and sweet, and ain't cruel to dumb brutes—now that's the girl-twin, but she loves boy-plays, and drums and fifes and soldiering, and rough-riding, and ain't afraid of anybody or anything—and that's the boy-twin; 'deed you needn't tell *me* she's only *one* child; no, sir, she's twins, and one of them got shet up out of sight. Out of sight, but that don't make any difference, that boy is in there, and you can see him look out of her eyes when her temper is up."

Then Dorcas went on, in her simple and earnest way, to furnish illustrations.

"Look at that raven, Marse Tom. Would anybody befriend a raven but that child? Of course they wouldn't; it ain't natural. Well, the Injun boy had the raven tied up, and was all the time plaguing it and starving it, and she pitied the po' thing, and tried to buy it from the boy, and the tears was in her eyes. That was the girl-twin, you see. She offered him her thimble, and he flung it down; she offered him all the doughnuts she had, which was two, and he flung them down; she offered him half a paper of pins, worth forty ravens, and he made a mouth at her and jabbed one of them in the raven's back. That was the limit, you know.

It called for the other twin. Her eyes blazed up, and she jumped for him like a wild-cat, and when she was done with him she was rags and he wasn't anything but an allegory. That was most undoubtedly the other twin, you see, coming to the front. No, sir; don't tell *me* he ain't in there. I've seen him with my own eyes—and plenty of times, at that."

"Allegory? What is an allegory?"

"I don't know, Marse Tom, it's one of her words; she loves the big ones, you know, and I pick them up from her; they sound good and I can't help it."

"What happened after she had converted the boy into an allegory?"

"Why, she untied the raven and confiscated him by force and fetched him home, and left the doughnuts and things on the ground. Petted him, of course, like she does with every creature. In two days she had him so stuck after her that she—well, *you* know how he follows her everywhere, and sets on her shoulder often when she rides her breakneck rampages—all of which is the girl-twin to the front, you see—and he does what he pleases, and is up to all kinds of devilment, and is a perfect nuisance in the kitchen. Well, they all stand it, but they wouldn't if it was another person's bird."

Here she began to chuckle comfortably, and presently she said:

"Well, you know, she's a nuisance herself, Miss Cathy is, she *is* so busy, and into everything, like that bird. It's all just as innocent, you know, and she don't mean any harm, and is so good and dear; and it ain't her fault, it's her nature; her interest is always a-working and always red-hot, and she *can't* keep quiet. Well, yesterday it was 'Please, Miss Cathy, don't do that'; and, 'Please, Miss Cathy, let that alone'; and, 'Please, Miss Cathy, don't make so much noise'; and so on and so on, till I reckon I had found fault fourteen times in fifteen minutes; then she looked up at me with her big brown eyes that can plead so, and said in that odd little foreign way that goes to your heart,

"'Please, mammy, make me a compliment.'"

"And of course you did it, you old fool?"

"Marse Tom, I just grabbed her up to my breast and says, 'Oh, you po' dear little motherless thing, you ain't got a fault in the world, and you can do anything you want to, and tear the house down, and yo' old black mammy won't say a word!'"

"Why, of course, of course—*I* knew you'd spoil the child."

She brushed away her tears, and said with dignity:

"Spoil the child? spoil *that* child, Marse Tom? There can't *anybody* spoil her. She's the king bee of this post, and everybody pets her and is her slave, and yet, as you know, your own self, she ain't the least little bit spoiled." Then she eased her mind with this retort: "Marse Tom, she makes you do anything she wants to, and you can't deny it; so if she could be spoilt, she'd been spoilt long ago, because you are the very *worst!* Look at that pile of cats in your chair, and you sitting on a candle-box, just as patient; it's because they're her cats."

If Dorcas were a soldier, I could punish her for such large frankness as that. I changed the subject, and made her resume her illustrations. She had scored against me fairly, and I wasn't going to cheapen her victory by disputing it. She proceeded to offer this incident in evidence on her twin theory:

"Two weeks ago when she got her finger mashed open, she turned pretty pale with the pain, but she never said a word. I took her in my lap, and the surgeon sponged off the blood and took a needle and thread and began to sew it up; it had to have a lot of stitches, and each one made her scrunch a little, but she never let go a sound. At last the surgeon was so full of admiration that he said, 'Well, you *are* a brave little thing!' and she said, just as ca'm and simple as if she was talking about the weather, 'There isn't anybody braver but the Cid!' You see? it was the boy-twin that the surgeon was a-dealing with."

"Who is the Cid?"

"I don't know, sir—at least only what she says. She's always talking about him, and says he was the bravest hero Spain ever had, or any other country. They have it up and down, the children do, she standing up for the Cid, and they working George Washington for all he is worth."

"Do they quarrel?"

"No; it's only disputing, and bragging, the way children do. They want her to be an American, but she can't be anything but a Spaniard, she says. You see, her mother was always longing for home, po' thing! and thinking about it, and so the child is just as much a Spaniard as if she'd always lived there. She thinks she remembers how Spain looked, but I reckon she don't, because she was only a baby when they moved to France. She is very proud to be a Spaniard."

Does that please you, Mercedes? Very well, be content; your niece is loyal to her allegiance: her mother laid deep the foundations of her love for Spain, and she will go back to you as good a Spaniard as you are yourself. She had made me promise to take her to you for a long visit when the War Office retires me.

I attend to her studies myself; has she told you that? Yes, I am her school-master, and she makes pretty good progress, I think, everything considered. Everything considered—being translated—means holidays. But the fact is, she was not born for study, and it comes hard. Hard for me, too; it hurts me like a physical pain to see that free spirit of the air and the sunshine laboring and grieving over a book; and sometimes when I find her gazing far away towards the plains and the blue mountains with the longing in her eyes, I have to throw open the prison doors; I can't help it. A quaint little scholar she is, and makes plenty of blunders. Once I put the question:

"What does the Czar govern?"

She rested her elbow on her knee and her chin on her hand and took that problem under deep consideration. Presently she looked up and answered, with a rising inflection implying a shade of uncertainty,

"The dative case?"

Here are a couple of her expositions which were delivered with tranquil confidence:

"*Chaplain*, diminutive of chap. *Lass* is masculine, *lassie* is feminine."

She is not a genius, you see, but just a normal child; they all make mistakes of that sort. There is a glad light in her eye which is pretty to see when she finds herself able to answer a question promptly and accurately, without any hesitation; as, for instance, this morning:

"Cathy dear, what is a cube?"

"Why, a native of Cuba."

She still drops a foreign word into her talk now and then, and there is still a subtle foreign flavor or fragrance about even her exactest English—and long may this abide! for it has for me a charm that is very pleasant. Sometimes her English is daintily prim and bookish and captivating. She has a child's sweet tooth, but for her health's sake I try to keep its inspirations under check. She is obedient—as is proper for a titled and recognized military personage, which she is—but the chain presses sometimes. For instance, we were out for a walk, and passed by some bushes that were freighted with wild gooseberries. Her face brightened and she put her hands together and delivered herself of this speech, most feelingly:

"Oh, if I was permitted a vice it would be the *gourmandise!*"

Could I resist that? No. I gave her a gooseberry.

You ask about her languages. They take care of themselves; they will not get rusty here; our regiments are not made up of natives alone—far from it. And she is picking up Indian tongues diligently.

# CHAPTER VI

## SOLDIER BOY AND THE MEXICAN PLUG

"WHEN did you come?"

"Arrived at sundown."

"Where from?"

"Salt Lake."

"Are you in the service?"

"No. Trade."

"Pirate trade, I reckon."

"What do you know about it?"

"I saw you when you came. I recognized your master. He is a bad sort. Trap-robber, horse-thief, squaw-man, renegado—Hank Butters—I know him very well. Stole you, didn't he?"

"Well, it amounted to that."

"I thought so. Where is his pard?"

"He stopped at White Cloud's camp."

"He is another of the same stripe, is Blake Haskins." (*Aside.*) They are laying for Buffalo Bill again, I guess. (*Aloud.*) "What is your name?"

"Which one?"

"Have you got more than one?"

"I get a new one every time I'm stolen. I used to have an honest name, but that was early; I've forgotten it. Since then I've had thirteen *aliases.*"

"Aliases? What is alias?"

"A false name."

"Alias. It's a fine large word, and is in my line;

it has quite a learned and cerebrospinal incandescent sound. Are you educated?"

"Well, no, I can't claim it. I can take down bars, I can distinguish oats from shoe-pegs, I can blaspheme a saddle-boil with the college-bred, and I know a few other things—not many; I have had no chance, I have always had to work; besides, I am of low birth and no family. You speak my dialect like a native, but you are not a Mexican Plug, you are a gentleman, I can see that; and educated, of course."

"Yes, I am of old family, and not illiterate. I am a fossil."

"A which?"

"Fossil. The first horses were fossils. They date back two million years."

"Gr-eat sand and sage-brush! do you mean it?"

"Yes, it is true. The bones of my ancestors are held in reverence and worship, even by men. They do not leave them exposed to the weather when they find them, but carry them three thousand miles and enshrine them in their temples of learning, and worship them."

"It is wonderful! I knew you must be a person of distinction, by your fine presence and courtly address, and by the fact that you are not subjected to the indignity of hobbles, like myself and the rest. Would you tell me your name?"

"You have probably heard of it—Soldier Boy."

"What!—the renowned, the illustrious?"

"Even so."

"It takes my breath! Little did I dream that

ever I should stand face to face with the possessor of that great name. Buffalo Bill's horse! Known from the Canadian border to the deserts of Arizona, and from the eastern marches of the Great Plains to the foot-hills of the Sierra! Truly this is a memorable day. You still serve the celebrated Chief of Scouts?"

"I am still his property, but he has lent me, for a time, to the most noble, the most gracious, the most excellent, her Excellency Catherine, Corporal-General Seventh Cavalry and Flag-Lieutenant Ninth Dragoons, U. S. A.,—on whom be peace!"

"Amen. Did you say *her* Excellency?"

"The same. A Spanish lady, sweet blossom of a ducal house. And truly a wonder; knowing everything, capable of everything; speaking all the languages, master of all sciences, a mind without horizons, a heart of gold, the glory of her race! On whom be peace!"

"Amen. It is marvelous!"

"Verily. I knew many things, she has taught me others. I am educated. I will tell you about her."

"I listen—I am enchanted."

"I will tell a plain tale, calmly, without excitement, without eloquence. When she had been here four or five weeks she was already erudite in military things, and they made her an officer—a double officer. She rode the drill every day, like any soldier; and she could take the bugle and direct the evolutions herself. Then, on a day, there was a grand race, for prizes—none to enter but the children. Seventeen children entered, and she was the youngest. Three girls, fourteen boys—good riders all. It was a steeplechase, with four hurdles, all pretty high. The first prize was a most cunning half-grown silver bugle, and mighty pretty, with red silk cord and tassels. Buffalo Bill was very anxious; for he had taught her to ride, and he did most dearly want her to win that race, for the glory of it. So he wanted her to ride me, but she wouldn't; and she reproached him, and said it was unfair and unright, and taking advantage; for what horse in this post or any other could stand a chance against me? and she was very severe with him, and said, 'You ought to be ashamed —you are proposing to me conduct unbecoming an officer and a gentleman.' So he just tossed her up in the air about thirty feet and caught her as she came down, and said he *was* ashamed; and put up his handkerchief and pretended to cry, which nearly broke her heart, and she petted him, and begged him to forgive her, and said she would do anything in the world he could ask but that; but he said he ought to go hang himself, and he *must*, if he could get a rope; it was nothing but right he should, for he never, never could forgive himself; and then *she* began to cry, and they both sobbed, the way you could hear him a mile, and she clinging around his neck and pleading, till at last he was comforted a little, and gave his solemn promise he wouldn't hang himself till after the race; and wouldn't do it at all if she won it, which made her happy, and she said she would win it or die in the saddle; so then everything was pleasant again and both of them content. He can't help playing jokes on her, he is so fond of her and she is so innocent and unsuspecting; and when she finds it out she cuffs him and is in a fury, but presently forgives him because it's *him;* and maybe the very next day she's caught with another joke; you see she can't learn any better, because she hasn't any deceit in her, and that kind aren't ever expecting it in another person.

"It was a grand race. The whole post was there, and there was such another whooping and shouting when the seventeen kids came flying down the turf and sailing over the hurdles—oh, beautiful to see! Half-way down, it was kind of neck and neck, and anybody's race and nobody's. Then, what should happen but a cow steps out and puts her head down to munch grass, with her broadside to the battalion, and they a-coming like the wind; they split apart to flank her, but *she?*—why, she drove the spurs home and soared over that cow like a bird! and on she went, and cleared the last hurdle solitary and alone, the army letting loose the grand yell, and she skipped from the horse the same as if he had been standing still, and made her bow, and everybody crowded around to congratulate, and they gave her the bugle, and she put it to her lips and blew 'boots and saddles' to see how it would go, and BB was as proud as you can't think! And he said, 'Take Soldier Boy, and don't pass him back till I ask for him!' and I can tell you he wouldn't have said that to any other person on this planet. That was two months and more ago, and nobody has been on my back since but the Corporal-General Seventh Cavalry and Flag-Lieutenant of the Ninth Dragoons, U.S.A.,—on whom be peace!"

"Amen. I listen—tell me more."

"She set to work and organized the Sixteen, and called it the First Battalion Rocky Mountain Rangers, U.S.A., and she wanted to be bugler, but they elected her Lieutenant-General *and* Bugler. So she ranks her uncle the commandant, who is only a Brigadier. And doesn't she train those little people! Ask the Indians, ask the traders, ask the soldiers; they'll tell you. She has been at it from the first day. Every morning they go clattering down into the plain, and there she sits on my back with her bugle at her mouth and sounds the orders and puts them through the evolutions for an hour or more; and it is too beautiful for anything to see those ponies dissolve from one formation into another, and waltz about, and break, and scatter, and form again, always moving, always graceful, now trotting, now galloping, and so on, sometimes near by, sometimes in the distance, all just like a state ball, you know, and sometimes she can't hold herself any longer, but sounds the 'charge,' and turns me loose! and you can take my word for it, if the battalion hasn't *too* much of a start we catch up and go over the breastworks with the front line.

"Yes, they are soldiers, those little people; and healthy, too, not ailing any more, the way they used to be sometimes. It's because of her drill. She's got a fort, now—Fort Fanny Marsh. Major-General Tommy Drake planned it out, and the Seventh and Dragoons built it. Tommy is the Colonel's son, and is fifteen and the oldest in the Battalion; Fanny Marsh is Brigadier-General, and is next oldest—

over thirteen. She is daughter of Captain Marsh, Company B, Seventh Cavalry. Lieutenant-General Alison is the youngest by considerable; I think she is about nine and a half or three-quarters. Her military rig, as Lieutenant-General, isn't for business, it's for dress parade, because the ladies made it. They say they got it out of the Middle Ages—out of a book—and it is all red and blue and white silks and satins and velvets; tights, trunks, sword, doublet with slashed sleeves, short cape, cap with just one feather in it; I've heard them name these things; they got them out of the book; she's dressed like a page, of old times, they say. It's the daintiest outfit that ever was—you will say so, when you see it. She's lovely in it—oh, just a dream! In some ways she is just her age, but in others she's as old as her uncle, I think. She is very learned. She teaches her uncle his book. I have seen her sitting by with the book and reciting to him what is in it, so that he can learn to do it himself.

"Every Saturday she hires little Injuns to garrison her fort; then she lays siege to it, and makes military approaches by make-believe trenches in make-believe night, and finally at make-believe dawn she draws her sword and sounds the assault and takes it by storm. It is for practice. And she has invented a bugle-call all by herself, out of her own head, and it's a stirring one, and the prettiest in the service. It's to call *me*—it's never used for anything else. She taught it to me, and told me what it says: '*It is I, Soldier—come!*' and when those thrilling notes come floating down the distance I hear them without fail, even if I am two miles away; and then —oh, then you should see my heels get down to business!

"And she has taught me how to say good-morning and good-night to her, which is by lifting my right hoof for her to shake; and also how to say good-by; I do that with my left foot—but only for practice, because there hasn't been any but make-believe good-bying yet, and I hope there won't ever be. It would make me cry if I ever had to put up my left foot in earnest. She has taught me how to salute, and I can do it as well as a soldier. I bow my head low, and lay my right hoof against my cheek. She taught me that because I got into disgrace once, through ignorance. I am privileged, because I am known to be honorable and trustworthy, and because I have a distinguished record in the service; so they don't hobble me nor tie me to stakes or shut me tight in stables, but let me wander around to suit myself. Well, trooping the colors is a very solemn ceremony, and everybody must stand uncovered when the flag goes by, the commandant and all; and once I was there, and ignorantly walked across right in front of the band, which was an awful disgrace. Ah, the Lieutenant-General was so ashamed, and so distressed that I should have done such a thing before all the world, that she couldn't keep the tears back; and then she taught me the salute, so that if I ever did any other unmilitary act through ignorance I could do my salute and she believed everybody would think it was apology enough and would not press the matter. It is very nice and distinguished; no other horse can do it; often the men salute me, and I return it. I am privileged to be present when the Rocky Mountain Rangers troop the colors and I stand solemn, like the children, and I salute when the flag goes by. Of course when she goes to her fort her sentries sing out 'Turn out the guard!' and then . . . do you catch that refreshing early-morning whiff from the mountain-pines and the wild flowers? The night is far spent; we'll hear the bugles before long. Dorcas, the black woman, is very good and nice; she takes care of the Lieutenant-General, and is Brigadier-General Alison's mother, which makes her mother-in-law to the Lieutenant-General. That is what Shekels says. At least it is what I think he says, though I never can understand him quite clearly. He—"

"Who is Shekels?"

"The Seventh Cavalry dog. I mean, if he *is* a dog. His father was a coyote and his mother was a wild-cat. It doesn't really make a dog out of him, does it?"

"Not a real dog, I should think. Only a kind of a general dog, at most, I reckon. Though this is a matter of ichthyology, I suppose; and if it is, it is out of my depth, and so my opinion is not valuable, and I don't claim much consideration for it."

"It isn't ichthyology; it is dogmatics, which is still more difficult and tangled up. Dogmatics always are."

"Dogmatics is quite beyond me, quite; so I am not competing. But on general principles it is my opinion that a colt out of a coyote and a wild-cat is no square dog, but doubtful. That is my hand, and I stand pat."

"Well, it is as far as I can go myself, and be fair and conscientious. I have always regarded him as a doubtful dog, and so has Potter. Potter is the great Dane. Potter says he is no dog, and not even poultry—though I do not go quite so far as that."

"And I wouldn't, myself. Poultry is one of those things which no person can get to the bottom of, there is so much of it and such variety. It is just wings, and wings, and wings, till you are weary: turkeys, and geese, and bats, and butterflies, and angels, and grasshoppers, and flying-fish, and—well, there is really no end to the tribe; it gives me the heaves just to think of it. But this one hasn't any wings, has he?"

"No."

"Well, then, in my belief he is more likely to be dog than poultry. I have not heard of poultry that hadn't wings. Wings is the *sign* of poultry; it is what you tell poultry by. Look at the mosquito."

"What do you reckon he is, then? He must be something."

"Why, he could be a reptile; anything that hasn't wings is a reptile."

"Who told you that?"

"Nobody told me, but I overheard it."

"Where did you overhear it?"

"Years ago. I was with the Philadelphia Institute expedition in the Bad Lands under Professor Cope, hunting mastodon bones, and I overheard him say, his own self, that any plantigrade circumflex vertebrate bacterium that hadn't wings and was uncertain was a reptile. Well, then, has this dog any wings?

No. Is he a plantigrade circumflex vertebrate bacterium? Maybe so, maybe not; but without ever having seen him, and judging only by his illegal and spectacular parentage, I will bet the odds of a bale of hay to a bran mash that he looks it. Finally, is he uncertain? That is the point—is he uncertain? I will leave it to you if you have ever heard of a more uncertainer dog than what this one is?"

"No, I never have."

"Well, then, he's a reptile. That's settled."

"Why, look here, whatsyourname—"

"Last alias, Mongrel."

"A good one, too. I was going to say, you are better educated than you have been pretending to be. I like cultured society, and I shall cultivate your acquaintance. Now as to Shekels, whenever you want to know about any private thing that is going on at this post or in White Cloud's camp or Thunder-Bird's, he can tell you; and if you make friends with him he'll be glad to, for he is a born gossip, and picks up all the tittle-tattle. Being the whole Seventh Cavalry's reptile, he doesn't belong to anybody in particular, and hasn't any military duties; so he comes and goes as he pleases, and is popular with all the house cats and other authentic sources of private information. He understands all the languages, and talks them all, too. With an accent like gritting your teeth, it is true, and with a grammar that is no improvement on blasphemy—still, with practice you get at the meat of what he says, and it serves. . . . Hark! That's the reveille. . . .

# A HORSE'S TALE

THE REVEILLE *

*At West Point the bugle is supposed to be saying:
"I can't get 'em up,
I can't get 'em up,
I can't get 'em up in the morning!"

"Faint and far, but isn't it clear, isn't it sweet? There's no music like the bugle to stir the blood, in the still solemnity of the morning twilight, with the dim plain stretching away to nothing and the spectral mountains slumbering against the sky. You'll hear another note in a minute—faint and far and clear, like the other one, and sweeter still, you'll notice. Wait . . . listen. There it goes! It says, '*It is I, Soldier—come!*' . . .

SOLDIER BOY'S BUGLE CALL

. . . Now then, watch me leave a blue streak behind!"

## CHAPTER VII

### SOLDIER BOY AND SHEKELS

DID you do as I told you? Did you look up the Mexican Plug?"

"Yes, I made his acquaintance before night and got his friendship."

"I liked him. Did you?"

"Not at first. He took me for a reptile, and it troubled me, because I didn't know whether it was a compliment or not. I couldn't ask him, because it would look ignorant. So I didn't say anything, and soon I liked him very well indeed. Was it a compliment, do you think?"

"Yes, that is what it was. They are very rare, the reptiles; very few left, now-a-days."

"Is that so? What is a reptile?"

"It is a plantigrade circumflex vertebrate bacterium that hasn't any wings and is uncertain."

"Well, it—it sounds fine, it surely does."

"And it *is* fine. You may be thankful you are one."

"I am. It seems wonderfully grand and elegant for a person that is so humble as I am; but I am thankful, I am indeed, and will try to live up to it. It is hard to remember. Will you say it again, please, and say it slow?"

"Plantigrade circumflex vertebrate bacterium that hasn't any wings and is uncertain."

"It *is* beautiful, anybody must grant it; beautiful, and of a noble sound. I hope it will not make me proud and stuck-up—I should not like to be that. It is much more distinguished and honorable to be a reptile than a dog, don't you think, Soldier?"

"Why, there's no comparison. It is awfully aristocratic. Often a duke is called a reptile; it is set down so, in history."

"Isn't that grand! Potter wouldn't ever associate with me, but I reckon he'll be glad to when he finds out what I am."

"You can depend upon it."

"I will thank Mongrel for this. He is a very good sort, for a Mexican Plug. Don't you think he is?"

"It is my opinion of him; and as for his birth, he cannot help that. We cannot all be reptiles, we cannot all be fossils; we have to take what comes and be thankful it is no worse. It is the true philosophy."

"For those others?"

"Stick to the subject, please. Did it turn out that my suspicions were right?"

"Yes, perfectly right. Mongrel has heard them planning. They are after BB's life, for running them out of Medicine Bow and taking their stolen horses away from them."

"Well, they'll get him yet, for sure."

"Not if he keeps a sharp lookout."

"*He* keep a sharp lookout! He never does; he despises them, and all their kind. His life is always being threatened, and so it has come to be monotonous."

"Does he know they are here?"

"Oh yes, he knows it. He is always the earliest to know who comes and who goes. But he cares nothing for them and their threats; he only laughs when people warn him. They'll shoot him from behind a tree the first he knows. Did Mongrel tell you their plans?"

"Yes. They have found out that he starts for Fort Clayton day after to-morrow, with one of his scouts; so they will leave to-morrow, letting on to go south, but they will fetch around north all in good time."

"Shekels, I don't like the look of it."

# CHAPTER VIII

## THE SCOUT-START. BB AND LIEUTENANT-GENERAL ALISON

BB (*saluting*). "Good! handsomely done! The Seventh couldn't beat it! You do certainly handle your Rangers like an expert, General. And where are you bound?"

"Four miles on the trail to Fort Clayton."

"Glad am I, dear! What's the idea of it?"

"Guard of honor for you and Thorndike."

"Bless—your—*heart!* I'd rather have it from you than from the Commander-in-Chief of the armies of the United States, you incomparable little soldier!—and I don't need to take any oath to that, for you believe it."

"I *thought* you'd like it, BB."

"*Like* it? Well, I should say so! Now then—all ready—sound the advance, and away we go!"

# CHAPTER IX

## SOLDIER BOY AND SHEKELS AGAIN

WELL, this is the way it happened. We did the escort duty; then we came back and struck for the plain and put the Rangers through a rousing drill—oh, for hours! Then we sent them home under Brigadier-General Fanny Marsh; then the Lieutenant-General and I went off on a gallop over the plains for about three hours, and were lazying along home in the middle of the afternoon, when we met Jimmy Slade, the drummer-boy, and he saluted and asked the Lieutenant-General if she had heard the news, and she said no, and he said:

"'Buffalo Bill has been ambushed and badly shot this side of Clayton, and Thorndike the scout, too; Bill couldn't travel, but Thorndike could, and he brought the news, and Sergeant Wilkes and six men of Company B are gone, two hours ago, hotfoot, to get Bill. And they say—'

" '*Go!*' she shouted to me—and I went."

"Fast?"

"Don't ask foolish questions. It was an awful pace. For four hours nothing happened, and not a word said, except that now and then she said, 'Keep it up, Boy, keep it up, sweetheart; we'll save him!' I kept it up. Well, when the dark shut down, in the rugged hills, that poor little chap had been tearing around in the saddle all day, and I noticed by the slack knee-pressure that she was tired and tottery, and I got dreadfully afraid; but every time I tried to slow down and let her go to sleep, so I could stop, she hurried me up again; and so, sure enough, at last over she went!

"Ah, that was a fix to be in! for she lay there and didn't stir, and what was I to do? I couldn't leave her to fetch help, on account of the wolves. There was nothing to do but stand by. It was dreadful. I was afraid she was killed, poor little thing! But she wasn't. She came to, by and by, and said, 'Kiss me, Soldier,' and those were blessed words. I kissed her—often; I am used to that, and we like it. But she didn't get up, and I was worried. She fondled my nose with her hand, and talked to me, and called me endearing names—which is her way—but she caressed with the same hand all the time. The other arm was broken, you see, but I didn't know it, and she didn't mention it. She didn't want to distress me, you know.

"Soon the big gray wolves came, and hung around, and you could hear them snarl, and snap at each other, but you couldn't see anything of them except their eyes, which shone in the dark like sparks and stars. The Lieutenant-General said, 'If I had the Rocky Mountain Rangers here, we would make those creatures climb a tree.' Then she made believe that the Rangers were in hearing, and put up her bugle and blew the 'assembly'; and then, 'boots and saddles'; then the 'trot'; 'gallop'; '*charge!*' Then she blew the 'retreat,' and said, 'That's for you, you rebels; the Rangers don't ever retreat!'

"The music frightened them away, but they were hungry, and kept coming back. And of course they got bolder and bolder, which is their way. It went on for an hour, then the tired child went to sleep, and it was pitiful to hear her moan and nestle, and I couldn't do anything for her. All the time I was laying for the wolves. They are in my line; I have had experience. At last the boldest one ventured within my lines, and I landed him among his friends with some of his skull still on him, and they did the rest. In the next hour I got a couple more, and they went the way of the first one, down the throats of the detachment. That satisfied the survivors, and they went away and left us in peace.

"We hadn't any more adventures, though I kept awake all night and was ready. From midnight on the child got very restless, and out of her head, and moaned, and said, 'Water, water—thirsty'; and now and then, 'Kiss me, Soldier'; and sometimes she was in her fort and giving orders to her garrison; and once she was in Spain, and thought her mother was with her. People say a horse can't cry; but they don't know, because we cry inside.

"It was an hour after sunup that I heard the boys coming, and recognized the hoof-beats of Pomp and Cæsar and Jerry, old mates of mine; and a welcomer sound there couldn't ever be.

"Buffalo Bill was in a horse-litter, with his leg broken by a bullet, and Mongrel and Blake Haskins's horse were doing the work. Buffalo Bill and Thorndike had killed both of those toughs.

"When they got to us, and Buffalo Bill saw the child lying there so white, he said, 'My God!' and the sound of his voice brought her to herself, and she gave a little cry of pleasure and struggled to get up, but couldn't, and the soldiers gathered her up like the tenderest women, and their eyes were wet and they were not ashamed, when they saw her arm dangling; and so were Buffalo Bill's, and when they laid her in his arms he said, 'My darling, how does this come?' and she said, 'We came to save you, but I was tired, and couldn't keep awake, and fell off and hurt myself, and couldn't get on again.' 'You came to save me, you dear little rat? It was too lovely of you!' 'Yes, and Soldier stood by me, which you know he would, and protected me from the wolves; and if he got a chance he kicked the life out of some of them—for you know he would, BB.' The sergeant said, 'He laid out three of them, sir, and here's the bones to show for it.' 'He's a grand horse,' said BB; 'he's the grandest horse that ever was! and has saved your life, Lieutenant-General Alison, and shall protect it the rest of his life—he's yours for a kiss!' He got it, along with a passion of delight, and he said, 'You are feeling better now, little Spaniard—do you think you could blow the advance?' She put up the bugle to do it, but he said wait a minute first. Then he and the sergeant set her arm and put it in splints, she wincing but not whimpering; then we took up the march for home, and that's the end of the tale; and I'm her horse. Isn't she a brick, Shekels?"

"Brick? She's more than a brick, more than a thousand bricks—she's a reptile!"

"It's a compliment out of your heart, Shekels. God bless you for it!"

# CHAPTER X

## GENERAL ALISON AND DORCAS

TOO much company for her, Marse Tom. Betwixt you, and Shekels, and the Colonel's wife, and the Cid—"

"The Cid? Oh, I remember—the raven."

"—and Mrs. Captain Marsh and Famine and Pestilence the baby *coyotes*, and Sour-Mash and her pups, and Sardanapalus and her kittens—hang these names she gives the creatures, they warp my jaw—and Potter: you—all sitting around *in* the house, and Soldier Boy at the window the entire time, it's a wonder to me she comes along as well as she does. She—"

"You want her all to yourself, you stingy old thing!"

"Marse Tom, you know better. It's too much company. And then the idea of her receiving reports all the time from her officers, and acting upon them, and giving orders, the same as if she was well! It ain't good for her, and the surgeon don't like it, and tried to persuade her not to and couldn't; and when he *ordered* her, she was that outraged and indignant, and was very severe on him, and accused him of insubordination, and said it didn't become him to give orders to an officer of her rank. Well, he saw he had excited her more and done more harm than all the rest put together, so he was vexed at himself and wished he had kept still. Doctors *don't* know much, and that's a fact. She's too much interested in things—she ought to rest more. She's all the time sending messages to BB, and to soldiers and Injuns and whatnot, and to the animals."

"To the animals?"

"Yes, sir."

"Who carries them?"

"Sometimes Potter, but mostly it's Shekels."

"Now come! who can find fault with such pretty make-believe as that?"

"But it ain't make-believe, Marse Tom. She does send them."

"Yes, I don't doubt that part of it."

"Do you doubt they get them, sir?"

"Certainly. Don't you?"

"No, sir. Animals talk to one another. I know it perfectly well, Marse Tom, and I ain't saying it by guess."

"What a curious superstition!"

"It ain't a superstition, Marse Tom. Look at that Shekels—look at him, *now.* Is he listening, or ain't he? *Now* you see! he's turned his head away. It's because he was caught—caught in the act. I'll ask you—could a Christian look any more ashamed than what he looks now?—*lay down!* You see? he was going to sneak out. Don't tell *me*, Marse Tom! If animals don't talk, I miss *my* guess. And Shekels is the worst. He goes and tells the animals everything that happens in the officers' quarters; and if he's short of facts, he invents them. He hasn't any more principle than a blue jay; and as for morals, he's empty. Look at him now; look at him grovel. He knows what I am saying, and he knows it's the truth. You see, yourself, that he can feel shame; it's the only virtue he's got. It's wonderful how they find out everything that's going on—the animals. They—"

"Do you really believe they do, Dorcas?"

"I don't only just believe it, Marse Tom, I know it. Day before yesterday they knew something was going to happen. They were that excited, and whispering around together; why, anybody could see that they— But my! I must get back to her, and I haven't got to my errand yet."

"What is it, Dorcas?"

"Well, it's two or three things. One is, the doctor don't salute when he comes . . . Now, Marse Tom, it ain't anything to laugh at, and so—

"Well, then, forgive me; I didn't mean to laugh—I got caught unprepared."

"You see, she don't want to hurt the doctor's feelings, so she don't say anything to him about it; but she is always polite, herself, and it hurts that kind for people to be rude to them."

"I'll have that doctor hanged."

"Marse Tom, she don't *want* him hanged. She—"

"Well, then, I'll have him boiled in oil."

"But she don't *want* him boiled. I—"

"Oh, very well, very well, I only want to please her; I'll have him skinned."

"Why, *she* don't want him skinned; it would break her heart. Now—"

"Woman, this is perfectly unreasonable. What in the nation *does* she want?"

"Marse Tom, if you would only be a little patient, and not fly off the handle at the least little thing. Why, she only wants you to speak to him."

"Speak to him! Well, upon my word! All this unseemly rage and row about such a—a— Dorcas, I never saw you carry on like this before. You have alarmed the sentry; he thinks I am being assassinated; he thinks there's a mutiny, a revolt, an insurrection; he—"

"Marse Tom, you are just putting on; you know it perfectly well; *I* don't know what makes you act like that—but you always did, even when you was little, and you can't get over it, I reckon. Are you over it now, Marse Tom?"

"Oh, well, yes; but it would try anybody to be doing the best he could, offering every kindness he could think of, only to have it rejected with contumely and . . . Oh, well, let it go; it's no matter—I'll talk to the doctor. Is that satisfactory, or are you going to break out again?"

"Yes, sir, it is; and it's only right to talk to him, too, because it's just as she says; she's trying to keep up discipline in the Rangers, and this insubordination of his is a bad example for them—now ain't it so, Marse Tom?"

"Well, there *is* reason in it, I can't deny it; so I will speak to him, though at bottom I think hanging would be more lasting. What is the rest of your errand, Dorcas?"

"Of course her room is Ranger headquarters now, Marse Tom, while she's sick. Well, soldiers of the cavalry and the dragoons that are off duty come and get her sentries to let them relieve them and serve in their place. It's only out of affection, sir, and because they know military honors please her, and please the children too, for her sake; and they don't bring their muskets; and so—"

"I've noticed them there, but didn't twig the idea. They are standing guard, are they?"

"Yes, sir, and she is afraid you will reprove them and hurt their feelings, if you see them there; so she begs, if—if you don't mind coming in the back way—"

"Bear me up, Dorcas; don't let me faint."

"There—sit up and behave, Marse Tom. You are not going to faint; you are only pretending—you used to act just so when you was little; it does seem a long time for you to get grown up."

"Dorcas, the way the child is progressing, I shall be out of my job before long—she'll have the whole post in her hands. I must make a stand, I must not go down without a struggle. These encroachments. . . . Dorcas, what do you think she will think of next?"

"Marse Tom, she don't mean any harm."

"Are you sure of it?"

"Yes, Marse Tom."

"You feel sure she has no ulterior designs?"

"I don't know what that is, Marse Tom, but I know she hasn't."

"Very well, then, for the present I am satisfied. What else have you come about?"

"I reckon I better tell you the whole thing first, Marse Tom, then tell you what she wants. There's been an emeute, as she calls it. It was before she got back with BB. The officer of the day reported it to her this morning. It happened at her fort. There was a fuss betwixt Major-General Tommy Drake and Lieutenant-Colonel Agnes Frisbie, and he snatched her doll away, which is made of white kid stuffed with sawdust, and tore every rag of its clothes off, right before them all, and is under arrest, and the charge is conduct un—"

"Yes, I know—conduct unbecoming an officer and a gentleman—a plain case, too, it seems to me. This is a serious matter. Well, what is her pleasure?"

"Well, Marse Tom, she has summoned a court-martial, but the doctor don't think she is well enough to preside over it, and she says there ain't anybody competent but her, because there's a major-general concerned; and so she—she—well, she says, would you preside over it for her? . . . Marse Tom, *sit* up! You ain't any more going to faint than Shekels is."

"Look here, Dorcas, go along back, and be tactful. Be persuasive; don't fret her; tell her it's all right, the matter is in my hands, but it isn't good form to hurry so grave a matter as this. Explain to her that we have to go by precedent, and that I believe this one to be new. In fact, you can say I know that nothing just like it has happened in our army, therefore I must be guided by European precedents, and must go cautiously and examine them carefully. Tell her not to be impatient, it will take me several days, but it will all come out right, and I will come over and report progress as I go along. Do you get the idea, Dorcas?"

"I don't know as I do, sir."

"Well, it's this. You see, it won't ever do for me, a brigadier in the regular army, to preside over that infant court-martial—there isn't any precedent for it, don't you see. Very well. I will go on examining authorities and reporting progress until she is well enough to get me out of this scrape by presiding herself. Do you get it now?"

"Oh, yes, sir, I get it, and it's good, I'll go and fix it with her. *Lay down!* and stay where you are."

"Why, what harm is he doing?"

"Oh, it ain't any harm, but it just vexes me to see him act so."

"What was he doing?"

"Can't you see, and him in such a sweat? He was starting out to spread it all over the post. *Now* I reckon you won't deny, any more, that they go and tell everything they hear, now that you've seen it with yo' own eyes."

"Well, I don't like to acknowledge it, Dorcas, but I don't see how I can consistently stick to my doubts in the face of such overwhelming proof as this dog is furnishing."

"There, now, you've got in yo' right mind at last! I wonder you can be so stubborn, Marse Tom. But you always was, even when you was little. I'm going now."

"Look here; tell her that in view of the delay, it is my judgment that she ought to enlarge the accused on his parole."

"Yes, sir, I'll tell her. Marse Tom?"

"Well?"

"She can't get to Soldier Boy, and he stands there all the time, down in the mouth and lonesome; and she says will you shake hands with him and comfort him? Everybody does."

"It's a curious kind of lonesomeness; but, all right, I will."

## CHAPTER XI

SEVERAL MONTHS LATER. ANTONIO AND THORNDIKE

THORNDIKE, isn't that Plug you're riding an asset of the scrap you and Buffalo Bill had with the late Blake Haskins and his pal a few months back?"

"Yes, this is Mongrel—and not a half-bad horse, either."

"I've noticed he keeps up his lick first-rate. Say—isn't it a gaudy morning?"

"Right you are!"

"Thorndike, it's Andalusian! and when that's said, all's said."

"Andalusian *and* Oregonian, Antonio! Put it that way, and you have my vote. Being a native up there, I know. You being Andalusian-born—"

"Can speak with authority for that patch of paradise? Well, I can. Like the Don! like Sancho! This is the correct Andalusian dawn now—crisp, fresh, dewy, fragrant, pungent—"

> " 'What though the spicy breezes
> Blow soft o'er Ceylon's isle—'

—*git* up, you old cow! stumbling like that when we've just been praising you! out on a scout and can't live up to the honor any better than that? Antonio, how long have you been out here in the Plains and the Rockies?"

"More than thirteen years."

"It's a long time. Don't you ever get homesick?"

"Not till now."

"Why *now?*—after such a long cure."

"These preparations of the retiring commandant's have started it up."

"Of course. It's natural."

"It keeps me thinking about Spain. I know the region where the Seventh's child's aunt lives; I know all the lovely country for miles around; I'll bet I've seen her aunt's villa many a time; I'll bet I've been in it in those pleasant old times when I was a Spanish gentleman."

"They say the child is wild to see Spain."

"It's so; I know it from what I hear."

"Haven't you talked with her about it?"

"No. I've avoided it. I should soon be as wild as she is. That would not be comfortable."

"I wish I was going, Antonio. There's two things I'd give a lot to see. One's a railroad."

"She'll see one when she strikes Missouri."

"The other's a bull-fight."

"I've seen lots of them; I wish I could see another."

"I don't know anything about it, except in a mixed-up, foggy way, Antonio, but I know enough to know it's grand sport."

"The grandest in the world! There's no other sport that begins with it. I'll tell you what I've seen, then you can judge. It was my first, and it's as vivid to me now as it was when I saw it. It was a Sunday afternoon, and beautiful weather, and my uncle, the priest, took me as a reward for being a good boy and because of my own accord and without anybody asking me I had bankrupted my savings-box and given the money to a mission that was civilizing the Chinese and sweetening their lives and softening their hearts with the gentle teachings of our religion, and I wish you could have seen what we saw that day, Thorndike.

"The amphitheater was packed, from the bull-ring to the highest row—twelve thousand people in one circling mass, one slanting, solid mass—royalties, nobles, clergy, ladies, gentlemen, state officials, generals, admirals, soldiers, sailors, lawyers, thieves, merchants, brokers, cooks, housemaids, scullery-maids, doubtful women, dudes, gamblers, beggars, loafers, tramps, American ladies, gentlemen, preachers, English ladies, gentlemen, preachers, German ditto, French ditto, and so on and so on, all the world represented: Spaniards to admire and praise, foreigners to enjoy and go home and find fault—there they were, one solid, sloping, circling sweep of rippling and flashing color under the downpour of the summer sun—just a garden, a gaudy, gorgeous flower-garden! Children munching oranges, six thousand fans fluttering and glimmering, everybody happy, everybody chatting gayly with their intimates, lovely girl-faces smiling recognition and salutation to other lovely girl-faces, gray old ladies and gentlemen dealing in the like exchanges with each other—ah, such a picture of cheery contentment and glad anticipation! not a mean spirit, nor a sordid soul, nor a sad heart there—ah, Thorndike, I wish I could see it again.

"Suddenly, the martial note of a bugle cleaves the hum and murmur—clear the ring!

"They clear it. The great gate is flung open, and the procession marches in, splendidly costumed and glittering: the marshals of the day, then the picadores on horseback, then the matadores on foot, each surrounded by his quadrille of *chulos*. They march to the box of the city fathers, and formally salute. The key is thrown, the bull-gate is unlocked. Another bugle blast—the gate flies open, the bull plunges in, furious, trembling, blinking in the blinding light, and stands there, a magnificent creature, center of those multitudinous and admiring eyes, brave, ready for battle, his attitude a challenge. He sees his enemy: horsemen sitting motionless, with long spears in rest, upon blindfolded broken-down nags, lean and starved, fit only for sport and sacrifice, then the carrion-heap.

"The bull makes a rush, with murder in his eye, but a picador meets him with a spear-thrust in the shoulder. He flinches with the pain, and the picador skips out of danger. A burst of applause for the picador, hisses for the bull. Some shout "Cow!" at the bull, and call him offensive names. But he is not listening to them, he is there for business; he is not minding the cloak-bearers that come fluttering around to confuse him; he chases this way, he chases that way, and hither and yon, scattering the nimble banderillos in every direction like a spray, and receiving their maddening darts in his neck as they dodge and fly—oh, but it's a lively spectacle, and brings down the house! Ah, you should hear the thundering roar that goes up when the game is at its wildest and brilliant things are done!

"Oh, that first bull, that day, was great! From the moment the spirit of war rose to flood-tide in him and he got down to his work, he began to do wonders. He tore his way through his persecutors, flinging one of them clear over the parapet; he bowled a horse and his rider down, and plunged straight for the next, got home with his horns, wounding both horse and man; on again, here and there and this way and that; and one after another he tore the bowels out of two horses so that they gushed to the ground, and ripped a third one so badly that although they rushed him to cover and shoved his bowels back and stuffed the rents with tow and rode him against the bull again, he couldn't make the trip; he tried to gallop, under the spur, but soon reeled and tottered and fell, all in a heap. For a while, that bull-ring was the most thrilling and glorious and inspiring sight that ever was seen. The bull absolutely cleared it, and stood there alone! monarch of the place. The people went mad for pride in him, and joy and delight, and you couldn't hear yourself think, for the roar and boom and crash of applause."

"Antonio, it carries me clear out of myself just to hear you tell it; it must have been perfectly splendid. If I live, I'll see a bull-fight yet before I die. Did they kill him?"

"Oh yes; that is what the bull is for. They tired him out, and got him at last. He kept rushing the matador, who always slipped smartly and gracefully aside in time, waiting for a sure chance; and at last it came; the bull made a deadly plunge for him—

was avoided neatly, and as he sped by, the long sword glided silently into him, between left shoulder and spine—in and in, to the hilt. He crumpled down, dying."

"Ah, Antonio, it *is* the noblest sport that ever was. I would give a year of my life to see it. Is the bull always killed?"

"Yes. Sometimes a bull is timid, finding himself in so strange a place, and he stands trembling, or tries to retreat. Then everybody despises him for his cowardice and wants him punished and made ridiculous; so they hough him from behind, and it is the funniest thing in the world to see him hobbling around on his severed legs; the whole vast house goes into hurricanes of laughter over it; I have laughed till the tears ran down my cheeks to see it. When he has furnished all the sport he can, he is not any longer useful, and is killed."

"Well, it is perfectly grand, Antonio, perfectly beautiful. Burning a nigger don't begin."

## CHAPTER XII

### MONGREL AND THE OTHER HORSE

SAGE-BRUSH, you have been listening?"

"Yes."

"Isn't it strange?"

"Well, no, Mongrel, I don't know that it is."

"Why don't you?"

"I've seen a good many human beings in my time. They are created as they are; they cannot help it. They are only brutal because that is their make; brutes would be brutal if it was *their* make."

"To me, Sage-Brush, man is most strange and unaccountable. Why should he treat dumb animals that way when they are not doing any harm?"

"Man is not always like that, Mongrel; he is kind enough when he is not excited by religion."

"Is the bull-fight a religious service?"

"I think so. I have heard so. It is held on Sunday."

(*A reflective pause, lasting some moments.*) Then:

"When we die, Sage-Brush, do we go to heaven and dwell with man?"

"My father thought not. He believed we do not have to go there unless we deserve it."

# Part II

# IN SPAIN

## CHAPTER XIII

### GENERAL ALISON TO HIS MOTHER

IT was a prodigious trip, but delightful, of course, through the Rockies and the Black Hills and the mighty sweep of the Great Plains to civilization and the Missouri border—where the railroading began and the delightfulness ended. But no one is the worse for the journey; certainly not Cathy, nor Dorcas, nor Soldier Boy; and as for me, I am not complaining.

Spain is all that Cathy had pictured it—and more, she says. She is in a fury of delight, the maddest little animal that ever was, and all for joy. She thinks she remembers Spain, but that is not very likely, I suppose. The two—Mercedes and Cathy—devour each other. It is a rapture of love, and beautiful to see. It is Spanish; that describes it. Will this be a short visit?

No. It will be permanent. Cathy has elected to abide with Spain and her aunt. Dorcas says she (Dorcas) foresaw that this would happen; and also says that she wanted it to happen, and says the child's own country is the right place for her, and that she ought not to have been sent to me, I ought to have gone to her. I thought it insane to take Soldier Boy to Spain, but it was well that I yielded to Cathy's pleadings; if he had been left behind, half of her heart would have remained with him, and she would not have been contented. As it is, everything has fallen out for the best, and we are all satisfied and comfortable. It may be that Dorcas and I will see America again some day; but also it is a case of maybe not.

We left the post in the early morning. It was an affecting time. The women cried over Cathy, so did even those stern warriors the Rocky Mountain Rangers; Shekels was there, and the Cid, and Sardanapalus, and Potter, and Mongrel, and Sour-Mash, Famine, and Pestilence, and Cathy kissed them all and wept; details of the several arms of the garrison were present to represent the rest, and say good-by and God bless you for all the soldiery; and there was a special squad from the Seventh, with the oldest veteran at its head, to speed the Seventh's Child with grand honors and impressive ceremonies; and the veteran had a touching speech by heart, and put up his hand in salute and tried to say it, but his lips trembled and his voice broke, but Cathy bent down from the saddle and kissed him on the mouth and turned his defeat to victory, and a cheer went up.

The next act closed the ceremonies, and was a moving surprise. It may be that you have discovered, before this, that the rigors of military law and custom melt insensibly away and disappear when a soldier or a regiment or the garrison wants to do something that will please Cathy. The bands conceived the idea of stirring her soldierly heart with a farewell which would remain in her memory always, beautiful and unfading, and bring back the past and its love for her whenever she should think of it; so they got their project placed before General Burnaby, my successor, who is Cathy's newest slave, and in spite of poverty of precedents they got his permission. The bands knew the child's favorite military airs. By this hint you know what is coming, but Cathy didn't. She was asked to sound the "reveille," which she did.

**REVEILLE**

With the last note the bands burst out with a crash: and woke the mountains with the "Star-Spangled Banner" in a way to make a body's heart swell and thump and his hair rise! It was enough to break a person all up, to see Cathy's radiant face shining out through her gladness and tears. By request she blew the "assembly," now. . . .

**THE ASSEMBLY**

. . . Then the bands thundered in, with "Rally round the flag, boys, rally once again!" Next, she blew another call ("to the Standard") . . . .

**TO THE STANDARD**

. . . and the bands responded with "When we were marching through Georgia." Straightway she sounded "boots and saddles," that thrilling and most expediting call. . . .

**BOOTS AND SADDLES**

. . . and the bands could hardly hold in for the final note; then they turned their whole strength loose on "Tramp, tramp, tramp, the boys are marching," and everybody's excitement rose to blood-heat.

Now an impressive pause—then the bugle sang "Taps"—translatable, this time, into "Good-by, and God keep us all!" for taps is the soldier's nightly release from duty, and farewell: plaintive, sweet, pathetic, for the morning is never sure, for him; always it is possible that he is hearing it for the last time. . . .

TAPS

. . . Then the bands turned their instruments towards Cathy and burst in with that rollicking frenzy of a tune, "Oh, we'll all get blind drunk when Johnny comes marching home—yes, we'll all get blind drunk when Johnny comes marching home!" and followed it instantly with "Dixie," that antidote for melancholy, merriest and gladdest of all military music on any side of the ocean—and that was the end. And so—farewell!

I wish you could have been there to see it all, hear it all, and feel it: and get yourself blown away with the hurricane huzza that swept the place as a finish.

When we rode away, our main body had already been on the road an hour or two—I speak of our camp equipage; but we didn't move off alone: when Cathy blew the "advance" the Rangers cantered out in column of fours, and gave us escort, and were joined by White Cloud and Thunder-Bird in all their gaudy bravery, and by Buffalo Bill and four subordinate scouts. Three miles away, in the Plains, the Lieutenant-General halted, sat her horse like a military statue, the bugle at her lips, and put the Rangers through the evolutions for half an hour; and finally, when she blew the "charge," she led it herself. "Not for the last time," she said, and got a cheer, and we said good-by all around, and faced eastward and rode away.

*Postscript. A Day Later.* Soldier Boy was stolen last night. Cathy is almost beside herself, and we cannot comfort her. Mercedes and I are not much alarmed about the horse, although this part of Spain is in something of a turmoil, politically, at present, and there is a good deal of lawlessness. In ordinary times the thief and the horse would soon be captured. We shall have them before long, I think.

# CHAPTER XIV

## SOLDIER BOY—TO HIMSELF

IT is five months. Or is it six? My troubles have clouded my memory. I think I have been all over this land, from end to end, and now I am back again since day before yesterday, to that city which we passed through, that last day of our long journey, and which is near her country home. I am a tottering ruin and my eyes are dim, but I recognized it. If she could see me she would know me and sound my call. I wish I could hear it once more; it would revive me, it would bring back her face and the mountains and the free life, and I would come—if I were dying I would come! She would not know *me*, looking as I do, but she would know me by my star. But she will never see me, for they do not let me out of this shabby stable—a foul and miserable place, with most two wrecks like myself for company.

How many times have I changed hands? I think it is twelve times—I cannot remember; and each time it was down a step lower, and each time I got a harder master. They have been cruel, every one; they have worked me night and day in degraded employments, and beaten me; they have fed me ill and some days not at all. And so I am but bones, now, with a rough and frowsy skin humped and cornered upon my shrunken body—that skin which was once so glossy, that skin which she loved to stroke with her hand. I was the pride of the mountains and the Great Plains; now I am a scarecrow and despised. These piteous wrecks that are my comrades here say we have reached the bottom of the scale, the final humiliation; they say that when a horse is no longer worth the weeds and discarded rubbish they feed to him, they sell him to the bull-ring for a glass of brandy, to make sport for the people and perish for their pleasure.

To die—that does not disturb me; we of the service never care for death. But if I could see her once more! if I could hear her bugle sing again and say, "It is I, Soldier—come!"

## CHAPTER XV

### GENERAL ALISON TO MRS. DRAKE, THE COLONEL'S WIFE

TO return, now, to where I was, and tell you the rest. We shall never know how she came to be there; there is no way to account for it. She was always watching for black and shiny and spirited horses—watching, hoping, despairing, hoping again; always giving chase and sounding her call, upon the meagerest chance of a response, and breaking her heart over the disappointment; always inquiring, always interested in sales-stables and horse accumulations in general. How she got there must remain a mystery.

At the point which I had reached in a preceding paragraph of this account, the situation was as follows: two horses lay dying; the bull had scattered his persecutors for the moment, and stood raging, panting, pawing the dust in clouds over his back, when the man that had been wounded returned to the ring on a remount, a poor blindfolded wreck that yet had something ironically military about his bearing—and the next moment the bull had ripped him open and his bowels were dragging upon the ground and the bull was charging his swarm of pests again. Then came pealing through the air a bugle-call that froze my blood—"*It is I, Soldier—come!*" I turned; Cathy was flying down through the massed people; she cleared the parapet at a bound, and sped towards that riderless horse, who staggered forward towards the remembered sound; but his strength failed, and he fell at her feet, she lavishing kisses upon him and sobbing, the house rising with one impulse, and white with horror! Before help could reach her the bull was back again—

She was never conscious again in life. We bore her home, all mangled and drenched in blood, and knelt by her and listened to her broken and wandering words, and prayed for her passing spirit, and there was no comfort—nor ever will be, I think. But she was happy, for she was far away under another sky, and comrading again with her Rangers, and her animal friends, and the soldiers. Their names fell softly and caressingly from her lips, one by one, with pauses between. She was not in pain, but lay with closed eyes, vacantly murmuring, as one who dreams. Sometimes she smiled, saying nothing; sometimes she smiled when she uttered a name—such as Shekels, or BB, or Potter. Sometimes she was at her fort, issuing commands; sometimes she was careering over the plains at the head of her men; sometimes she was training her horse; once she said, reprovingly, "You are giving me the wrong foot; give me the left—don't you know it is good-by?"

After this, she lay silent some time; the end was near. By and by she murmured, "Tired . . . sleepy . . . take Cathy, mamma." Then, "Kiss me, Soldier." For a little time she lay so still that we were doubtful if she breathed. Then she put out her hand and began to feel gropingly about;

then said, "I cannot find it; blow 'taps.'"* It was the end.

TAPS

* "Lights out."

# EXTRACT FROM CAPTAIN STORMFIELD'S VISIT TO HEAVEN

# EXTRACT FROM CAPTAIN STORMFIELD'S VISIT TO HEAVEN*

## CHAPTER I

WELL, when I had been dead about thirty years, I begun to get a little anxious. Mind you, I had been whizzing through space all that time, like a comet. *Like* a comet! Why, Peters, I laid over the lot of them! Of course there warn't any of them going my way, as a steady thing, you know, because they travel in a long circle like the loop of a lasso, whereas I was pointed as straight as a dart for the Hereafter; but I happened on one every now and then that was going my way for an hour or so, and then we had a bit of a brush together. But it was generally pretty one-sided, because I sailed by them the same as if they were standing still. An ordinary comet don't make more than about 200,000 miles a minute. Of course when I came across one of that sort—like Encke's and Halley's comets, for instance—it warn't anything but just a flash and a vanish, you see. You couldn't rightly call it a race. It was as if the comet was a gravel-train and I was a telegraph despatch. But after I got outside of our astronomical system, I used to flush a comet occasionally that was something *like.* *We* haven't got any such comets—ours don't begin. One night I was swinging along at a good round gait, everything taut and trim, and the wind in my favor—I judged I was going about a million miles a minute—it might have been more, it couldn't have been less—when I flushed a most uncommonly big one about three points off my starboard bow. By his stern lights I judged he was bearing about northeast-and-by-north-half-east. Well, it was so near my course that I wouldn't throw away the chance; so I fell off a point, steadied my helm, and went for him. You should have heard me whiz, and seen the electric fur fly! In about a minute and a half I was fringed out with an electrical nimbus that flamed around for miles and miles and lit up all space like broad day. The comet was burning blue in the distance, like a sickly torch, when I first sighted him, but he begun to grow bigger and bigger as I crept up on him. I slipped up on him so fast that when I had gone about 150,000,000 miles I was close enough to be swallowed up in the phosphorescent glory of his wake, and I couldn't see anything for the glare. Thinks I, it won't do to run into him, so I shunted to one side and tore along. By and by I closed up abreast of his tail. Do you know what it was like? It was like a gnat closing up on the continent of America. I forged along. By and by I had sailed along his coast for a little upwards of a hundred and fifty million miles, and then I could see by the shape of him that I hadn't even got up to his waistband yet. Why, Peters, *we* don't know anything about comets, down here. If you want to see comets that *are* comets, you've got to go outside of our solar system—where there's room for them, you understand. My friend, I've seen comets out there that couldn't even lay down inside the *orbits* of our noblest comets without their tails hanging over.

Well, I boomed along another hundred and fifty million miles, and got up abreast his shoulder, as you may say. I was feeling pretty fine, I tell you; but just then I noticed the officer of the deck come to the side and hoist his glass in my direction. Straight off I heard him sing out—

"Below there, ahoy! Shake her up, shake her up! Heave on a hundred million billion tons of brimstone!"

"Ay—ay, sir!"

"Pipe the stabboard watch! All hands on deck!"

"Ay—ay, sir!"

"Send two hundred thousand million men aloft to shake out royals and sky-scrapers!"

"Ay—ay, sir!"

"Hand the stuns'ls! Hang out every rag you've got! Clothe her from stem to rudder-post!"

"Ay—ay, sir!"

In about a second I begun to see I'd woke up a pretty ugly customer, Peters. In less than ten seconds that comet was just a blazing cloud of red-hot canvas. It was piled up into the heavens clean out of sight—the old thing seemed to swell out and occupy all space; the sulphur smoke from the furnaces—oh, well, nobody can describe the way it rolled and tumbled up into the skies, and nobody can half describe the way it smelt. Neither can anybody begin to describe the way that monstrous craft begun to crash along. And such another powwow—thousands of bo's'n's whistles screaming at once, and a crew like the populations of a hundred thousand worlds like ours all swearing at once. Well, I never heard the like of it before.

We roared and thundered along side by side, both doing our level best, because I'd never struck a comet before that could lay over me, and so I was bound to beat this one or break something. I judged I had some reputation in space, and I calculated to keep it. I noticed I wasn't gaining as fast, now, as I was before, but still I was gaining. There was a power of excitement on board the comet. Upwards of a hundred billion passengers swarmed up from below and rushed to the side and begun to bet on the race. Of course this careened her and damaged her speed. My, but wasn't the mate mad! He jumped at that crowd, with his trumpet in his hand, and sung out—

"Amidships! amidships, you——!* or I'll brain the last idiot of you!"

Well, sir, I gained and gained, little by little, till at last I went skimming sweetly by the magnificent old conflagration's nose. By this time the captain of the comet had been rousted out, and he stood there in the red glare for'ard, by the mate, in his shirtsleeves and slippers, his hair all rats' nests

* The captain could not remember what this word was. He said it was in a foreign tongue.

and one suspender hanging, and how sick those two men did look! I just simply couldn't help putting my thumb to my nose as I glided away and singing out:

"Ta-ta! ta-ta! Any word to send to your family?"

Peters, it was a mistake. Yes, sir, I've often regretted that—it was a mistake. You see, the captain had given up the race, but that remark was too tedious for him—he couldn't stand it. He turned to the mate, and says he—

"Have we got brimstone enough of our own to make the trip?"

"Yes, sir."

"Sure?"

"Yes, sir—more than enough."

"How much have we got in cargo for Satan?"

"Eighteen hundred thousand billion quintillions of kazarks."

"Very well, then, let his boarders freeze till the next comet comes. Lighten ship! Lively, now, lively, men! Heave the whole cargo overboard!"

Peters, look me in the eye, and be calm. I found out, over there, that a kazark is exactly the bulk of a *hundred and sixty-nine worlds like ours!* They hove all that load overboard. When it fell it wiped out a considerable raft of stars just as clean as if they'd been candles and somebody blowed them out. As for the race, that was at an end. The minute she was lightened the comet swung along by me the same as if I was anchored. The captain stood on the stern, by the after-davits, and put his thumb to his nose and sung out—

"Ta-ta! ta-ta! Maybe *you've* got some message to send your friends in the Everlasting Tropics!"

Then he hove up his other suspender and started for'ard, and inside of three-quarters of an hour his craft was only a pale torch again in the distance. Yes, it was a mistake, Peters—that remark of mine. I don't reckon I'll ever get over being sorry about it. I'd 'a' beat the bully of the firmament if I'd kept my mouth shut.

But I've wandered a little off the track of my tale; I'll get back on my course again. Now you see what kind of speed I was making. So, as I said, when I had been tearing along this way about thirty years I begun to get uneasy. Oh, it was pleasant enough, with a good deal to find out, but then it was kind of lonesome, you know. Besides, I wanted to get somewhere. I hadn't shipped with the idea of cruising forever. First off, I liked the delay, because I judged I was going to fetch up in pretty warm quarters when I got through; but towards the last I begun to feel that I'd rather go to—well, most any place, so as to finish up the uncertainty.

Well, one night—it was always night, except when I was rushing by some star that was occupying the whole universe with its fire and its glare—light enough then, of course, but I necessarily left it behind in a minute or two and plunged into a solid week of darkness again. The stars ain't so close together as they look to be. Where was I? Oh yes; one night I was sailing along, when I discovered a tremendous long row of blinking lights away on the horizon ahead.

As I approached, they begun to tower and swell and look like mighty furnaces. Says I to myself—

"By George, I've arrived at last—and at the wrong place, just as I expected!"

Then I fainted. I don't know how long I was insensible, but it must have been a good while, for, when I came to, the darkness was all gone and there was the loveliest sunshine and the balmiest, fragrantest air in its place. And there was such a marvelous world spread out before me—such a glowing, beautiful, bewitching country. The things I took for furnaces were gates, miles high, made all of flashing jewels, and they pierced a wall of solid gold that you couldn't see the top of, nor yet the end of, in either direction. I was pointed straight for one of these gates, and a-coming like a house afire. Now I noticed that the skies were black with millions of people, pointed for those gates. What a roar they made, rushing through the air! The ground was as thick as ants with people, too—billions of them, I judge.

I lit. I drifted up to a gate with a swarm of people, and when it was my turn the head clerk says, in a businesslike way—

"Well, quick! Where are you from?"

"San Francisco," says I.

"San Fran—*what?*" says he.

"San Francisco."

He scratched his head and looked puzzled, then he says—

"Is it a planet?"

By George, Peters, think of it! "*Planet?*" says

I; "it's a city. And moreover, it's one of the biggest and finest and—"

"There, there!" says he, "no time here for conversation. We don't deal in cities here. Where are you from in a *general* way?"

"Oh," I says, "I beg your pardon. Put me down for California."

I had him *again*, Peters! He puzzled a second, then he says, sharp and irritable—

"I don't know any such planet—is it a constellation?"

"Oh, my goodness!" says I. "Constellation, says you? No—it's a State."

"Man, we don't deal in States here. *Will* you tell me where you are from *in general—at large*, don't you understand?"

"Oh, now I get your idea," I says. "I'm from America,—the United States of America."

Peters, do you know I had him *again?* If I hadn't I'm a clam! His face was as blank as a target after a militia shooting-match. He turned to an under clerk and says—

"Where is America? *What* is America?"

The under clerk answered up prompt and says—

"There ain't any such orb."

"*Orb?*" says I. "Why, what are you talking about, young man? It ain't an orb; it's a country; it's a continent. Columbus discovered it; I reckon likely you've heard of *him*, anyway. America—why, sir, America—"

"Silence!" says the head clerk. "Once for all, where—are—you—*from?*"

"Well," says I, "I don't know anything more to say—unless I lump things, and just say I'm from the world."

"Ah," says he, brightening up, "now that's something like! *What* world?"

Peters, he had *me*, that time. I looked at him, puzzled, he looked at me, worried. Then he burst out—

"Come, come, what world?"

Says I, "Why, *the* world, of course."

"*The* world!" he says. "H'm! there's billions of them! . . . Next!"

That meant for me to stand aside. I done so, and a sky-blue man with seven heads and only one leg hopped into my place. I took a walk. It just occurred to me, then, that all the myriads I had seen swarming to that gate, up to this time, were just like that creature. I tried to run across somebody I was acquainted with, but they were out of acquaintances of mine just then. So I thought the thing all over and finally sidled back there pretty meek and feeling rather stumped, as you may say.

"Well?" said the head clerk.

"Well, sir," I says, pretty humble, "I don't seem to make out which world it is I'm from. But you may know it from this—it's the one the Saviour saved."

He bent his head at the Name. Then he says, gently—

"The worlds He has saved are like to the gates of heaven in number—none can count them. What astronomical system is your world in?—perhaps that may assist."

"It's the one that has the sun in it—and the moon —and Mars"—he shook his head at each name—hadn't ever heard of them, you see—"and Neptune —and Uranus—and Jupiter—"

"Hold on!" says he—"hold on a minute! Jupiter . . . Jupiter . . . Seems to me we had a man from there eight or nine hundred years ago—but people from that system very seldom enter by this gate." All of a sudden he begun to look me so straight in the eye that I thought he was going to bore through me. Then he says, very deliberate, "Did you come *straight here* from your system?"

"Yes, sir," I says—but I blushed the least little bit in the world when I said it.

He looked at me very stern, and says—

"That is not true; and this is not the place for prevarication. You wandered from your course. How did that happen?"

Says I, blushing again—

"I'm sorry, and I take back what I said, and confess. I raced a little with a comet one day—only just the least little bit—only the tiniest lit—"

"So—so," says he—and without any sugar in his voice to speak of.

I went on, and says—

"But I only fell off just a bare point, and I went right back on my course again the minute the race was over."

"No matter—that divergence has made all this trouble. It has brought you to a gate that is billions of leagues from the right one. If you had gone to your own gate they would have known all about your world at once and there would have been no delay. But we will try to accommodate you." He turned to an under clerk and says—

"What system is Jupiter in?"

"I don't remember, sir, but I think there is such a planet in one of the little new systems away out in one of the thinly worlded corners of the universe. I will see."

He got a balloon and sailed up and up and up, in front of a map that was as big as Rhode Island. He went on up till he was out of sight, and by and by he came down and got something to eat and went up again. To cut a long story short, he kept on doing this for a day or two, and finally he came down and said he thought he had found that solar system, but it might be fly-specks. So he got a microscope and went back. It turned out better than he feared. He had rousted out our system, sure enough. He got me to describe our planet and its distance from the sun, and then he says to his chief—

"Oh, I know the one he means, now, sir. It is on the map. It is called the Wart."

"Says I to myself, "Young man, it wouldn't be wholesome for you to go down *there* and call it the Wart."

Well, they let me in, then, and told me I was safe forever and wouldn't have any more trouble.

Then they turned from me and went on with their work, the same as if they considered my case all complete and shipshape. I was a good deal surprised at this, but I was diffident about speaking up and reminding them. I did so hate to do it, you know; it seemed a pity to bother them, they had so much on their hands. Twice I thought I would give up and let the thing go; so twice I started to leave, but immediately I thought what a figure I should cut stepping out amongst the redeemed in such a rig, and that made me hang back and come to anchor again. People got to eying me—clerks, you know—wondering why I didn't get under way. I couldn't stand this long—it was too uncomfortable. So at last I plucked up courage and tipped the head clerk a signal. He says—

"What! you here yet? What's wanting?"

Says I, in a low voice and very confidential, making a trumpet with my hands at his ear—

"I beg pardon, and you mustn't mind my reminding you, and seeming to meddle, but hain't you forgot something?"

He studied a second, and says—

"Forgot something? . . . No, not that I know of."

"Think," says I.

He thought. Then he says—

"No, I can't seem to have forgot anything. What is it?"

"Look at me," says I, "look me all over."

He done it.

"Well?" says he.

"Well," says I, "you don't notice anything? If I branched out amongst the elect looking like this, wouldn't I attract considerable attention?—wouldn't I be a little conspicuous?"

"Well," he says, "I don't see anything the matter. What do you lack?"

"Lack! Why, I lack my harp, and my wreath, and my halo, and my hymn-book, and my palm branch—I lack everything that a body naturally requires up here, my friend."

Puzzled? Peters, he was the worst puzzled man you ever saw. Finally he says—

"Well, you seem to be a curiosity every way a body takes you. I never heard of these things before."

I looked at the man awhile in solid astonishment; then I says—

"Now, I hope you don't take it as an offence, for I don't mean any, but really, for a man that has been in the Kingdom as long as I reckon you have, you do seem to know powerful little about its customs."

"Its customs!" says he. "Heaven is a large place, good friend. Large empires have many and diverse customs. Even small dominions have, as you doubtless know by what you have seen of the matter on a small scale in the Wart. How can you imagine I could ever learn the varied customs of the countless kingdoms of heaven? It makes my head ache to think of it. I know the customs that prevail in those portions inhabited by peoples that are appointed to enter by my own gate—and hark ye, that is quite enough knowledge for one individual to try to pack into his head in the thirty-seven millions of years I have devoted night and day to that study. But the idea of learning the customs of the whole appalling expanse of heaven—O man, how insanely you talk! Now I don't doubt that this odd costume you talk about is the fashion in that district of heaven you belong to, but you won't be conspicuous in this section without it."

I felt all right, if that was the case, so I bade him good-day and left. All day I walked towards the far end of a prodigious hall of the office, hoping to come out into heaven any moment, but it was a mistake. That hall was built on the general heavenly plan—it naturally couldn't be small. At last I got so tired I couldn't go any farther; so I sat down to rest, and begun to tackle the queerest sort of strangers and ask for information, but I didn't get any; they couldn't understand my language, and I could not understand theirs. I got dreadfully lonesome. I was so downhearted and homesick I wished a hundred times I never had died. I turned back, of course. About noon next day, I got back at last and was on hand at the booking-office once more. Says I to the head clerk—

"I begin to see that a man's got to be in his own heaven to be happy."

"Perfectly correct," says he. "Did you imagine the same heaven would suit all sorts of men?"

"Well, I had that idea—but I see the foolishness of it. Which way am I to go to get to my district?"

He called the under clerk that had examined the map, and he gave me general directions. I thanked him and started; but he says—

"Wait a minute; it is millions of leagues from here. Go outside and stand on that red wishing-carpet; shut your eyes, hold your breath, and wish yourself there."

"I'm much obliged," says I; "why didn't you dart me through when I first arrived?"

"We have a good deal to think of here; it was your place to think of it and ask for it. Good-by; we probably sha'n't see you in this region for a thousand centuries or so."

"In that case, *o revoor*," says I.

I hopped onto the carpet and held my breath and shut my eyes and wished I was in the booking-office of my own section. The very next instant a voice I knew sung out in a business kind of a way—

"A harp and a hymn-book, pair of wings and a halo, size 13, for Cap'n Eli Stormfield, of San Francisco!—make him out a clean bill of health, and let him in."

I opened my eyes. Sure enough, it was a Pi Ute Injun I used to know in Tulare County; mighty good fellow—I remembered being at his funeral, which consisted of him being burnt and the other Injuns gauming their faces with his ashes and howling like wild-cats. He was powerful glad to see me, and you may make up your mind I was just as glad to see him, and felt that I was in the right kind of a heaven at last.

Just as far as your eye could reach, there was swarms of clerks, running and bustling around, tricking out thousands of Yanks and Mexicans and English and Arabs, and all sorts of people in their new outfits; and when they gave me my kit and I put on my halo and I took a look in the glass, I could have jumped over a house for joy, I was so happy. "Now *this* is something like!" says I. "Now," says I, "I'm all right—show me a cloud."

Inside of fifteen minutes I was a mile on my way

towards the cloud-banks and about a million people along with me. Most of us tried to fly, but some got crippled and nobody made a success of it. So we concluded to walk, for the present, till we had had some wing practice.

We begun to meet swarms of folks who were coming back. Some had harps and nothing else; some had hymn-books and nothing else; some had nothing at all; all of them looked meek and uncomfortable; one young fellow hadn't anything left but his halo, and he was carrying that in his hand; all of a sudden he offered it to me and says—

"Will you hold it for me a minute?"

Then he disappeared in the crowd. I went on. A woman asked me to hold her palm branch, and then *she* disappeared. A girl got me to hold her harp for her, and by George, *she* disappeared; and so on and so on, till I was about loaded down to the guards. Then comes a smiling old gentleman and asked me to hold *his* things. I swabbed off the perspiration and says, pretty tart—

"I'll have to get you to excuse me, my friend,—*I* ain't no hat-rack."

About this time I begun to run across piles of those traps, lying in the road. I just quietly dumped my extra cargo along with them. I looked around, and, Peters, that whole nation that was following me were loaded down the same as I'd been. The return crowd had got them to hold their things a minute, you see. They all dumped their loads, too, and we went on.

When I found myself perched on a cloud, with a

million other people, I never felt so good in my life. Says I, "Now this is according to the promises; I've been having my doubts, but now I *am* in heaven, sure enough." I gave my palm branch a wave or two, for luck, and then I tautened up my harp-strings and struck in. Well, Peters, you can't imagine anything like the row we made. It was grand to listen to, and made a body thrill all over, but there was considerable many tunes going on at once, and that was a drawback to the harmony, you understand; and then there was a lot of Injun tribes, and they kept up such another war-whooping that they kind of took the tuck out of the music. By and by I quit performing, and judged I'd take a rest. There was quite a nice mild old gentleman sitting next me, and I noticed he didn't take a hand; I encouraged him, but he said he was naturally bashful, and was afraid to try before so many people. By and by the old gentleman said he never could seem to enjoy music somehow. The fact was, I was beginning to feel the same way; but I didn't say anything. Him and I had a considerable long silence, then, but of course it warn't noticeable in that place. After about sixteen or seventeen hours, during which I played and sung a little, now and then—always the same tune, because I didn't know any other—I laid down my harp and begun to fan myself with my palm branch. Then we both got to sighing pretty regular. Finally, says he—

"Don't you know any tune but the one you've been pegging at all day?"

"Not another blessed one," says I.

"Don't you reckon you could learn another one?" says he.

"Never," says I; "I've tried to, but I couldn't manage it."

"It's a long time to hang to the one—eternity, you know."

"Don't break my heart," says I; "I'm getting low-spirited enough already."

After another long silence, says he—

"Are you glad to be here?"

Says I, "Old man, I'll be frank with you. This *ain't* just as near my idea of bliss as I thought it was going to be, when I used to go to church."

Says he, "What do you say to knocking off and calling it half a day?"

"That's me," says I. "I never wanted to get off watch so bad in my life."

So we started. Millions were coming to the cloud-bank all the time, happy and hosannahing; millions were leaving it all the time, looking mighty quiet, I tell you. We laid for the new-comers, and pretty soon I'd got them to hold all my things a minute, and then I was a free man again and most outrageously happy. Just then I ran across old Sam Bartlett, who had been dead a long time, and stopped to have a talk with him. Says I—

"Now tell me—is this to go on forever? Ain't there anything else for a change?"

Says he—

"I'll set you right on that point very quick. People take the figurative language of the Bible and the allegories for literal, and the first thing they ask for when they get here is a halo and a harp, and so on. Nothing that's harmless and reasonable is refused a body here, if he asks it in the right spirit. So they are outfitted with these things without a word. They go and sing and play just about one day, and that's the last you'll ever see them in the choir. They don't need anybody to tell them that that sort of thing wouldn't make a heaven—at least not a heaven that a sane man could stand a week and remain sane. That cloud-bank is placed where the noise can't disturb the old inhabitants, and so there ain't any harm in letting everybody get up there and cure himself as soon as he comes.

"Now you just remember this—heaven is as blissful and lovely as it can be; but it's just the busiest place you ever heard of. There ain't any idle people here after the first day. Singing hymns and waving palm branches through all eternity is pretty when you hear about it in the pulpit, but it's as poor a way to put in valuable time as a body could contrive. It would just make a heaven of warbling ignoramuses, don't you see? Eternal Rest sounds comforting in the pulpit, too. Well, you try it once, and see how heavy time will hang on your hands. Why, Stormfield, a man like you, that had been active and stirring all his life, would go mad in six months in a heaven where he hadn't anything to do. Heaven is the very last place to come to *rest* in,—and don't you be afraid to bet on that!"

Says I—

"Sam, I'm as glad to hear it as I thought I'd be sorry I'm glad I come, now."

Says he—

"Cap'n, ain't you pretty physically tired?"

Says I—

"Sam, it ain't any name for it! I'm dog-tired."

"Just so—just so. You've earned a good sleep, and you'll get it. You've earned a good appetite, and you'll enjoy your dinner. It's the same here as it is on earth—you've got to earn a thing, square and honest, before you enjoy it. You can't enjoy first and earn afterwards. But there's this difference, here: you can choose your own occupation, and all the powers of heaven will be put forth to help you make a success of it, if you do your level best. The shoemaker on earth that had the soul of a poet in him won't have to make shoes here."

"Now that's all reasonable and right," says I. "Plenty of work, and the kind you hanker after; no more pain, no more suffering—"

"Oh, hold on; there's plenty of pain here—but it don't kill. There's plenty of suffering here, but it don't last. You see, happiness ain't a *thing in itself*—it's only a *contrast* with something that ain't pleasant. That's all it is. There ain't a thing you can mention that is happiness in its own self—it's only so by contrast with the other thing. And so, as soon as the novelty is over and the force of the contrast dulled, it ain't happiness any longer, and you have to get something fresh. Well, there's plenty of pain and suffering in heaven—consequently there's plenty of contrasts, and just no end of happiness."

Says I, "It's the sensiblest heaven I've heard of yet, Sam, though it's about as different from the one I was brought up on as a live princess is different from her own wax figger."

Along in the first months I knocked around about the Kingdom, making friends and looking at the country, and finally settled down in a pretty likely region, to have a rest before taking another start. I went on making acquaintances and gathering up information. I had a good deal of talk with an old bald-headed angel by the name of Sandy McWilliams. He was from somewhere in New Jersey. I went about with him, considerable. We used to lay around, warm afternoons, in the shade of a rock, on some meadow-ground that was pretty high and out of the marshy slush of his cranberry-farm, and there we used to talk about all kinds of things, and smoke pipes. One day, says I—

"About how old might you be, Sandy?"

"Seventy-two."

"I judged so. How long you been in heaven?"

"Twenty-seven years, come Christmas."

"How old was you when you come up?"

"Why, seventy-two, of course."

"You can't mean it!"

"Why can't I mean it?"

"Because, if you was seventy-two then, you are naturally ninety-nine now."

"No, but I ain't. I stay the same age I was when I come."

"Well," says I, "come to think, there's something just here that I want to ask about. Down below, I always had an idea that in heaven we would all be young, and bright, and spry."

"Well, you *can* be young if you want to. You've only got to wish."

"Well, then, why didn't you wish?"

"I did. They all do. You'll try it, some day, like enough; but you'll get tired of the change pretty soon."

"Why?"

"Well, I'll tell you. Now you've always been a sailor; did you ever try some other business?"

"Yes, I tried keeping grocery, once, up in the mines; but I couldn't stand it; it was too dull—no stir, no storm, no life about it; it was like being part dead and part alive, both at the same time. I wanted to be one thing or t'other. I shut up shop pretty quick and went to sea."

"That's it. Grocery people like it, but you couldn't. You see you wasn't used to it. Well, I wasn't used to being young, and I couldn't seem to take any interest in it. I was strong, and handsome, and had curly hair,—yes, and wings, too!—gay wings like a butterfly. I went to picnics and dances and parties with the fellows, and tried to carry on and talk nonsense with the girls, but it wasn't any use; I couldn't take to it—fact is, it was an awful bore. What I wanted was early to bed and early to rise, and something to *do;* and when my work was done, I wanted to sit quiet, and smoke and think—not tear around with a parcel of giddy young kids. You can't think what I suffered whilst I was young."

"How long was you young?"

"Only two weeks. That was plenty for me. Laws, I was so lonesome! You see, I was full of the knowledge and experience of seventy-two years; the deepest subject those young folks could strike was only *a-b-c* to me. And to hear them argue—oh, my! it would have been funny, if it hadn't been so pitiful. Well, I was so hungry for the ways and the sober talk I was used to, that I tried to ring in with the old people, but they wouldn't have it. They considered me a conceited young upstart, and gave me the cold shoulder. Two weeks was a-plenty for me. I was glad to get back my bald head again, and my pipe, and my old drowsy reflections in the shade of a rock or a tree."

"Well," says I, "do you mean to say you're going to stand still at seventy-two, forever?"

"I don't know, and I ain't particular. But I ain't going to drop back to twenty-five any more—I know that, mighty well. I know a sight more than I did twenty-seven years ago, and I enjoy learning, all the time, but I don't seem to get any older. That is, bodily—my mind gets older, and stronger, and better seasoned, and more satisfactory."

Says I, "If a man comes here at ninety, don't he ever set himself back?"

"Of course he does. He sets himself back to fourteen; tries it a couple of hours, and feels like a fool; sets himself forward to twenty; it ain't much improvement; tries thirty, fifty, eighty, and finally ninety—finds he is more at home and comfortable at the same old figure he is used to than any other way. Or, if his mind begun to fail him on earth at eighty, that's where he finally sticks up here. He sticks at the place where his mind was last at its best, for there's where his enjoyment is best, and his ways most set and established."

"Does a chap of twenty-five stay always twenty-five, and look it?"

"If he is a fool, yes. But if he is bright, and ambitious and industrious, the knowledge he gains and the experience he has, change his ways and thoughts and likings, and make him find his best pleasure in the company of people above that age; so he allows his body to take on that look of as many added years as he needs to make him comfortable and proper in that sort of society; he lets his body go on taking the look of age, according as he progresses, and by and by he will be bald and wrinkled outside, and wise and deep within."

"Babies the same?"

"Babies the same. Laws, what asses we used to be, on earth, about these things! We said we'd be always young in heaven. We didn't say *how* young—we didn't think of that, perhaps—that is, we didn't all think alike, anyway. When I was a boy of seven, I suppose I thought we'd all be twelve, in heaven; when I was twelve, I suppose I thought we'd all be eighteen or twenty in heaven; when I was forty, I begun to go back; I remember I hoped we'd all be about *thirty* years old in heaven. Neither a man nor a boy ever thinks the age he *has* is exactly the best one—he puts the *right* age a few years older or a few years younger than he is. Then he makes the ideal age the general age of the heavenly people. And he expects everybody to *stick* at that age—stand stock-still—and expects them to enjoy it!—

Now just think of the idea of standing still in heaven! Think of a heaven made up entirely of hoop-rolling, marble-playing cubs of seven years!—or of awkward, diffident, sentimental immaturities of nineteen!—or of vigorous people of thirty, healthy-minded, brimming with ambition, but chained hand and foot to that one age and its limitations like so many helpless galley-slaves! Think of the dull sameness of a society made up of people all of one age and one set of looks, habits, tastes and feelings. Think how superior to it earth would be, with its variety of types and faces and ages, and the enlivening attrition of the myriad interests that come into pleasant collision in such a variegated society."

"Look here," says I, "do you know what you're doing?"

"Well, what am I doing?"

"You are making heaven pretty comfortable in one way, but you are playing the mischief with it in another."

"How d'you mean?"

"Well," I says, "take a young mother that's lost her child, and—"

"'Sh!" he says. "Look!"

It was a woman. Middle-aged, and had grizzled hair. She was walking slow, and her head was bent down, and her wings hanging limp and droopy; and she looked ever so tired, and was crying, poor thing! She passed along by, with her head down, that way, and the tears running down her face, and didn't see us. Then Sandy said, low and gentle, and full of pity:

"*She's* hunting for her child! No, *found* it, I

reckon. Lord, how she's changed! But I recognized her in a minute, though it's twenty-seven years since I saw her. A young mother she was, about twenty-two or four, or along there; and blooming and lovely and sweet? oh, just a flower! And all her heart and all her soul was wrapped up in her child, her little girl, two years old. And it died, and she went wild with grief, just wild! Well, the only comfort she had was that she'd see her child again, in heaven—'never more to part,' she said, and kept on saying it over and over, 'never more to part.' And the words made her happy; yes, they did; they made her joyful; and when I was dying, twenty-seven years ago, she told me to find her child the first thing, and say she was coming—'soon, soon, *very* soon, she hoped and believed!'"

"Why, it's pitiful, Sandy."

He didn't say anything for a while, but sat looking at the ground, thinking. Then he says, kind of mournful:

"And now she's come!"

"Well? Go on."

"Stormfield, maybe she hasn't found the child, but *I* think she has. Looks so to me. I've seen cases before. You see, she's kept that child in her head just the same as it was when she jounced it in her arms a little chubby thing. But here it didn't elect to *stay* a child. No, it elected to grow up, which it did. And in these twenty-seven years it has learned all the deep scientific learning there is to learn, and is studying and studying and learning and learning more and more, all the time, and don't give a damn for anything *but* learning; just learning, and discussing gigantic problems with people like herself."

"Well?"

"Stormfield, don't you see? Her mother knows *cranberries*, and how to tend them, and pick them, and put them up, and market them; and not another blamed thing! Her and her daughter can't be any more company for each other *now* than mud turtle and bird o' paradise. Poor thing, she was looking for a baby to jounce; *I* think she's struck a disapp'intment."

"Sandy, what will they do—stay unhappy forever in heaven?"

"No, they'll come together and get adjusted by and by. But not this year, and not next. By and by."

## CHAPTER II

I HAD been having considerable trouble with my wings. The day after I helped the choir I made a dash or two with them, but was not lucky. First off, I flew thirty yards, and then fouled an Irishman and brought him down—brought us both down, in fact. Next, I had a collision with a Bishop—and bowled him down, of course. We had some sharp words, and I felt pretty cheap, to come banging into a grave old person like that, with a million strangers looking on and smiling to themselves.

I saw I hadn't got the hang of the steering, and so couldn't rightly tell where I was going to bring up when I started. I went afoot the rest of the day, and let my wings hang. Early next morning I went to a private place to have some practice. I got up on a pretty high rock, and got a good start, and went swooping down, aiming for a bush a little over three hundred yards off; but I couldn't seem to calculate for the wind, which was about two points abaft my beam. I could see I was going considerable to looard of the bush, so I worked my starboard wing slow and went ahead strong on the port one, but it wouldn't answer; I could see I was going to broach to, so I slowed down on both, and lit. I went back to the rock and took another chance at it. I aimed two or three points to starboard of the bush—yes, more than that—enough so as to make it nearly a head-wind. I done well enough, but made pretty poor time. I could see, plain enough, that on a head-wind, wings was a mistake. I could see that a body could sail pretty close to the wind, but he couldn't go in the wind's eye. I could see that if I wanted to go a-visiting any distance from home, and the wind was ahead, I might have to wait days, maybe, for a change; and I could see, too, that these things could not be any use at all in a gale; if you tried to run before the wind, you would make a mess of it, for there isn't any way to shorten sail—like reefing, you know—you have to take it *all* in—shut your feathers down flat to your sides. That would *land* you, of course. You could lay to, with your head to the wind—that is the best you could do, and right hard work you'd find it, too. If you tried any other game, you would founder, sure.

I judge it was about a couple of weeks or so after this that I dropped old Sandy McWilliams a note one day—it was a Tuesday—and asked him to come over and take his manna and quails with me next day; and the first thing he did when he stepped in was to twinkle his eye in a sly way, and say,—

"Well, Cap, what you done with your wings?"

I saw in a minute that there was some sarcasm done up in that rag somewheres, but I never let on. I only says,—

"Gone to the wash."

"Yes," he says, in a dry sort of way, "they mostly go to the wash—about this time—I've often noticed it. Fresh angels are powerful neat. When do you look for 'em back?"

"Day after to-morrow," says I.

He winked at me, and smiled.

Says I,—

"Sandy, out with it. Come—no secrets among friends. I notice you don't ever wear wings—and plenty others don't. I've been making an ass of myself—is that it?"

"That is about the size of it. But it is no harm. We all do it at first. It's perfectly natural. You see, on earth we jumped to such foolish conclusions as to things up here. In the pictures we always saw the angels with wings on—and that was all right; but we jumped to the conclusion that that was their way of getting around—and that was all wrong. The wings ain't anything but a uniform, that's all. When they are in the field—so to speak,—they always wear them; you never see an angel going with a message anywhere without his wings, any more than you would see a military officer presiding at a court-martial without his uniform, or a postman delivering letters, or a policeman walking his beat, in plain clothes. But they ain't to *fly* with! The wings are for show, not for use. Old experienced angels are like officers of the regular army—they dress plain, when they are off duty. New angels are like the militia—never shed the uniform—always fluttering and floundering around in their wings, butting people down, flapping here, and there, and everywhere, always imagining they are attracting the admiring eye—well, they just think they are the very most important people in heaven. And when you see one of them come sailing around with one wing tipped up and t'other down, you make up your mind he is saying to himself: 'I wish Mary Ann in Arkansaw could see me now. I reckon she'd wish she hadn't shook me.' No, they're just for show, that's all—only just for show."

"I judge you've got it about right, Sandy," says I.

"Why, look at it yourself," says he. "*You* ain't built for wings—no man is. You know what a grist of years it took you to come here from the earth—and yet you were booming along faster than any cannon-ball could go. Suppose you had to fly that distance with your wings—wouldn't eternity have been over before you got here? Certainly. Well, angels have to go to the earth every day—millions of them—to appear in visions to dying children and good people, you know—it's the heft of their business. They appear with their wings, of course, because they are on official service, and because the dying persons wouldn't know they were angels if they hadn't wings—but do you reckon they fly with them? It stands to reason they don't. The wings would wear out before they got half-way; even the pin-feathers would be gone; the wing frames would be as bare as kite sticks before the paper is pasted on. The distances in heaven are billions of times greater; angels have to go all over heaven every day; could they do it with their wings alone? No, indeed; they wear the wings for style, but they travel any distance in an instant by *wishing*. The wishing-carpet of the Arabian Nights was a sensible idea—but our earthly idea of angels flying these awful distances with their clumsy wings was foolish.

"Our young saints, of both sexes, wear wings all

the time—blazing red ones, and blue and green, and gold, and variegated, and rainbowed, and ring-streaked-and-striped ones—and nobody finds fault. It is suitable to their time of life. The things are beautiful, and they set the young people off. They are the most striking and lovely part of their outfit —a halo don't *begin.*"

"Well," says I, "I've tucked mine away in the cupboard, and I allow to let them lay there till there's mud."

"Yes—or a reception."

"What's that?"

"Well, you can see one to-night if you want to. There's a barkeeper from Jersey City going to be received."

"Go on—tell me about it."

"This barkeeper got converted at a Moody and Sankey meeting, in New York, and started home on the ferryboat, and there was a collision and he got drowned. He is of a class that think all heaven goes wild with joy when a particularly hard lot like him is saved; they think all heaven turns out hosannah-ing to welcome them; they think there isn't anything talked about in the realms of the blest but their case, for that day. This barkeeper thinks there hasn't been such another stir here in years, as his coming is going to raise.—And I've always noticed this peculiarity about a dead barkeeper—he not only expects all hands to turn out when he arrives, but he expects to be received with a torchlight procession."

"I reckon he is disappointed, then."

"No, he isn't. No man is allowed to be disappointed here. Whatever he wants, when he comes—that is, any reasonable and unsacrilegious thing—he can have. There's always a few millions or billions of young folks around who don't want any better entertainment than to fill up their lungs and swarm out with their torches and have a high time over a barkeeper. It tickles the barkeeper till he can't rest, it makes a charming lark for the young folks, it don't do anybody any harm, it don't cost a rap, and it keeps up the place's reputation for making all comers happy and content."

"Very good. I'll be on hand and see them land the barkeeper."

"It is manners to go in full dress. You want to wear your wings, you know, and your other things."

"Which ones?"

"Halo, and harp, and palm branch, and all that."

"Well," says I, "I reckon I ought to be ashamed of myself, but the fact is I left them laying around that day I resigned from the choir. I haven't got a rag to wear but this robe and the wings."

"That's all right. You'll find they've been raked up and saved for you. Send for them."

"I'll do it, Sandy. But what was it you was saying about unsacrilegious things, which people expect to get, and will be disappointed about?"

"Oh, there are a lot of such things that people expect and don't get. For instance, there's a Brooklyn preacher by the name of Talmage, who is laying up a considerable disappointment for himself. He says, every now and then in his sermons, that the first thing he does when he gets to heaven, will be to fling his arms around Abraham, Isaac and Jacob, and kiss them and weep on them. There's millions of people down there on earth that are promising themselves the same thing. As many as sixty thousand people arrive here every single day, that want to run straight to Abraham, Isaac and Jacob, and hug them and weep on them. Now mind you, sixty thousand a day is a pretty heavy contract for those old people. If they were a mind to allow it, they wouldn't ever have anything to do, year in and year out, but stand up and be hugged and wept on thirty-two hours in the twenty-four. They would be tired out and as wet as muskrats all the time. What would heaven be, to *them?* It would be a mighty good place to get out of—you know that, yourself. Those are kind and gentle old Jews, but they ain't any fonder of kissing the emotional high-lights of Brooklyn than you be. You mark my words, Mr. T.'s endearments are going to be declined, with thanks. There are limits to the privileges of the elect, even in heaven. Why, if Adam was to show himself to every new comer that wants to call and gaze at him and strike him for his autograph, he would never have time to do anything else but just that. Talmage has said he is going to give Adam some of his attentions, as well as A., I. and J. But he will have to change his mind about that."

"Do you think Talmage will really come here?"

"Why, certainly, he will; but don't you be alarmed; he will run with his own kind, and there's plenty of them. That is the main charm of heaven—

there's all kinds here—which wouldn't be the case if you let the preachers tell it. Anybody can find the sort he prefers, here, and he just lets the others alone, and they let him alone. When the Deity builds a heaven, it is built right, and on a liberal plan."

Sandy sent home for his things, and I sent for mine, and about nine in the evening we begun to dress. Sandy says,—

"This is going to be a grand time for you, Stormy. Like as not some of the patriarchs will turn out."

"No, but will they?"

"Like as not. Of course they are pretty exclusive. They hardly ever show themselves to the common public. I believe they never turn out except for an eleventh-hour convert. They wouldn't do it then, only earthly tradition makes a grand show pretty necessary on that kind of an occasion."

"Do they all turn out, Sandy?"

"Who?—all the patriarchs? Oh, no—hardly ever more than a couple. You will be here fifty thousand years—maybe more—before you get a glimpse of all the patriarchs and prophets. Since I have been here, Job has been to the front once, and once Ham and Jeremiah both at the same time. But the finest thing that has happened in my day was a year or so ago; that was Charles Peace's reception—him they called 'the Bannercross Murderer'—an Englishman. There were four patriarchs and two prophets on the Grand Stand that time—there hasn't been anything like it since Captain Kidd came; Abel was there—the first time in twelve hundred years. A report got around that Adam was coming; well, of course, Abel was enough to bring a crowd, all by himself, but there is nobody that can draw like Adam. It was a false report, but it got around, anyway, as I say, and it will be a long day before I see the like of it again. The reception was in the English department, of course, which is eight hundred and eleven million miles from the New Jersey line. I went, along with a good many of my neighbors, and it was a sight to see, I can tell you. Flocks came from all the departments. I saw Esquimaux there, and Tartars, Negroes, Chinamen—people from everywhere. You see a mixture like that in the Grand Choir, the first day you land here, but you hardly ever see it again. There were billions of people; when they were singing or hosannahing, the noise was wonderful; and even when their tongues were still the drumming of the wings was nearly enough to burst your head, for all the sky was as thick as if it was snowing angels. Although Adam was not there, it was a great time anyway, because we had three archangels on the Grand Stand—it is a seldom thing that even one comes out."

"What did they look like, Sandy?"

"Well, they had shining faces, and shining robes, and wonderful rainbow wings, and they stood eighteen feet high, and wore swords, and held their heads up in a noble way, and looked like soldiers."

"Did they have halos?"

"No—anyway, not the hoop kind. The archangels and the upper-class patriarchs wear a finer thing than that. It is a round, solid, splendid glory of gold, that is blinding to look at. You have often seen a patriarch in a picture, on earth, with that thing on—you remember it?—he looks as if he had his head in a brass platter. That don't give you the right idea of it at all—it is much more shining and beautiful."

"Did you talk with those archangels and patriarchs, Sandy?"

"Who—*I?* Why, what can you be thinking about, Stormy? I ain't worthy to speak to such as they."

"Is Talmage?"

"Of course not. You have got the same mixed-up idea about these things that everybody has down there. I had it once, but I got over it. Down there they talk of the heavenly King—and that is right—but then they go right on speaking as if this was a republic and everybody was on a dead level with everybody else, and privileged to fling his arms around anybody he comes across, and be hail-fellow-well-met with all the elect, from the highest down. How tangled up and absurd that is! How are you going to have a republic under a king? How are you going to have a republic at all, where the head of the government is absolute, holds his place forever, and has no parliament, no council to meddle or make in his affairs, nobody voted for, nobody elected, nobody in the whole universe with a voice in the government, nobody asked to take a hand in its matters, and nobody *allowed* to do it? Fine republic, ain't it?"

"Well, yes—it *is* a little different from the idea I had—but I thought I might go around and get acquainted with the grandees, anyway—not exactly splice the main-brace with them, you know, but shake hands and pass the time of day."

"Could Tom, Dick and Harry call on the Cabinet of Russia and do that?—on Prince Gortschakoff, for instance?"

"I reckon not, Sandy."

"Well, this is Russia—only more so. There's not the shadow of a republic about it anywhere. There are ranks, here. There are viceroys, princes, governors, sub-governors, sub-sub-governors, and a hundred orders of nobility, grading along down from grand-ducal archangels, stage by stage, till the general level is struck, where there ain't any titles. Do you know what a prince of the blood is, on earth?"

"No."

"Well, a prince of the blood don't belong to the royal family exactly, and he don't belong to the mere nobility of the kingdom; he is lower than the one, and higher than t'other. That's about the position of the patriarchs and prophets here. There's some mighty high nobility here—people that you and I ain't worthy to polish sandals for—and *they* ain't worthy to polish sandals for the patriarchs and prophets. That gives you a kind of an idea of their rank, don't it? You begin to see how high up they are, don't you? Just to get a two-minute glimpse of one of them is a thing for a body to remember and tell about for a thousand years. Why, Captain, just think of this: if Abraham was to set his foot down here by this door, there would be a railing set up around that foot-track right away, and a shelter put over it, and people would flock here from all over heaven, for hundreds and hundreds of years, to look at it. Abraham is one of the parties that Mr. Talmage, of Brooklyn, is going to embrace, and kiss, and weep on, when he comes. He wants to lay in a good stock of tears, you know, or five to one he will go dry before he gets a chance to do it."

"Sandy," says I, "I had an idea that *I* was going to be equal with everybody here, too, but I will let that drop. It don't matter, and I am plenty happy enough anyway."

"Captain, you are happier than you would be, the other way. These old patriarchs and prophets have got ages the start of you; they know more in two minutes than you know in a year. Did you ever try to have a sociable improving-time discussing winds, and currents and variations of compass with an undertaker?"

"I get your idea, Sandy. He couldn't interest me. He would be an ignoramus in such things—he would bore me, and I would bore him."

"You have got it. You would bore the patriarchs when you talked, and when they talked they would shoot over your head. By and by you would say, 'Good morning, your Eminence, I will call again'—but you wouldn't. Did you ever ask the slush-boy to come up in the cabin and take dinner with you?"

"I get your drift again, Sandy. I wouldn't be used to such grand people as the patriarchs and prophets, and I would be sheepish and tongue-tied in their company, and mighty glad to get out of it. Sandy, which is the highest rank, patriarch or prophet?"

"Oh, the prophets hold over the patriarchs. The newest prophet, even, is of a sight more consequence than the oldest patriarch. Yes, sir, Adam himself has to walk behind Shakespeare."

"Was Shakespeare a prophet?"

"Of course he was; and so was Homer, and heaps more. But Shakespeare and the rest have to walk behind a common tailor from Tennessee, by the name of Billings; and behind a horse-doctor named Sakka, from Afghanistan. Jeremiah, and Billings and Buddha walk together, side by side, right behind a crowd from planets not in our astronomy; next come a dozen or two from Jupiter and other worlds; next come Daniel, and Sakka and Confucius; next a lot from systems outside of ours; next come Ezekiel, and Mahomet, Zoroaster, and a knife-grinder from ancient Egypt; then there is a long string, and after them, away down toward the bottom, come Shakespeare and Homer, and a shoemaker named Marais, from the back settlements of France."

"Have they really rung in Mahomet and all those other heathens?"

"Yes—they all had their message, and they all get their reward. The man who don't get his reward on earth, needn't bother—he will get it here, sure."

"But why did they throw off on Sheakespeare, that way, and put him away down there below those shoemakers and horse-doctors and knife-grinders—a lot of people nobody ever heard of?"

"That is the heavenly justice of it—they warn't

rewarded according to their deserts, on earth, but here they get their rightful rank. That tailor Billings, from Tennessee, wrote poetry that Homer and Shakespeare couldn't begin to come up to; but nobody would print it, nobody read it but his neighbors, an ignorant lot, and they laughed at it. Whenever the village had a drunken frolic and a dance, they would drag him in and crown him with cabbage leaves, and pretend to bow down to him; and one night when he was sick and nearly starved to death, they had him out and crowned him, and then they rode him on a rail about the village, and everybody followed along, beating tin pans and yelling. Well, he died before morning. He wasn't ever expecting to go to heaven, much less that there was going to be any fuss made over him, so I reckon he was a good deal surprised when the reception broke on him."

"Was you there, Sandy?"

"Bless you, no!"

"Why? Didn't you know it was going to come off?"

"Well, I judge I did. It was the talk of these realms—not for a day, like this barkeeper business, but for twenty years before the man died."

"Why the mischief didn't you go, then?"

"Now how you talk! The like of me go meddling around at the reception of a prophet? A mudsill like me trying to push in and help receive an awful grandee like Edward J. Billings? Why, I should have been laughed at for a billion miles around. I shouldn't ever heard the last of it."

"Well, who did go, then?"

"Mighty few people that you and I will ever get a chance to see, Captain. Not a solitary commoner ever has the luck to see a reception of a prophet, I can tell you. All the nobility, and all the patriarchs and prophets—every last one of them—and all the archangels, and all the princes and governors and viceroys, were there,—and *no* small fry—not a single one. And mind you, I'm not talking about only the grandees from *our* world, but the princes and patriarchs and so on from *all* the worlds that shine in our sky, and from billions more that belong in systems upon systems away outside of the one our sun is in. There were some prophets and patriarchs there that ours ain't a circumstance to, for rank and illustriousness and all that. Some were from Jupiter and other worlds in our own system, but the most celebrated were three poets, Saa, Bo and Soof, from great planets in three different and very remote systems. These three names are common and familiar in every nook and corner of heaven, clear from one end of it to the other—fully as well known as the eighty Supreme Archangels, in fact—whereas our Moses, and Adam, and the rest, have not been heard of outside of our world's little corner of heaven, except by a few very learned men scattered here and there—and they always spell their names wrong, and get the performances of one mixed up with the doings of another, and they almost always locate them simply *in our solar system*, and think that is enough without going into little details such as naming the particular world they are from. It is like a learned

Hindoo showing off how much he knows by saying Longfellow lived in the United States—as if he lived all over the United States, and as if the country was so small you couldn't throw a brick there without hitting him. Between you and me, it does gravel me, the cool way people from those monster worlds outside our system snub our little world, and even our system. Of course we think a good deal of Jupiter, because our world is only a potato to it, for size; but then there are worlds in other systems that Jupiter isn't even a mustard-seed to—like the planet Goobra, for instance, which you couldn't squeeze inside the orbit of Halley's comet without straining the rivets. Tourists from Goobra (I mean parties that lived and died there—natives) come here, now and then, and inquire about our world, and when they find out it is so little that a streak of lightning can flash clear around it in the eighth of a second, they have to lean up against something to laugh. Then they screw a glass into their eye and go to examining *us*, as if we were a curious kind of foreign bug, or something of that sort. One of them asked me how long our day was; and when I told him it was twelve hours long, as a general thing, he asked me if people where I was from considered it worth while to get up and wash for such a day as that. That is the way with those Goobra people—they can't seem to let a chance go by to throw it in your face that their day is three hundred and twenty-two of our years long. This young snob was just of age—he was six or seven thousand of his days old—say two million of our years—and he had all the puppy airs that belong to that time of life—that turning-point when a person has got over being a boy and yet ain't quite a man exactly. It if had been anywhere else but in heaven, I would have given him a piece of my mind. Well, anyway, Billings had the grandest reception that has been seen in thousands of centuries, and I think it will have a good effect. His name will be carried pretty far, and it will make our system talked about, and maybe our world, too, and raise us in the respect of the general public of heaven. Why, look here—Shakespeare walked backwards before that tailor from Tennessee, and scattered flowers for him to walk on, and Homer stood behind his chair and waited on him at the banquet. Of course that didn't go for much *there*, amongst all those big foreigners from other systems, as they hadn't heard of Shakespeare or Homer either, but it would amount to considerable down there on our little earth if they could know about it. I wish there was something *in* that miserable spiritualism, so we could send them word. That Tennessee village would set up a monument to Billings, then, and his autograph would outsell Satan's. Well, they had grand times at that reception—a small-fry noble from Hoboken told me all about it—Sir Richard Duffer, Baronet."

"What, Sandy, a nobleman from Hoboken? How is that?"

"Easy enough. Duffer kept a sausage-shop and never saved a cent in his life because he used to give all his spare meat to the poor, in a quiet way. Not tramps,—no, the other sort—the sort that will starve before they will beg—honest square people out of work. Dick used to watch hungry-looking men and women and children, and track them home, and find out all about them from the neighbors, and then feed them and find them work. As nobody ever *saw* him give anything to anybody, he had the reputation of being mean; he died with it, too, and everybody said it was a good riddance; but the minute he landed here, they made him a baronet, and the very first words Dick the sausage-maker of Hoboken heard when he stepped upon the heavenly shore were, 'Welcome, Sir Richard Duffer!' It surprised him some, because he thought he had reasons to believe he was pointed for a warmer climate than this one."

All of a sudden the whole region fairly rocked under the crash of eleven hundred and one thunder blasts, all let off at once, and Sandy says,—

"There, that's for the barkeep."

I jumped up and says,—

"Then let's be moving along, Sandy; we don't want to miss any of this thing, you know."

"Keep your seat," he says; "he is only just telegraphed, that is all."

"How?"

"That blast only means that he has been sighted from the signal-station. He is off Sandy Hook. The committees will go down to meet him, now, and escort him in. There will be ceremonies and delays; they won't be coming up the Bay for a considerable time, yet. It is several billion miles away, anyway."

"*I* could have been a barkeeper and a hard lot

just as well as not," says I, remembering the lonesome way I arrived, and how there wasn't any committee nor anything.

"I notice some regret in your voice," says Sandy, "and it is natural enough; but let bygones be bygones; you went according to your lights, and it is too late now to mend the thing."

"No, let it slide, Sandy, I don't mind. But you've got a Sandy Hook *here*, too, have you?"

"We've got everything here, just as it is below. All the States and Territories of the Union, and all the kingdoms of the earth and the islands of the sea are laid out here just as they are on the globe—all the same shape they are down there, and all graded to the relative size, only each State and realm and island is a good many billion times bigger here than it is below. There goes another blast."

"What is that one for?"

"That is only another fort answering the first one. They each fire eleven hundred and one thunder blasts at a single dash—it is the usual salute for an eleventh-hour guest; a hundred for each hour and an extra one for the guest's sex; if it was a woman we would know it by their leaving off the extra gun."

"How do we know there's eleven hundred and one, Sandy, when they all go off at once?—and yet we certainly do know."

"Our intellects are a good deal sharpened up, here, in some ways, and that is one of them. Numbers and sizes and distances are so great, here, that we have to be made so we can *feel* them—our old ways of counting and measuring and ciphering wouldn't ever give us an idea of them, but would only confuse us and oppress us and make our heads ache."

After some more talk about this, I says: "Sandy, I notice that I hardly ever see a white angel; where I run across one white angel, I strike as many as a hundred million copper-colored ones—people that can't speak English. How is that?"

"Well, you will find it the same in any State or Territory of the American corner of heaven you choose to go to. I have shot along, a whole week on a stretch, and gone millions and millions of miles, through perfect swarms of angels, without ever seeing a single white one, or hearing a word I could understand. You see, America was occupied a billion years and more, by Injuns and Aztecs, and that sort of folks, before a white man ever set his foot in it. During the first three hundred years after Columbus's discovery, there wasn't ever more than one good lecture audience of white people, all put together, in America—I mean the whole thing, British Possessions and all; in the beginning of our century there were only 6,000,000 or 7,000,000—say seven; 12,000,000 or 14,000,000 in 1825; say 23,000,000 in 1850; 40,000,000 in 1875. Our death-rate has always been 20 in 1000 per annum. Well, 140,000 died the first year of the century; 280,000 the twenty-fifth year; 500,000 the fiftieth year; about a million the seventy-fifth year. Now I am going to be liberal about this thing, and consider that fifty million whites have died in America from the beginning up to to-day—make it sixty, if you want to; make it a hundred million—it's no difference about a few millions one way or t'other. Well, now, you can see, yourself, that when you come to spread a little dab of people like that over these hundreds of billions of miles of American territory here in heaven, it is like scattering a ten-cent box of homœopathic pills over the Great Sahara and expecting to find them again. You can't expect us to amount to anything in heaven, and we *don't*—now that is the simple fact, and we have got to do the best we can with it. The learned men from other planets and other systems come here and hang around a while, when they are touring around the Kingdom, and then go back to their own section of heaven and write a book of travels, and they give America about five lines in it. And what do they say about us? They say this wilderness is populated with a scattering few hundred thousand billions of red angels, with now and then a curiously complected *diseased* one. You see, they think we whites and the occasional nigger are Injuns that have been bleached out or blackened by some leprous disease or other—for some peculiarly rascally *sin*, mind you. It is a mighty sour pill for us all, my friend—even the modestest of us, let alone the other kind, that think they are going to be received like a long-lost government bond, and hug Abraham into the bargain. I haven't asked you any of the particulars, Captain, but I judge it goes without saying—if my experience is worth anything—that there wasn't much of a hooraw made over you when you arrived—now was there?"

"Don't mention it, Sandy," says I, coloring up a little; "I wouldn't have had the family see it for any amount you are a mind to name. Change the subject, Sandy, change the subject."

"Well, do you think of settling in the California department of bliss?"

"I don't know. I wasn't calculating on doing anything really definite in that direction till the family come. I thought I would just look around, meantime, in a quiet way, and make up my mind. Besides, I know a good many dead people, and I was calculating to hunt them up and swap a little gossip with them about friends, and old times, and one thing or another, and ask them how they like it here, as far as they have got. I reckon my wife will want to camp in the California range, though, because most all her departed will be there, and she likes to be with folks she knows."

"Don't you let her. You see what the Jersey district of heaven is, for whites; well, the California district is a thousand times worse. It swarms with a mean kind of leather-headed mud-colored angels—and your nearest white neighbors is likely to be a million miles away. *What a man mostly misses, in heaven, is company*—company of his own sort and color and language. I have come near settling in the European part of heaven once or twice on that account."

"Well, why didn't you, Sandy?"

"Oh, various reasons. For one thing, although you *see* plenty of whites there, you can't understand any of them hardly, and so you go about as hungry for talk as you do here. I like to look at a Russian or a German or an Italian—I even like to look at a

Frenchman if I ever have the luck to catch him engaged in anything that ain't indelicate—but *looking* don't cure the hunger—what you want is talk."

"Well, there's England, Sandy—the English district of heaven."

"Yes, but it is not so very much better than this end of the heavenly domain. As long as you run across Englishmen born this side of three hundred years ago, you are all right; but the minute you get back of Elizabeth's time the language begins to fog up, and the further back you go the foggier it gets. I had some talk with one Langland and a man by the name of Chaucer—old-time poets—but it was no use, I couldn't quite understand them and they couldn't quite understand me. I have had letters from them since, but it is such broken English I can't make it out. Back of those men's time the English are just simply foreigners, nothing more, nothing less; they talk Danish, German, Norman French, and sometimes a mixture of all three; back of *them*, they talk Latin, and ancient British, Irish, and Gaelic; and then back of these come billions and billions of pure savages that talk a gibberish that Satan himself couldn't understand. The fact is, where you strike one man in the English settlements that you can understand, you wade through awful swarms that talk something you can't make head nor tail of. You see, every country on earth has been overlaid so often, in the course of a billion years, with different kinds of people and different sorts of languages, that this sort of mongrel business was bound to be the result in heaven."

"Sandy," says I, "did you see a good many of the great people history tells about?"

"Yes—plenty. I saw kings and all sorts of distinguished people."

"Do the kings rank just as they did below?"

"No; a body can't bring his rank up here with him. Divine right is a good-enough earthly romance, but it don't go, here. Kings drop down to the general level as soon as they reach the realms of grace. I knew Charles the Second very well—one of the most popular comedians in the English section—draws first rate. There are better, of course—people that were never heard of on earth—but Charles is making a very good reputation indeed, and is considered a rising man. Richard the Lion-hearted is in the prize-ring, and coming into considerable favor. Henry the Eighth is a tragedian, and the scenes where he kills people are done to the very life. Henry the Sixth keeps a religious-book stand."

"Did you ever see Napoleon, Sandy?"

"Often—sometimes in the Corsican range, sometimes in the French. He always hunts up a conspicuous place, and goes frowning around with his arms folded and his field-glass under his arm, looking as grand, gloomy and peculiar as his reputation calls for, and very much bothered because he don't stand as high, here, for a soldier, as he expected to."

"Why, who stands higher?"

"Oh, a *lot* of people *we* never heard of before—the shoemaker and horse-doctor and knife-grinder kind, you know—clodhoppers from goodness knows where, that never handled a sword or fired a shot in their lives—but the soldiership was in them, though they never had a chance to show it. But here they take their right place, and Cæsar and Napoleon and Alexander have to take a back seat. The greatest military genius our world ever produced was a bricklayer from somewhere back of Boston—died during the Revolution—by the name of Absalom Jones. Wherever he goes, crowds flock to see him. You see, everybody knows that if he had had a chance he would have shown the world some generalship that would have made all generalship before look like child's play and 'prentice work. But he never got a chance; he tried heaps of times to enlist as a private, but he had lost both thumbs and a couple of front teeth, and the recruiting sergeant wouldn't pass him. However, as I say, everybody knows, now, what he *would* have been, and so they flock by the million to get a glimpse of him whenever they hear he is going to be anywhere. Cæsar, and Hannibal, and Alexander, and Napoleon are all on his staff, and ever so many more great generals; but the public hardly care to look at *them* when *he* is around. Boom! There goes another salute. The barkeeper's off quarantine now."

Sandy and I put on our things. Then we made a wish, and in a second we were at the reception-place. We stood on the edge of the ocean of space, and looked out over the dimness, but couldn't make out anything. Close by us was the Grand Stand—tier on tier of dim thrones rising up toward the zenith. From each side of it spread away the tiers of seats for the general public. They spread away for leagues and leagues—you couldn't see the ends. They were empty and still, and hadn't a cheerful look, but looked dreary, like a theater before anybody comes—gas turned down. Sandy says,—

"We'll sit down here and wait. We'll see the head of the procession come in sight away off yonder pretty soon, now."

Says I,—

"It's pretty lonesome, Sandy; I reckon there's a hitch somewheres. Nobody but just you and me—it ain't much of a display for the barkeeper."

"Don't you fret, it's all right. There'll be one more gun-fire—then you'll see."

In a little while we noticed a sort of a lightish flush, away off on the horizon.

"Head of the torchlight procession," says Sandy.

It spread, and got lighter and brighter; soon it had a strong glare like a locomotive headlight; it kept on getting brighter and brighter till it was like the sun peeping above the horizon-line at sea—the big red rays shot high up into the sky.

"Keep your eyes on the Grand Stand and the miles of seats—sharp!" says Sandy, "and listen for the gun-fire."

Just then it burst out, "Boom-boom-boom!" like a million thunderstorms in one, and made the whole heavens rock. Then there was a sudden and awful glare of light all about us, and in that very instant every one of the millions of seats was occupied, and as far as you could see, in both directions, was just a solid pack of people, and the place was all splendidly lit up! It was enough to take a body's breath away. Sandy says,—

"That is the way we do it here. No time fooled away; nobody straggling in after the curtain's up. Wishing is quicker work than traveling. A quarter of a second ago these folks were millions of miles from here. When they heard the last signal, all they had to do was to wish, and here they are."

The prodigious choir struck up,—

> We long to hear thy voice,
> To see thee face to face.

It was noble music, but the uneducated chipped in and spoilt it, just as the congregations used to do on earth.

The head of the procession began to pass, now, and it was a wonderful sight. It swept along, thick and solid, five hundred thousand angels abreast, and every angel carrying a torch and singing—the whirring thunder of the wings made a body's head ache. You could follow the line of the procession back, and slanting upward into the sky, far away in a glittering snaky rope, till it was only a faint streak in the distance. The rush went on and on, for a long time, and at last, sure enough, along comes the barkeeper, and then everybody rose, and a cheer went up that made the heavens shake, I tell you! He was all smiles, and had his halo tilted over one ear in a cocky way, and was the most satisfied-looking saint I ever saw. While he marched up the steps of the Grand Stand, the choir struck up,—

The whole wide heaven groans,
And waits to hear that voice.

There were four gorgeous tents standing side by side in the place of honor, on a broad railed platform in the center of the Grand Stand, with a shining guard of honor round about them. The tents had been shut up all this time. As the barkeeper climbed along up, bowing and smiling to everybody, and at last got to the platform, these tents were jerked up aloft all of a sudden, and we saw four noble thrones of gold, all caked with jewels, and in the two middle ones sat old white-whiskered men, and in the two others a couple of the most glorious and gaudy giants, with platter halos and beautiful armor. All the millions went down on their knees, and stared, and looked glad, and burst out into a joyful kind of murmurs. They said,—

"Two archangels!—that is splendid. Who can the others be?"

The archangels gave the barkeeper a stiff little military bow; the two old men rose; one of them said, "Moses and Esau welcome thee!" and then all the four vanished, and the thrones were empty.

The barkeeper looked a little disappointed, for he was calculating to hug those old people, I judge; but it was the gladdest and proudest multitude you ever saw—because they had seen Moses and Esau. Everybody was saying, "Did you see them?—I did—Esau's side face was to me, but I saw Moses full in the face, just as plain as I see you this minute!"

The procession took up the barkeeper and moved

on with him again, and the crowd broke up and scattered. As we went along home, Sandy said it was a great success, and the barkeeper would have a right to be proud of it forever. And he said *we* were in luck, too; said we might attend receptions for forty thousand years to come, and not have a chance to see a brace of such grand moguls as Moses and Esau. We found afterwards that we had come near seeing another patriarch, and likewise a genuine prophet besides, but at the last moment they sent regrets. Sandy said there would be a monument put up there, where Moses and Esau had stood, with the date and circumstances, and all about the whole business, and travelers would come for thousands of years and gawk at it, and climb over it, and scribble their names on it.

# A FABLE

# A FABLE*

ONCE upon a time an artist who had painted a small and very beautiful picture placed it so that he could see it in the mirror. He said, "This doubles the distance and softens it, and it is twice as lovely as it was before."

The animals out in the woods heard of this through the housecat, who was greatly admired by them because he was so learned, and so refined and civilized, and so polite and high-bred, and could tell them so much which they didn't know before, and were not certain about afterward. They were much excited about this new piece of gossip, and they asked questions, so as to get at a full understanding of it. They asked what a picture was, and the cat explained.

"It is a flat thing," he said; "wonderfully flat, marvelously flat, enchantingly flat and elegant. And, oh, so beautiful!"

That excited them almost to a frenzy, and they said they would give the world to see it. Then the bear asked:

"What is it that makes it so beautiful?"

"It is the looks of it," said the cat.

This filled them with admiration and uncertainty, and they were more excited than ever. Then the cow asked:

* Copyright, 1909, by Harper & Brothers.

"What is a mirror?"

"It is a hole in the wall," said the cat. "You look in it, and there you see the picture, and it is so dainty and charming and ethereal and inspiring in its unimaginable beauty that your head turns round and round, and you almost swoon with ecstasy."

The ass had not said anything as yet; he now began to throw doubts. He said there had never been anything as beautiful as this before, and probably wasn't now. He said that when it took a whole basketful of sesquipedalian adjectives to whoop up a thing of beauty, it was time for suspicion.

It was easy to see that these doubts were having an effect upon the animals, so the cat went off offended. The subject was dropped for a couple of days, but in the meantime curiosity was taking a fresh start, and there was a revival of interest perceptible. Then the animals assailed the ass for spoiling what could possibly have been a pleasure to them, on a mere suspicion that the picture was not beautiful, without any evidence that such was the case. The ass was not troubled; he was calm, and said there was one way to find out who was in the right, himself or the cat: he would go and look in that hole, and come back and tell what he found there. The animals felt relieved and grateful, and asked him to go at once—which he did.

But he did not know where he ought to stand; and so, through error, he stood between the picture and the mirror. The result was that the picture had no chance, and didn't show up. He returned home and said:

"The cat lied. There was nothing in that hole but an ass. There wasn't a sign of a flat thing visible. It was a handsome ass, and friendly, but just an ass, and nothing more."

The elephant asked:

"Did you see it good and clear? Were you close to it?"

"I saw it good and clear, O Hathi, King of Beasts. I was so close that I touched noses with it."

"This is very strange," said the elephant; "the cat was always truthful before—as far as we could make out. Let another witness try. Go, Baloo, look in the hole, and come and report."

So the bear went. When he came back, he said:

"Both the cat and the ass have lied; there was nothing in the hole but a bear."

Great was the surprise and puzzlement of the animals. Each was now anxious to make the test himself and get at the straight truth. The elephant sent them one at a time.

First, the cow. She found nothing in the hole but a cow.

The tiger found nothing in it but a tiger.

The lion found nothing in it but a lion.

The leopard found nothing in it but a leopard.

The camel found a camel, and nothing more.

Then Hathi was wroth, and said he would have the truth, if he had to go and fetch it himself. When he returned, he abused his whole subjectry for liars, and was in an unappeasable fury with the moral and mental blindness of the cat. He said that anybody but a near-sighted fool could see that there was nothing in the hole but an elephant.

MORAL, BY THE CAT

You can find in a text whatever you bring, if you will stand between it and the mirror of your imagination. You may not see your ears, but they will be there.

# MY PLATONIC SWEETHEART

# MY PLATONIC SWEETHEART*

*Mark Twain was always interested in those psychic phenomena which we call dreams. His own sleep fancies were likely to be vivid, and it was his habit to recall them and to find interest, and sometimes amusement, in their detail. In the story which follows he set down, and not without some fidelity to circumstance—dream circumstance—a phase of what we call recurrent dreams. As the tale progressed he felt an inclination to treat the subject more fully—more philosophically—and eventually he laid the manuscript away. The time did not come when he was moved to rewrite it; and for the pure enjoyment of it as a delicate fancy it may be our good fortune that he left it unchanged.*—Albert Bigelow Paine.

I MET her first when I was seventeen and she fifteen. It was in a dream. No, I did not meet her; I overtook her. It was in a Missourian village which I had never been in before, and was not in at that time, except dreamwise; in the flesh I was on the Atlantic seaboard ten or twelve hundred miles away. The thing was sudden, and without preparation—after the custom of dreams. There I was, crossing a wooden bridge that had a wooden rail and was untidy with scattered wisps of hay, and there she was, five steps in front of me; half a second previously neither of us was there. This was the exit of the village, which lay immediately behind us. Its last house was the blacksmith-shop; and the peaceful clinking of the hammers—a sound which nearly always seems remote, and is always touched with a spirit of loneliness and a feeling of soft regret for something, you don't know what—was wafted to my ears over my shoulder; in front of us was the winding country road, with woods on one side, and on the other a rail fence, with blackberry vines and hazel bushes crowding its angles; on an upper rail a bluebird, and scurrying toward him along the same rail a fox-squirrel with his tail bent high like a shepherd's crook; beyond the fence a rich field of grain, and far away a farmer in shirtsleeves and straw hat wading knee-deep through it; no other representatives of life, and no noise at all; everywhere a Sabbath stillness.

I remember it all—and the girl, too, and just how she walked, and how she was dressed. In the first moment I was five steps behind her; in the next one I was at her side—without either stepping or gliding; it merely happened; the transfer ignored space. I noticed that, but not with any surprise; it seemed a natural process.

I was at her side. I put my arm around her waist and drew her close to me, for I loved her; and although I did not know her, my behavior seemed to me quite natural and right, and I had no misgivings about it. She showed no surprise, no distress, no displeasure, but put an arm around my waist, and turned up her face to mine with a happy welcome in it, and when I bent down to kiss her she received the kiss as if she was expecting it, and as if it was quite natural for me to offer it and her to take it and have pleasure in it. The affection which I felt for her and which she manifestly felt for me was a quite simple fact; but the quality of it was another matter. It was not the affection of brother and sister—it was closer than that, more clinging, more endearing, more reverent; and it was not the love of sweethearts, for there was no fire in it. It was somewhere between the two, and was finer than either, and more exquisite, more profoundly contenting. We often experience this strange and gracious thing in our dream-loves; and we remember it as a feature of our childhood-loves, too.

We strolled along, across the bridge and down the road, chatting like the oldest friends. She called me George, and that seemed natural and right, though it was not my name; and I called her Alice, and she did not correct me, though without doubt it was not her name. Everything that happened seemed just natural and to be expected. Once I said, "What a dear little hand it is!" and without any words she laid it gracefully in mine for me to examine it. I did it, remarking upon its littleness, its delicate beauty, and its satin skin, then kissed it; she put it up to her lips without saying anything and kissed it in the same place.

Around a curve of the road, at the end of half a mile, we came to a log house, and entered it and found the table set and everything on it steaming hot—a roast turkey, corn in the ear, butterbeans, and the rest of the usual things—and a cat curled up asleep in a splint-bottomed chair by the fireplace; but no people; just emptiness and silence. She said she would look in the next room if I would wait for her. So I sat down, and she passed through a door, which closed behind her with a click of the latch. I waited and waited. Then I got up and followed, for I could not any longer bear to have her out of my sight. I passed through the door, and found myself in a strange sort of cemetery, a city of innumerable tombs and monuments stretching far and wide on every hand, and flushed with pink and gold lights flung from the sinking sun. I turned around, and the log house was gone. I ran here and there and yonder down the lanes between the rows of tombs, calling Alice; and presently the night closed down, and I could not find my way. Then I woke, in deep distress over my loss, and was in my bed in Philadelphia. And I was not seventeen, now, but nineteen.

Ten years afterward, in another dream, I found her. I was seventeen again, and she was still fifteen. I was in a grassy place in the twilight deeps of a magnolia forest some miles above Natchez, Mississippi; the trees were snowed over with great blossoms, and the air was loaded with their rich and strenuous fragrance; the ground was high, and through a rift in the wood a burnished patch of the river was visible in the distance. I was sitting on the grass, absorbed in thinking, when an arm was laid around my neck, and there was Alice sitting by my side and looking into my face. A deep and satisfied happiness and an unwordable gratitude rose in me, but with it there was no feeling of surprise; and there was no sense of a time-lapse; the ten years amounted to hardly even a yesterday; indeed, to hardly even a noticeable fraction of it. We dropped in the tranquilest way into affectionate caressings and pettings, and chatted along without a reference to the separation; which was natural, for I think we did not know there had been any that one might measure with either clock or almanac. She called me Jack and I called her Helen, and those seemed the right and proper names, and perhaps neither of us suspected that we had ever borne others; or, if we did suspect it, it was probably not a matter of consequence.

She had been beautiful ten years before; she was just as beautiful still; girlishly young and sweet and innocent, and she was still that now. She had blue eyes, a hair of flossy gold before; she had black hair now, and dark-brown eyes. I noted these differences, but they did not suggest change; to me she was the same girl she was before, absolutely. It never occurred to me to ask what became of the log house; I doubt if I even thought of it. We were living in a simple and natural and beautiful world where everything that happened was natural and right, and was not perplexed with the unexpected or with any forms of surprise, and so there was no occasion for explanations and no interest attaching to such things.

We had a dear and pleasant time together, and were like a couple of ignorant and contented children. Helen had a summer hat on. She took it off presently and said, "It was in the way; now you can kiss me better." It seemed to me merely a bit of courteous and considerate wisdom, nothing more; and a natural thing for her to think of and do. We went wandering through the woods, and came to a limpid and shallow stream a matter of three yards wide. She said:

"I must not get my feet wet, dear; carry me over."

I took her in my arms and gave her my hat to hold. This was to keep my own feet from getting wet. I did not know why this should have that effect; I merely knew it; and she knew it, too. I crossed the stream, and said I would go on carrying her, because it was so pleasant; and she said it was pleasant to her, too, and wished we had thought of it sooner. It seemed to me a pity that we should have walked so far, both of us on foot, when we could have been having this higher enjoyment; and I spoke of it regretfully, as a something lost which could never be got back. She was troubled about it, too, and said there must be some way to get it back; and she would think. After musing deeply a little while she looked up radiant and proud, and said she had found it.

"Carry me back and start over again."

I can see, now, that that was no solution, but at the time it seemed luminous with intelligence, and I believed that there was not another little head in the world that could have worked out that difficult problem with such swiftness and success. I told her that, and it pleased her; and she said she was glad it all happened, so that I could see how capable she was. After thinking a moment she added that it was "quite atreous." The words seemed to mean something, I do not know why: in fact, it seemed to cover the whole ground and leave nothing more to say; I admired the nice aptness and the flashing felicity of the phrase, and was filled with respect for the marvelous mind that had been able to engender it. I think less of it now. It is a noticeable fact that the intellectual coinage of Dreamland often passes for more there than it would fetch here. Many a time in after years my dream-sweetheart threw off golden sayings which crumbled to ashes under my pencil when I was setting them down in my note-book after breakfast.

I carried her back and started over again; and all the long afternoon I bore her in my arms, miles upon miles, and it never occurred to either of us that there was anything remarkable in a youth like me being able to carry that sweet bundle around half a day without some sense of fatigue or need of rest. There are many dream-worlds, but none is so rightly and reasonably and pleasantly arranged as that one.

After dark we reached a great plantation-house, and it was her home. I carried her in, and the family knew me and I knew them, although we had not met before; and the mother asked me with ill disguised anxiety how much twelve times fourteen was, and I said a hundred and thirty-five, and she put it down on a piece of paper, saying it was her habit in the process of perfecting her education not to trust important particulars to her memory; and her husband was offering me a chair, but noticed that Helen was asleep, so he said it would be best not to disturb her; and he backed me softly against a wardrobe and said I could stand more easily now;

then a negro came in, bowing humbly, with his slouch-hat in his hand, and asked me if I would have my measure taken. The question did not surprise me, but it confused me and worried me, and I said I should like to have advice about it. He started toward the door to call advisers; then he and the family and the lights began to grow dim, and in a few moments the place was pitch dark; but straightway there came a flood of moonlight and a gust of cold wind, and I found myself crossing a frozen lake, and my arms were empty. The wave of grief that swept through me woke me up, and I was sitting at my desk in the newspaper office in San Francisco, and I noticed by the clock that I had been asleep less than two minutes. And what was of more consequence, I was twenty-nine years old.

That was 1864. The next year and the year after I had momentary glimpses of my dream-sweetheart, but nothing more. These are set down in my note-books under their proper dates, but with no talks nor other particulars added; which is sufficient evidence to me that there were none to add. In both of these instances there was the sudden meeting and recognition, the eager approach, then the instant disappearance, leaving the world empty and of no worth. I remember the two images quite well; in fact, I remember all the images of that spirit, and can bring them before me without help of my note-book. The habit of writing down my dreams of all sorts while they were fresh in my mind, and then studying them and rehearsing them and trying to find out what the source of dreams is, and which of the two or three separate persons inhabiting us is their architect, has given me a good dream-memory —a thing which is not usual with people, for few drill the dream-memory and, no memory can be kept strong without that.

I spent a few months in the Hawaiian Islands in 1866, and in October of that year I delivered my maiden lecture; it was in San Francisco. In the following January I arrived in New York, and had just completed my thirty-first year. In that year I saw my platonic dream-sweetheart again. In this dream I was again standing on the stage of the Opera House in San Francisco, ready to lecture, and with the audience vividly individualized before me in the strong light. I began, spoke a few words, and stopped, cold with fright; for I discovered that I had no subject, no text, nothing to talk about. I choked for a while, then got out a few words, a lame, poor attempt at humor. The house made no response. There was a miserable pause, then another attempt, and another failure. There were a few scornful laughs; otherwise the house was silent, unsmilingly austere, deeply offended. I was consuming with shame. In my distress I tried to work upon its pity. I began to make servile apologies, mixed with gross and ill-timed flatteries, and to beg and plead for forgiveness; this was too much, and the people broke into insulting cries, whistlings, hootings, and cat-calls, and in the midst of this they rose and began to struggle in a confused mass toward the door. I stood dazed and helpless, looking out over this spectacle, and thinking how everybody would be talking about it next day, and I could not show myself in the streets. When the house was become wholly empty and still, I sat down on the only chair that was on the stage and bent my head down on the reading-desk to shut out the look of that place. Soon that familiar dream-voice spoke my name, and swept all my troubles away:

"Robert!"

I answered:

"Agnes!"

The next moment we two were lounging up the blossomy gorge called the Iao Valley, in the Hawaiian Islands. I recognized, without any explanations, that Robert was not my name, but only a pet name, a common noun, and meant "dear"; and both of us knew that Agnes was not a name, but only a pet name, a common noun, whose spirit was affectionate, but not conveyable with exactness in any but the dream-language. It was about the equivalent of "dear," but the dream-vocabulary shaves meanings finer and closer than do the world's daytime dictionaries. We did not know why those words should have those meanings; we had used words which had no existence in any known language, and had expected them to be understood, and they were understood. In my note-books there are several letters from this dream-sweetheart, in some unknown tongue—presumably dream-tongue—with translations added. I should like to be master of that tongue, then I could talk in shorthand. Here is one of those letters—the whole of it:

"Rax oha tal."

Translation.—"When you receive this it will remind you that I long to see your face and touch your hand, for the comfort of it and the peace."

It is swifter than waking thought; for thought is not thought at all, but only a vague and formless fog until it is articulated into words.

We wandered far up the fairy gorge, gathering the beautiful flowers of the ginger-plant and talking affectionate things, and tying and retying each other's ribbons and cravats, which didn't need it; and finally sat down in the shade of a tree and climbed the vine-hung precipices with our eyes, up and up and up toward the sky to where the drifting scarfs of white mist clove them across and left the green summits floating pale and remote, like spectral islands wandering in the deeps of space; and then we descended to earth and talked again.

"How still it is—and soft, and balmy, and reposeful! I could never tire of it. You like it, don't you, Robert?"

"Yes, and I like the whole region—all the islands. Maui. It is a darling island. I have been here before. Have you?"

"Once, but it wasn't an island then."

"What was it?"

"It was a sufa."

I understood. It was the dream-word for "part of a continent."

"What were the people like?"

"They hadn't come yet. There weren't any."

"Do you know, Agnes—that is Haleakala, the dead volcano, over there across the valley; was it here in your friend's time?"

20

"Yes, but it was burning."

"Do you travel much?"

"I think so. Not here much, but in the stars a good deal."

"Is it pretty there?"

She used a couple of dream-words for "You will go with me some time and you will see." Non-committal, as one perceives now, but I did not notice it then.

A man-of-war-bird lit on her shoulder; I put out my hand and caught it. Its feathers began to fall out, and it turned into a kitten; then the kitten's body began to contract itself to a ball and put out hairy, long legs, and soon it was a tarantula; I was going to keep it, but it turned into a star-fish, and I threw it away. Agnes said it was not worth while to try to keep things; there was no stability about them. I suggested rocks; but she said a rock was like the rest; it wouldn't stay. She picked up a stone, and it turned into a bat and flew away. These curious matters interested me, but that was all; they did not stir my wonder.

While we were sitting there in the Iao gorge talking, a Kanaka came along who was wrinkled and bent and white-headed, and he stopped and talked to us in the native tongue, and we understood him without trouble and answered him in his own speech. He said he was a hundred and thirty years old, and he remembered Captain Cook well, and was present when he was murdered; saw it with his own eyes, and also helped. Then he showed us his gun, which was of strange make, and he said it was his own invention and was to shoot arrows with, though one loaded it with powder and it had a percussion lock. He said it would carry a hundred miles. It seemed a reasonable statement; I had no fault to find with it, and it did not in any way surprise me. He loaded it and fired an arrow aloft, and it darted into the sky and vanished. Then he went his way, saying that the arrow would fall near us in half an hour, and would go many yards into the earth, not minding the rocks.

I took the time, and we waited, reclining upon the mossy slant at the base of a tree, and gazing into the sky. By and by there was a hissing sound, followed by a dull impact, and Agnes uttered a groan. She said, in a series of fainting gasps:

"Take me to your arms—it passed through me—hold me to your heart—I am afraid to die—closer—closer. It is growing dark—I cannot see you. Don't leave me—where are you? You are not gone? You will not leave me? I would not leave you."

Then her spirit passed; she was clay in my arms.

The scene changed in an instant and I was awake and crossing Bond Street in New York with a friend, and it was snowing hard. We had been talking, and there had been no observable gaps in the conversation. I doubt if I had made any more than two steps while I was asleep. I am satisfied that even the most elaborate and incident-crowded dream is seldom more than a few seconds in length. It would not cost me very much of a strain to believe in Mohammed's seventy-year dream, which began when he knocked his glass over, and ended in time for him to catch it before the water was spilled.

Within a quarter of an hour I was in my quarters, undressed, ready for bed, and was jotting down my dream in my note-book. A striking thing happened now. I finished my notes, and was just going to turn out the gas when I was caught with a most strenuous gape, for it was very late and I was very drowsy. I fell asleep and dreamed again. What now follows occurred while I was asleep; and when I woke again the gape had completed itself, but not long before, I think, for I was still on my feet. I was in Athens—a city which I had not then seen, but I recognized the Parthenon from the pictures, although it had a fresh look and was in perfect repair. I passed by it and climbed a grassy hill toward a palatial sort of mansion which was built of red terra-cotta and had a spacious portico, whose roof was supported by a rank of fluted columns with Corinthian capitals. It was noonday, but I met no one. I passed into the house and entered the first room. It was very large and light, its walls were of polished and richly tinted and veined onyx, and its floor was a pictured pattern in soft colors laid in tiles. I noted the details of the furniture and the ornaments—a thing which I should not have been likely to do when awake—and they took sharp hold and remained in my memory; they are not really dim yet, and this was more than thirty years ago.

There was a person present—Agnes. I was not surprised to see her, but only glad. She was in the simple Greek costume, and her hair and eyes were different as to color from those she had had when she died in the Hawaiian Islands half an hour before, but to me she was exactly her own beautiful little self as I had always known her, and she was still fifteen, and I was seventeen once more. She was sitting on an ivory settee, crocheting something or other, and had her crewels in a shallow willow work-basket in her lap. I sat down by her and we began to chat in the usual way. I remembered her death, but the pain and the grief and the bitterness which had been so sharp and so desolating to me at the moment that it happened had wholly passed from me now, and had left not a scar. I was grateful to have her back, but there was no realizable sense that she had ever been gone, and so it did not occur to me to speak about it, and she made no reference to it herself. It may be that she had often died before, and knew that there was nothing lasting about it, and consequently nothing important enough in it to make conversation out of.

When I think of that house and its belongings, I recognize what a master in taste and drawing and color and arrangement is the dream-artist who resides in us. In my waking hours, when the inferior artist in me is in command, I cannot draw even the simplest picture with a pencil, nor do anything with a brush and colors; I cannot bring before my mind's eye the detail image of any building known to me except my own house at home; of St. Paul's, St. Peter's, the Eiffel Tower, the Taj, the Capitol at Washington, I can reproduce only portions, partial glimpses; the same with Niagara Falls, the Matterhorn, and other familiar things in nature; I cannot bring before my mind's eye the face or figure of any human being known to me; I have seen my family at breakfast within the past two hours; I cannot bring their images before me, I do not know how they look; before me, as I write, I see a little grove of young trees in the garden; high above them projects the slender lance of a young pine, beyond it is a glimpse of the upper half of a dull-white chimney covered by an A-shaped little roof shingled with brown-red tiles, and half a mile away is a hill-top densely wooded, and the red is cloven by a curved, wide vacancy, which is smooth and grass-clad; I cannot shut my eyes and reproduce that picture as a whole at all, nor any single detail of it except the grassy curve, and that but vaguely and fleetingly.

But my dream-artist can draw anything, and do it perfectly; he can paint with all the colors and all the shades, and do it with delicacy and truth; he can place before me vivid images of palaces, cities, hamlets, hovels, mountains, valleys, lakes, skies, glowing in sunlight or moonlight, or veiled in driving gusts of snow or rain, and he can set before me people who are intensely alive, and who feel, and express their feelings in their faces, and who also talk and laugh, sing and swear. And when I wake I can shut my eyes and bring back those people, and the scenery and the buildings; and not only in general view, but often in nice detail. While Agnes and I sat talking in that grand Athens house, several stately Greeks entered from another part of it, disputing warmly about something or other, and passed us by with courteous recognition; and among them was Socrates. I recognized him by his nose. A moment later the house and Agnes and Athens vanished away, and I was in my quarters in New York again and reaching for my note-book.

In our dreams—I know it!—we do make the journeys we seem to make; we do see the things we seem to see; the people, the horses, the cats, the dogs, the birds, the whales, are real, not chimeras; they are living spirits, not shadows; and they are immortal and indestructible. They go whither they will; they visit all resorts, all points of interest, even the twinkling suns that wander in the wastes of space. That is where those strange mountains are which slide from under our feet while we walk, and where those vast caverns are whose bewildering avenues close behind us and in front when we are lost, and shut us in. We know this because there are no such things here, and they must be there, because there is no other place.

This tale is long enough, and I will close it now. In the forty-four years that I have known my Dreamland sweetheart, I have seen her once in two years on an average. Mainly these were glimpses, but she was always immediately recognizable, notwithstanding she was so given to repair herself and getting up doubtful improvements in her hair and eyes. She was always fifteen, and looked it and acted it; and I was always seventeen, and never felt a day older. To me she is a real person, not a fiction, and her sweet and innocent society has been one of the prettiest and pleasantest experiences of my life. I know that to you her talk will not seem of the first intellectual order; but you should hear her in Dreamland—then you would see!

I saw her a week ago, just for a moment. Fifteen, as usual, and I seventeen, instead of going on sixty-three, as I was when I went to sleep. We were in India, and Bombay was in sight; also Windsor Castle, its towers and battlements veiled in a delicate haze, and from it the Thames flowed, curving and winding between its swarded banks, to our feet. I said:

"There is no question about it, England is the most beautiful of all the countries."

Her face lighted with approval, and she said, with that sweet and earnest irrelevance of hers:

"It is, because it is so marginal."

Then she disappeared. It was just as well; she could probably have added nothing to that rounded and perfect statement without damaging its symmetry.

This glimpse of her carries me back to Maui, and that time when I saw her gasp out her young life. That was a terrible thing to me at the time. It was preternaturally vivid; and the pain and the grief and the misery of it to me transcended many sufferings that I have known in waking life. For everything in a dream is more deep and strong and sharp and real than is ever its pale imitation in the unreal life which is ours when we go about awake and clothed with our artificial selves in this vague and dull-tinted artificial world. When we die we shall slough off this cheap intellect, perhaps, and go abroad into Dreamland clothed in our real selves, and aggrandized and enriched by the command over the mysterious mental magician who is here not our slave, but only our guest.

# HUNTING THE DECEITFUL TURKEY

# HUNTING THE DECEITFUL TURKEY*

WHEN I was a boy my uncle and his big boys hunted with the rifle, the youngest boy Fred and I with a shotgun—a small single-barrelled shotgun which was properly suited to our size and strength; it was not much heavier than a broom. We carried it turn about, half an hour at a time. I was not able to hit anything with it, but I liked to try. Fred and I hunted feathered small game, the others hunted deer, squirrels, wild turkeys, and such things. My uncle and the big boys were good shots. They killed hawks and wild geese and such like on the wing; and they didn't wound or kill squirrels, they *stunned* them. When the dogs treed a squirrel, the squirrel would scamper aloft and run out on a limb and flatten himself along it, hoping to make himself invisible in that way—and not quite succeeding. You could see his wee little ears sticking up. You couldn't see his nose, but you knew where it was. Then the hunter, despising a "rest" for his rifle, stood up and took offhand aim at the limb and sent a bullet into it immediately under the squirrel's nose, and down tumbled the animal, unwounded but unconscious; the dogs gave him a shake and he was dead. Sometimes when the distance was great and the wind not accurately allowed for, the bullet would hit the squirrel's head; the dogs could do as they pleased with that one—the hunter's pride was hurt, and he wouldn't allow it to go into the game-bag.

In the first faint gray of the dawn the stately wild turkeys would be stalking around in great flocks, and ready to be sociable and answer invitations to come and converse with other excursionists of their kind. The hunter concealed himself and imitated the turkey-call by sucking the air through the legbone of a turkey which had previously answered a call like that and lived only just long enough to regret it. There is nothing that furnishes a perfect turkey-call except that bone. Another of Nature's treacheries, you see. She is full of them; half the time she doesn't know which she likes best—to betray her child or protect it. In the case of the turkey she is badly mixed: she gives it a bone to be used in getting it into trouble, and she also furnishes it with a trick for getting itself out of the trouble again. When a mamma-turkey answers an invitation and finds she has made a mistake in accepting it, she does as the mamma-partridge does—remembers a previous engagement and goes limping and scrambling away, pretending to be very lame; and at the same time she is saying to her not-visible children, "Lie low, keep still, don't expose yourselves; I shall be back as soon as I have beguiled this shabby swindler out of the country."

When a person is ignorant and confiding, this immoral device can have tiresome results. I followed an ostensibly lame turkey over a considerable part of the United States one morning, because I believed in her and could not think she would deceive a mere boy, and one who was trusting her and considering her honest. I had the single-barrelled shotgun, but my idea was to catch her alive. I often got within rushing distance of her, and then made my rush; but always, just as I made my final plunge and put my hand down where her back had been, it wasn't there; it was only two or three inches from there and I brushed the tail-feathers as I landed on my stomach—a very close call, but still not quite close enough; that is, not close enough for success, but just close enough to convince me that I could do it next time. She always waited for me, a little piece away, and let on to be resting and greatly fatigued; which was a lie, but I believed it, for I still thought her honest long after I ought to have begun to doubt her, suspecting that this was no way for a high-minded bird to be acting. I followed, and followed, and followed, making my periodical rushes, and getting up and brushing the dust off, and resuming the voyage with patient confidence; indeed, with a confidence which grew, for I could see by the change of climate and vegetation that we were getting up into the high latitudes, and as she always looked a little tireder and a little more discouraged after each rush, I judged that I was safe to win, in the end, the competition being purely a matter of staying power and the advantage lying with me from the start because she was lame.

Along in the afternoon I began to feel fatigued

myself. Neither of us had had any rest since we first started on the excursion, which was upwards of ten hours before, though latterly we had paused awhile after rushes, I letting on to be thinking about something else; but neither of us sincere, and both of us waiting for the other to call game but in no real hurry about it, for indeed those little evanescent snatches of rest were very grateful to the feelings of us both; it would naturally be so, skirmishing along like that ever since dawn and not a bite in the meantime; at least for me, though sometimes as she lay on her side fanning herself with a wing and praying for strength to get out of this difficulty a grasshopper happened along whose time had come, and that was well for her, and fortunate, but I had nothing—nothing the whole day.

More than once, after I was very tired, I gave up taking her alive, and was going to shoot her, but I never did it, although it was my right, for I did not believe I could hit her; and besides, she always stopped and posed, when I raised the gun, and this made me suspicious that she knew about me and my marksmanship, and so I did not care to expose myself to remarks.

I did not get her, at all. When she got tired of the game at last, she rose from almost under my hand and flew aloft with the rush and whir of a shell and lit on the highest limb of a great tree and sat down and crossed her legs and smiled down at me, and seemed gratified to see me so astonished.

I was ashamed, and also lost; and it was while wandering the woods hunting for myself that I found a deserted log cabin and had one of the best meals there that in my life-days I have eaten. The weed-grown garden was full of ripe tomatoes, and I ate them ravenously, though I had never liked them before. Not more than two or three times since have I tasted anything that was so delicious as those tomatoes. I surfeited myself with them, and did not taste another one until I was in middle life. I can eat them now, but I do not like the look of them. I suppose we have all experienced a surfeit at one time or another. Once, in stress of circumstances, I ate part of a barrel of sardines, there being nothing else at hand, but since then I have always been able to get along without sardines.

# THE McWILLIAMSES AND THE BURGLAR ALARM

# THE McWILLIAMSES AND THE BURGLAR ALARM

THE conversation drifted smoothly and pleasantly along from weather to crops, from crops to literature, from literature to scandal, from scandal to religion; then took a random jump, and landed on the subject of burglar alarms. And now for the first time Mr. McWilliams showed feeling. Whenever I perceive this sign on this man's dial, I comprehend it, and lapse into silence, and give him opportunity to unload his heart. Said he, with but ill-controlled emotion:

"I do not go one single cent on burglar alarms, Mr. Twain—not a single cent—and I will tell you why. When we were finishing our house, we found we had a little cash left over, on account of the plumber not knowing it. I was for enlightening the heathen with it, for I was always unaccountably down on the heathen somehow; but Mrs. McWilliams said no, let's have a burglar alarm. I agreed to this compromise. I will explain that whenever I want a thing, and Mrs. McWilliams wants another thing, and we decide upon the thing that Mrs. McWilliams wants—as we always do—she calls that a compromise. Very well: the man came up from New York and put in the alarm, and charged three hundred and twenty-five dollars for it, and said we could sleep without uneasiness now. So we did for awhile—say a month. Then one night we smelled smoke, and I was advised to get up and see what the matter was. I lit a candle, and started toward the stairs, and met a burglar coming out of a room with a basket of tinware, which he had mistaken for solid silver in the dark. He was smoking a pipe. I said, 'My friend, we do not allow smoking in this room.' He said he was a stranger, and could not be expected to know the rules of the house: said he had been in many houses just as good as this one, and it had never been objected to before. He added that as far as his experience went, such rules had never been considered to apply to burglars, anyway.

"I said: 'Smoke along, then, if it is the custom, though I think that the conceding of a privilege to a burglar which is denied to a bishop is a conspicuous sign of the looseness of the times. But waiving all that, what business have you to be entering this house in this furtive and clandestine way, without ringing the burglar alarm?'

"He looked confused and ashamed, and said, with embarrassment: 'I beg a thousand pardons. I did not know you had a burglar alarm, else I would have rung it. I beg you will not mention it where my parents may hear of it, for they are old and feeble, and such a seemingly wanton breach of the hallowed conventionalities of our Christian civilization might all too rudely sunder the frail bridge which hangs darkling between the pale and evanescent present and the solemn great deeps of the eternities. May I trouble you for a match?'

"I said: 'Your sentiments do you honor, but if you

will allow me to say it, metaphor is not your best hold. Spare your thigh; this kind light only on the box, and seldom there, in fact, if my experience may be trusted. But to return to business: how did you get in here?'

"'Through a second-story window.'

"It was even so. I redeemed the tinware at pawnbroker's rates, less cost of advertising, bade the burglar good-night, closed the window after him, and retired to headquarters to report. Next morning we sent for the burglar-alarm man, and he came up and explained that the reason the alarm did not 'go off' was that no part of the house but the first floor was attached to the alarm. This was simply idiotic; one might as well have no armor on at all in battle as to have it only on his legs. The expert now put the whole second story on the alarm, charged three hundred dollars for it, and went his way. By and by, one night, I found a burglar in the third story, about to start down a ladder with a lot of miscellaneous property. My first impulse was to crack his head with a billiard cue; but my second was to refrain from this attention, because he was between me and the cue rack. The second impulse was plainly the soundest, so I refrained, and proceeded to compromise. I redeemed the property at former rates, after deducting ten per cent. for use of ladder, it being my ladder, and next day we sent down for the expert once more, and had the third story attached to the alarm, for three hundred dollars.

"By this time the 'annunciator' had grown to formidable dimensions. It had forty-seven tags on it, marked with the names of the various rooms and chimneys, and it occupied the space of an ordinary wardrobe. The gong was the size of a wash-bowl, and was placed above the head of our bed. There was a wire from the house to the coachman's quarters in the stable, and a noble gong alongside his pillow.

"We should have been comfortable now but for one defect. Every morning at five the cook opened the kitchen door, in the way of business, and rip went that gong! The first time this happened I thought the last day was come sure. I didn't think it *in* bed—no, but out of it—for the first effect of that frightful gong is to hurl you across the house, and slam you against the wall, and then curl you up, and squirm you like a spider on a stove lid, till somebody shuts the kitchen door. In solid fact, there is no clamor that is even remotely comparable to the dire clamor which that gong makes. Well, this catastrophe happened every morning regularly at five o'clock, and lost us three hours sleep; for, mind you, when that thing wakes you, it doesn't merely wake you in spots; it wakes you all over, conscience and all, and you are good for eighteen hours of wide-awakeness subsequently—eighteen hours of the very most inconceivable wide-awakeness that you ever experienced in your life. A stranger died on our hands one time, and we vacated and left him in our room overnight. Did that stranger wait for the general judgment? *No*, sir; he got up at five the next morning in the most prompt and unostentatious way. I knew he would; I knew it mighty well. He collected his life-insurance, and lived happy ever after, for there was plenty of proof as to the perfect squareness of his death.

"Well, we were gradually fading toward a better land, on account of the daily loss of sleep; so we finally had the expert up again, and he ran a wire to the outside of the door, and placed a switch there, whereby Thomas, the butler, always made one little mistake—he switched the alarm off at night when he went to bed, and switched it on again at daybreak in the morning, just in time for the cook to open the kitchen door, and enable that gong to slam us across the house, sometimes breaking a window with one or the other of us. At the end of a week we recognized that this switch business was a delusion and a snare. We also discovered that a band of burglars had been lodging in the house the whole time—not exactly to steal, for there wasn't much left now, but to hide from the police, for they were hot pressed, and they shrewdly judged that the detectives would never think of a tribe of burglars taking sanctuary in a house notoriously protected by the most imposing and elaborate burglar alarm in America.

"Sent down for the expert again, and this time he struck a most dazzling idea—he fixed the thing so that opening the kitchen door would take off the alarm. It was a noble idea, and he charged accordingly. But you already foresee the result. I switched on the alarm every night at bed-time, no longer trusting on Thomas's frail memory; and as soon as the lights were out the burglars walked in at the kitchen door, thus taking the alarm off without waiting for the cook to do it in the morning. You see how aggravatingly we were situated. For months we couldn't have any company. Not a spare bed in the house; all occupied by burglars.

"Finally, I got up a cure of my own. The expert answered the call, and ran another ground wire to the stable, and established a switch there, so that the coachman could put on and take off the alarm. That worked first rate, and a season of peace ensued, during which we got to inviting company once more and enjoying life.

"But by and by the irrepressible alarm invented a new kink. One winter's night we were flung out of bed by the sudden music of that awful gong, and when we hobbled to the annunciator, turned up the gas, and saw the word 'Nursery' exposed, Mrs. McWilliams fainted dead away, and I came precious near doing the same thing myself. I seized my shotgun, and stood timing the coachman whilst that appalling buzzing went on. I knew that his gong had flung him out, too, and that he would be along with his gun as soon as he could jump into his clothes. When I judged that the time was ripe, I crept to the room next the nursery, glanced through the window, and saw the dim outline of the coachman in the yard below, standing at present-arms and waiting for a chance. Then I hopped into the nursery and fired, and in the same instant the coachman fired at the red flash of my gun. Both of us were successful; I crippled a nurse, and he shot off all my back hair. We turned up the gas, and telephoned for a surgeon. There was not a sign of a burglar, and no window had been raised. One glass was absent, but that was where the coachman's charge had come through. Here was a fine mystery—a burglar alarm 'going off' at midnight of its own accord, and not a burglar in the neighborhood!

"The expert answered the usual call, and explained that it was a 'False alarm.' Said it was easily fixed. So he overhauled the nursery window, charged a remunerative figure for it, and departed.

"What we suffered from false alarms for the next three years no stylographic pen can describe. During the next three months I always flew with my gun to the room indicated, and the coachman always sallied forth with his battery to support me. But there was never anything to shoot at—windows all tight and secure. We always sent down for the expert next day, and he fixed those particular windows so they would keep quiet a week or so, and always remembered to send us a bill about like this:

| | |
|---|---|
| Wire | $2.15 |
| Nipple | .75 |
| Two hours' labor | 1.50 |
| Wax | .47 |
| Tape | .34 |
| Screws | .15 |
| Recharging battery | .98 |
| Three hours' labor | 2.25 |
| String | .02 |
| Lard | .66 |
| Pond's Extract | 1.25 |
| Springs at 50 | 2.00 |
| Railroad fares | 7.25 |
| | $19.77 |

"At length a perfectly natural thing came about—after we had answered three or four hundred false alarms—to wit, we stopped answering them. Yes, I simply rose up calmly, when slammed across the house by the alarm, calmly inspected the annunciator, took note of the room indicated, and then calmly disconnected that room from the alarm, and went back to bed as if nothing had happened. Moreover, I left that room off permanently, and did not send for the expert. Well, it goes without saying that in the course of time *all* the rooms were taken off, and the entire machine was out of service.

"It was at this unprotected time that the heaviest calamity of all happened. The burglars walked in one night and carried off the burglar alarm! yes, sir, every hide and hair of it: ripped it out, tooth and nail; springs, bells, gongs, battery, and all; they took a hundred and fifty miles of copper wire; they just cleaned her out, bag and baggage, and never left us a vestige of her to swear at—swear by, I mean.

"We had a time of it to get her back; but we accomplished it finally, for money. The alarm firm said that what we needed now was to have her put in right—with their new patent springs in the windows to make false alarms impossible, and their new patent clock attached to take off and put on the alarm morning and night without human assistance. That seemed a good scheme. They promised to have the whole thing finished in ten days. They began work, and we left for the summer. They worked a couple of days; then *they* left for the summer. After which the burglars moved in, and began *their* summer vacation. When we returned in the fall, the house was as empty as a beer closet in premises where painters have been at work. We refurnished, and then sent down to hurry up the expert. He came up and finished the job, and said: 'Now this clock is set to put on the alarm every night at 10, and take it off every morning at 5:45. All you've got to do is to wind her up every week, and then leave her alone—she will take care of the alarm herself.'

"After that we had a most tranquil season during three months. The bill was prodigious, of course, and I had said I would not pay it until the new machinery had proved itself to be flawless. The time stipulated was three months. So I paid the bill, and the very next day the alarm went to buzzing like ten thousand bee swarms at ten o'clock in the morning. I turned the hands around twelve hours, according to instructions, and this took off the alarm; but there was another hitch at night, and I had to set her ahead twelve hours once more to get her to put the alarm on again. That sort of nonsense went on a week or two, then the expert came up and put in a new clock. He came up every three months during the next three years, and put in a new clock. But it was always a failure. His clocks all had the same perverse defect: they would put the alarm on in the daytime, and they would *not* put it on at night; and if you forced it on yourself, they *would* take it off again the minute your back was turned.

"Now there is the history of that burglar alarm—everything just as it happened; nothing extenuated, and naught set down in malice. Yes, sir,—and when I had slept nine years with burglars, and maintained an expensive burglar alarm the whole time, for their protection, not mine, and at my sole cost—for not a d——d cent could I ever get *them* to contribute—I just said to Mrs. McWilliams that I had had enough of that kind of pie; so with her full consent I took the whole thing out and traded it off for a dog, and shot the dog. I don't know what *you* think about it, Mr. Twain; but *I* think those things are made solely in the interest of the burglars. Yes, sir, a burglar alarm combines in its person all that is objectionable about a fire, a riot, and a harem, and at the same time had none of the compensating advantages, of one sort or another, that customarily belong with that combination. Good-by: I get off here."

THE END